Skye

Lisa-Maree Patterson

Skye

The Caledonian Series

Book One

Dedication

For all those who left their hearts in Scotland.

And for those travelling through the stones.

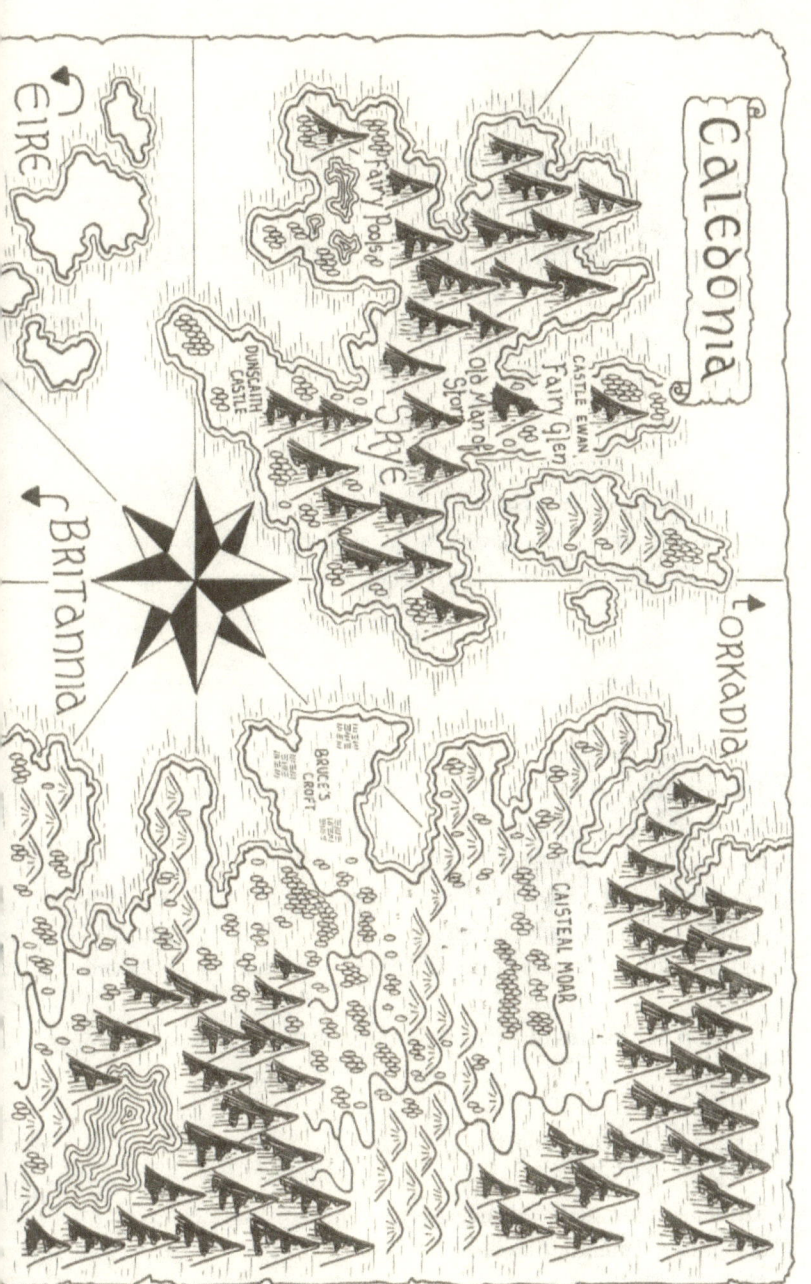

The Language of Auld

"Words carry power in our world, Claire. The Auld tongue still whispers through the glens and over the sea, in battle cries, love songs, and prayers to the Auld ones. Use them wisely. For they are both your future and your history."

Dún Scáith — Fortress of Shadows. The legendary home of Scáthach.

Valkyrie — Old Norse for "chooser of the slain."

Scáthach — The Shadowy One. A legendary and mystical female warrior from Celtic mythology.

Sgian Dubh (pronounced ski-an-DOO) — A small, single-edged knife.

A dhìon agus a dhìon — To protect and defend. Motto of Clan MacLeod.

Bairn — A child.

Ghillie Dhu (Gille Dubh) — A solitary male fairy in Scottish folklore.

Sithichean (pronounced shee-AN) — The fae; mischievous and sometimes dangerous beings.

Ifrinn — Hell.

M'iníon — My daughter.

Teampall na Ghealaich — Temple of the Moon.

Taranis — Celtic god of thunder, known as "The Thunderer."

Sorcha (pronounced SOR-uh-kah) — Brightness or radiance.

Bidh gaol agam ort gu bràth — I will love you forever.

Cat fiadhaich — Wild cat.

Phiuthar — Sister.

Mo phiuthar — My sister.

Mo bhràthair — My brother.

Mo ghràdh — My love.

Mackenzie Dùn — Ancestral home of the Clan Mackenzie. The Fortress

Beyla — In Norse mythology, the goddess of bees and fertility; associated with the earth. (Also, the name of my favourite gin from Orkney.)

Mo chridhe — My heart; also used as my darling.

Madainn mhath — Good morning.

Erasaid / Arisaid — A woman's belted plaid, worn with extra material draped over the shoulders or head.

A chuisle mo chroí — Beat of my heart; my everything.

Mo ghrá thú — You are my love.

Ghrá — Love.

Tá mé I ngrá leat (pronounced taw may I ngraw lat) — I am in love with you.

Maolraith — Inspired by Gàidhlig; King of the Sky.

Beòthach — Inspired by Gàidhlig; from Beò, meaning living – one with a free, untamed nature.

Eejit — Foolish person.

Burn — A small river or stream.

Teampall na Grèine — Temple of the Sun.

Mo nighean — My lass or my daughter.

Cèilidh — A dance or gathering with music and storytelling.

Mallachd dha — Curse him or to hell with him.

Gàidhlig — The Gaelic language.

Bannock — Traditional round oatcake or bread.

Éire — Ireland.

Fomórach — The giants; an ancient race from Celtic lore.

Na Fir-chlis (the Mirrie Dancers) — The northern lights.

Fiadh (pronounced FEE-ah) — Wild or untamed.
Ifrinn, mac na galla — Devil, son of a bitch. A coarse curse.
A chuisle mo chroi — Beat of my heart.

"The Auld words are not forgotten, though many of them were never written down. They endure in the hearts of our people, in love, in battle, and in song. And Claire... the Dragons will always remember, even if those who ride them are long gone."
T.M.P

Prologue

Mist. Staircase. Rocks. Hills. Fairy dunes. Stormy
mountains. Dew. Sulphur. Hair like fire. Eyes like the sea.
As time pauses, images flash behind my eyes.
A coppery river runs through my mouth.
The clash of iron shrieks through my ears, sending chills
climbing up my spine.
Those eyes—deeper and darker than any loch.
A scream. A blinding light.
What have I done?

Chapter One

THE CHIEFTAIN MACLEOD SAT AT THE head of the hall on a chair carved from the ash wood that hid the keep. It was remarkable— hundreds of years old, if the tales were to be believed, and carved by the first MacLeods who ruled this land. Along the edges, runes were carved with stars along the top—paused in time to guide a lost traveller home. Below the sky were the Munros, Corbetts, Moors, and Glens guiding the way. Underneath the chair, the names of the MacLeods and their heirs were carved as a reminder to those who came next — each tale passed down a warning a secret kept safe all these years. And a map to where the great chieftains lie, protecting their heirs and their secrets from the dark.

Again, if the tales were to be believed.

The current chieftain of the MacLeods did not need to be seated at the dais of the hall to tower above his people—his head sitting upon his strong, broad shoulders was already well above those in the room. His hair was the colour of a golden eagle, with streaks of copper, gold, and silver that were illuminated by the flickering hearth fires. A strong, sharp nose and chin, framed with a neat beard of that same light brown. Eyes of grey, which were framed by dark lashes.

Unlike the rest of him, his eyes, though well proportioned, appeared smaller and softer than they should be. He peered through his lashes, watching his people, as though looking for someone, or something. A glimmer of flame lit his eyes as he looked towards the door, and suddenly, it disappeared, leaving behind sadness that dulled the grey.

Four long tables lined the rest of the hall, overfilled with platters of different vegetables, meats, and fruits. Warm steam drifted above, filling the room with rich aromas that made my mouth water. His people, in groups of family and friends, sat gathered around these tables, lifting horned cups to their mouths while their arms energetically told the tales of the day to those around them. Running between two of those tables were two small children, hair of whispering flames, and three scruffy dogs following close behind. They halted suddenly at the Chieftain. MacLeod looked down his nose, eyes focused on all five creatures below. "Off with ya, laddies, go fill your bellies before your Da sees you running amok with the besties again."

The children nodded their fiery heads. "Yes, Granda," they say, and with tails between their legs, they disappeared to the far table for dinner.

The tall chair to his right remained empty; carvings of thistles and heather decorated it, with ancient ruins deeply carved in its sides. The Chieftain sipped his drink, his right hand balanced delicately along the arm of the empty chair. He sighed as his broad shoulders lowered with an invisible weight as he sipped. His table was filled with his family. A brawny, tall young man, a mirror of his father with the same nose, but with deep blue eyes and flaming red hair, laughed heartily. A large smile lined his face, one eyebrow raised with a glimmer in his eyes suggesting a cheeky tale, as the table roared in laughter.

The MacLeod's eyes moved from his son and towards the hall doorway again, meeting mine.

His head gave a small nod, and the right corner of his mouth twitched in the slightest smile. I nodded my head ever so slightly and walked through the middle of the hall to approach the dais.

Though made of stone, the walls glowed in the firelight of the hearths. Shadows danced to the lively tune of a bard's fiddle, their movements weaving in and out of the cracks in the stone.

I reached the MacLeod, whose smile changed to that of amusement and concern. "Why is it that my daughter returns home late, boots lined in mud, foxtails in her hair and smelling of pine and thistles, while the other lords' daughters are off having bairns, tending to their men and doing knitting?"

"Well, I guess those other lords didn't give their only daughter a broadsword for their tenth name day, did they?"

MacLeod's face dropped, pausing his breath for a minute, then he bellowed out a laugh that warmed my heart. "Aye, of course it be my own fault, would it not lassie. Come sit by me and tell me your tale, for I have naught but left the walls today, and I need some adventure."

He gestured to a servant who brought a chair, placing it to his left between himself and his son. The chair to his right remained empty, but his hand touched it gently and then rested on the table. Our heads close together, I began to explain my day.

I had left the keep in search of solitude, away from the bustle of the castle and the extra noise of people preparing for the gathering. With it coming in a couple of months, Auntie Genevieve had been nagging me again about a marriage match. I felt it would be best if I slipped out before I attacked her with the nearest chamber pot. I had decided to walk today rather than ride, leaving with just a dagger and bow. The woods were quieter than usual, the birds still chirping and small creatures rustling in the leaves. But the wind... the wind was silent, as though it, too, was listening.

The sounds of the small creeks as they ran down from the mountains masked my footsteps as I climbed the hill. When I reached the top, I sat in the heather. It was beginning to turn purple and thistles were beginning to bloom; as I watched the sun set, two amber eyes met mine, old, gentle, but concerned. The eyes belonged to a stag. It walked out from the pines towards me, stopping but not breaking eye contact. Its two broad antlers both had seven points each, its coat was not red but white instead, but not like milk, more like the moon with a silver liquid to it. The stag nodded its head low, then, turning to the west, it walked back to the pines.

It had approached me as though it knew me, not concerned that I could harm it. I just stared, mesmerised by its eyes, and when it bowed, I bowed my head in return.

I sat in the heather in silence until it became dark, then followed the stars home.

The MacLeod sat back in his chair, hands together and fingers as in prayer raised to his lips. He turned his head to the empty chair beside his for a moment, then towards me; his grey eyes met mine, liquid and dancing in the firelight.

"Well, *mo nighean, my daughter*, you say a grand white stag with seven points on each antler not only presented itself but walked up and bowed."

"I ken it's hard to believe, Da, but I swear it's the truth."

"Aye, Alix, I believe you, but for now let's keep this between us, eh? I'll think on this, but we may need to go visit your grandmother. Stay close, *mo nighean,* to the keep for now."

"Da, I hear ya, you're scared it's a bad omen, but I feel it's not a warning as such but is asking for help. The forest dinna seem right today and I'm not sure why, I cannot stay inside the keep if something is troubling it, can I?"

"*Mo nighean* for my sake, until we speak to your grandmother, stay close." His voice was firm, conversation over. He lifted his knife and began to eat.

A warm hand covered mine with a gentle squeeze. Turning my head, I met my brother, who had a kind smile on his face, though his deep blue eyes were dark pools in the hearthlight. He was giving me a warning: *not the right time or place, Alix.*

Callum, my eldest brother, wise beyond his years, had spent years training with the wisest teachers in our lands. He had a gift for languages, could read and speak most, and he was also one of the few who could write in ruins and the languages of Auld. He was, moreover, the sibling I had spent the most time with. As my other brothers spent more time on *Skye*, Callum had been here at *Caisteal Moar* learning from Da his responsibilities as heir. He had taken it upon himself to be my tutor and had a way of seeing through me, of understanding and showing kindness when I needed it most.

From where I sat at dinner, I could see the fire in the hearth, the flames slowly flickering in a mesmerising dance. Around me, the hall slowly emptied, leaving all but those too drunk to walk or those having a moment in thought. The MacLeod sat in his chair, silently swirling his whisky deep in thought. He didn't notice as I stood, bowing my head, and left. As I reached the doors, I turned to see a tear roll down his face, his hand gripping the empty chair beside him.

The door's iron handle was chilled like ice, stinging as I turned it. I walked through the door and up to my chambers, hoping the servants had warmed my bed.

***

The castle was alive with all the servants preparing for the gathering. Soon, members of the MacLeod clan would be arriving to pledge allegiance to the Chieftain. It had been ten years since the last, and for those who never ventured far from the keep it was an exciting time to meet other folk, pass on tales and—much to the delight of my aunt and the other ladies in the keep—explore marriage opportunities and match making. For this reason, I wanted to spend as little time as I could inside the keep where I could not be found. Not long after dawn, I strode into the kitchens to break my fast, hoping that fresh porridge and berries were ready.

"Ah, Lady Alix, eating down here again. You must be avoiding Lady Genevieve?"

Ms Mac had been running the keep for longer than the twenty-five years I had been alive. She was a short, round woman, with a frizzy head of hair, dull brown eyes, and the ability to make any problems go away with a bowl of warm broth and cakes if all else failed. Ms Mac knew the ins and outs of the keep and was an extremely helpful ally in avoiding my aunt's plans.

"Aye, I cannot wait until this gathering is over and she's off my back. Why she cannot meddle with someone else, I do not know."

"Well, my dear, she only wants what's best for you, especially with all her daughters being married with bairns, your eldest brother too, and Marcus, bless his heart, still thinks he's a young lad. I can't see him being ready for a wife just yet... You, on the other hand, I think she's worried you'll soon be stuck with no husband or bairns and be tending to your father in his old age or, worse, in the kitchens with us."

Her kind eyes gave me a gentle smile, and she softly patted my cheek. "Now, lass, let's get you a nice hot cup of tea, and after do you think you could go to the stables? I hear Auld Mac's not too well, coughing all night keeping the stable boys and the horses awake".

"Aye, of course I can, I'll grab my pack and head out soon," I said. "But if you see Aunt Genevieve, don't tell her you've seen me, aye."

Ms Mac gave me one of her big smiles, reaching out and touching my cheeks. "You remind me so much of your father when he was young, lass, but it was your mother who always had a thistle or two in her hair."

Ms Mac turned to grab the boiling cauldron, her skirts twisting as she walked towards the hearth. The other maids were busy kneading bread. I watched, thinking of the safe knowledge that whatever might be happening, the castle's kitchens would not change—nothing here had changed since before my grandparents were bairns and the previous Ms Mac was in charge.

I left the kitchens, grabbed my small pack and slid through the back doors, making my way to the stables. The sun had risen, and the keep was beginning to wake, filled with noises of the animals, servants rushing around, the stream crackling as it flowed its fresh water in and around the front tower. I could smell the oak of the trees coming in on the mist and the homely smell of the hay as I approached the stables.

Auld Mac had spent his whole life in these stables, breeding and raising fine horses for the laird and the laird before. No matter his age, he was always the first to wake, cleaning the stables, freshening up the hay, and nicking an apple from the tree to treat his loved old mare. Auld Mac was tall and strong, even with his hands frozen and bent inwards from years of riding horses. On cold nights, I knew it pained him, but he was always reluctant to tell me, not wanting to be a nuisance. I could hear his coughing before I saw him, leaning against the fence, softly speaking in the auld language a tale to his mare.

"I ken there, lass." His soft voice reached me.

I brought out an apple from my pack and gave it to Merideth. She nuzzled me and took the gesture.

"I should have expected my sister to send you up sooner than later, Lady Alix." His hand was brushing Merideth's fringe. He turned his head to look at me. "I'm fine, lass. Not be a wee cough."

"Have you been putting the herbs into your pipe like I told ya, it will help you ken with your breathing?"

I smiled and followed him into the small room on the side of the stable. His face was flushed and felt on fire.

"As it does fine but…. Well, I don't mean to trouble you, lass, but you see, I had them in my pocket, and well, the new foal took the lot."

Old Mac's face filled with shame and embarrassment.

"Oh, Mac, you should have said. It's no trouble to bring you more, here, let's fill your pipe and we will make a wee brew to warm your throat."

***

I left the stables mid-morning, keen to sneak past the main gates and through the keep walls. As I reached the wall, a body dropped down in front of me, dark hair flowing down on impact.

Taken aback, I almost fell, before strong hands grabbed me.

"And here I was thinking you might actually listen to Da and stay inside the keep."

"I do not ken what you are talking about, Marcus," I said.

I pushed past him, making my way over to the strong oak tree between the wall and the stream. Gripping the trunk and upper branch, I was able to pull myself up, climbing around until I got to the branches above the wall. With a wink to my brother, I balanced myself and walked across with the grace of a cat; my feet sure, my body taut with the familiar thrill of danger. Without hesitation, I leapt from the branch, landing softly in a crouch. I straightened with a grin, feeling the rush of freedom already. Turning over my shoulder, I could see Marcus also climbing and leaping out, landing further along than I did. I did not stop my pace but continued onwards towards the woods. After walking in silence for an hour or so, we reached a saint's pool. I stopped and took a drink.

"Alix, are you going to tell me what you are playing at? Da does not want you out here, and here you are walking through the woods with no weapons and by yourself. Are you daft?" I could feel Marcus's eyes glowing at my back. He was pissed, and it was more because he was not told why.

"I'm not out here with no weapons, ya Nonie, I've got my *Sgian Dubh* hidden in my coat and my dirk, plus, I'm not alone. You're here."

Marcus gave a loud snort and rolled his eyes.

"Right then, what is it I'm here to protect you from?" he said.

"Oh, the usual: giants, rogue clansmen, and witches most likely."

"Did Mrs Mac at least give you some food in that pack of yours? I'm famished."

As he spoke, his stomach answered.

"Aye, she must have known you'd follow; she's packed your favourite tart."

We sat by the pool, eating a blackberry tart and drinking ale, the birds around us singing, and the trees whispering between them. Marcus was stretched out on the grass, enjoying the sunlight that peeped through the canopy. Though we looked like strangers—him dark as night, me pale as day—Marcus and I shared something no one else did. We'd always been two halves of a whole. He understood me in a way no one else could. It was in the way he looked at me, the way he spoke without words. He didn't need to say a thing for me to know what he was thinking. When I climbed a tree, he followed without hesitation, like we'd done it a hundred times before, even though we'd only just discovered the escape route. I knew his thoughts as clearly as I knew my own—he was worried, he was angry, but he'd never let me see it. He'd sooner die than let me face anything alone, even though all I wanted was for him to leave me be sometimes.

My hair fell in flowing waves, like my father's, the colour of autumn leaves; a light brown that revealed streaks of gold, silver, and copper in the sun. He told me that when the light hit just right, the strands shimmered like the flicker of flames, echoing the untamed spirit of my mother.

Marcus was everything I was not. His skin was the colour of the earth after a summer storm, golden and warm, as if he had been kissed by the sun at birth. His hair was dark, like nightfall, and his indigo eyes were as deep as the midnight sea. There was a weight to them, a depth and grounding that I envied. My eyes were silver: cold, pale, almost unnatural, like the sky before dawn. I noticed the way strangers looked at me when they caught my gaze, even some in the castle avoided it. They were hesitant, as if unsure whether they looked at something too strange, too unnatural. We were born under the moonless night, and sometimes I wondered if my eyes were a mark of that strange birth, a sign of the things I was tied to but couldn't quite understand. Where my eyes were silver and strange, his were full of certainty, as if they'd already seen everything the world had to offer.

Most of the folk were fine, usually, until they got a look at our eyes, gifts from the fairies or the devil himself. When we were babes, one of the maids, believing us to be changelings, left us beneath a fairy hill. Thankfully, Auld Mac found us in the dead of the night before any harm had come to us. The maid who had abandoned us… Well, she disappeared shortly after. Some say the fairies took her as punishment, but none of the adults ever spoke of it much. It's just one of those strange things we didn't talk about— like our eyes. No one ever really explained them, but they all noticed them. I told Marcus of the white stag as we lay there. He turned to me, his head tilted slightly to the right as he was thinking.

"Were you up past the heather meadows and the top cleft—the spot mother used to take us?"

"Aye, I was." Not realising it at the time, it was a spot I often went to think and enjoy the peace. A magical spot, we called it. Where, although surrounded by hundreds of creatures, you felt completely alone, safe, and at peace.

"Strange that, I was up there a week past, late in the evening when I came home from the islands and camped the night. I woke, looking out across the meadow and saw a giant wolf, amber eyes and a coat of purest silver. I could have sworn he was trying to tell me something."

"Did you tell Da?"

Marcus was silent. "*Mo phiuthar ghaoil* only you." No, my darling sister, only you.

"What does this mean? Da did not want me coming back here until we saw Grannie; he looks afraid."

"That, Alix, is what makes me afraid. Come now, let's go back before they notice you're missing. Well, before Aunt Genevieve does." A wide grin spread across his face.

I let out a loud snort, then threw my cup at his head. Marcus jumped up and laughed, curtsying as he left off. I followed behind, curiously looking around for any sign of the wee folk as we walked. We strode through the clearing, reaching the keep walls. In a hidden crevice, we found our rope, Marcus threw it up into the oak tree, looping it round in tension. I gripped my boots into the wall and began to climb, Marcus following behind. As my hands reached the top, I pulled myself up only to come face to face with grey eyes. *Beyla*, we were in trouble.

The MacLeod stuck his head over the wall, making eye contact with Marcus. We were caught, both of us frozen, and my heart skipped a beat. There was a moment when I looked at Marcus, and it was like we were speaking without words—his eyes locked on mine, and suddenly, I knew he was as much in trouble as I was. I could see the uncertainty on his face. He wasn't sure what to do next. Should he run or stay? Should he keep me from whatever came next, or let me face it on my own?

So much for the secret route out of the keep walls.

As though he read my mind, the MacLeod looked down his long nose at us both.

"Aye, you forget I also escaped the keep one time or another, who'd you think hid the rope?" And he backhanded Marcus over his head. "You clot."

The MacLeod lifted himself into the oak and then dropped down into the grounds. Marcus gave me a push to go first. I turned to give him a look, letting him know whose fault this was, as clearly I would not be reckless enough to let Da know we knew this spot. The MacLeod bellowed up, "If you two clotheads don't come down now, you can stay up there and miss your supper, and I'll send Aunt Genevieve up to get you."

At that moment, we both jumped into the tree, pushing each other, and then tumbled in a pile on the ground right at the MacLeod's feet.

"Lady Alix, is that you? That is no way for a lady to behave!"

A loud female voice bellowed across the grounds. No, please no.

"Alastair Callum Brian Fitzpatrick MacLeod," she continued, "how dare you let your daughter run around like one of the stable lads, roughhousing with her brothers, climbing trees, wearing trousers It's bad enough you got her that broadsword, then arrows—she's as wild as anything. Here I am trying to find a suitable match, and how can I do that with her looking like a *cat-fiadhaich, wild cat*, Alastair? *Bhràthair, brother*, you expect me to work miracles. And then there's you two."

Aunt Genevieve and her flying skirts had reached us, the three of us frozen still, hoping the she-devil might not see us.

I could feel the heat of her glare on my back. She'd never been shy about her plans for me and it felt like there was no escape. I tried to hide behind my father, but it was no use. Aunt Genevieve was relentless.

"You two, move it. Alix wash now, Marcus, you look like you have not washed in weeks. Go, Alastair."

"Aye, sister, I'm going to wash too."

"I'm not too proud to grab your bollocks, laird or not, if you roll your eyes at me again, lad."

I shoved Marcus over and fled. Da was laughing as he ran. Auntie Genevieve's voice carried through the open grounds. "Alexandria, you get right upstairs! I expect to find you looking like a lady tonight, or I'll tie you up and marry you off to auld laird Fraser's son." And with that threat, I was gone, round the corner and into the castle.

Da stuck his head out to see Aunt Genevieve giving some horrid talking to Marcus, who looked like his gizzards were being twisted. We looked at each other and sank onto the floor laughing.

"Oh, Alix, *mo nighean*, it has been some time since I have seen my sister that angry or laughed that hard. Poor Marcus, I should rescue him, but… her face, she does not listen to a word anyone says, stubborn fiend." He continued to laugh, tears running down his face. It had been a long time since I had seen him laugh like that. I heard boots approaching. Ms Mac came round the corner, stopping as she saw us.

"Well, that explains the noise I heard. I should have thought himself had stopped stirring his sister by now, thought you'd have learned your lesson the last time when she put the wee froggies in your bed." Da's face paled to a sheet of white as he remembered. I fell back on the ground laughing, hands on my belly.

"Now get up, the two of you, and scally. Lady Genevieve is making her way here, dragging young Marcus behind her."

Wasting no time, we jumped up and split up the dividing staircases to our chambers. Ms Mac shook her head as I turned to her with a smile. She walked about, throwing a block of lye soap at Marcus, who was about to be tortured by the Lady Genevieve MacLeod.

***

Reluctant as I was to be dressed as a prized mare, the dinner prepared by Ms Mac was delicious—a grand feast of potatoes, pheasant, venison, and trout. My aunt had guests from a nearby clan to visit, three sons in tow, each bragging about the strength and girth they possessed. My aunt's foot pressed down on mine as she recognised my facial expression and the remarks that may or may not have come to mind. Instead, with the gentle reminder of her large and heavy foot, I answered with delicate smiles perfectly respectful of a laird's daughter. Looking down the table, I saw Marcus, face scrunched up and miserable, being seated between two ladies who were also this prominent laird's daughters, easily recognised by the matching pinched noses of their mother.

My eldest brother, Callum, sat next to our aunt. He was happily married with bairns, having a wonderful dinner, and could not help but ask intriguing questions of our guests about life at their dull castle and their fond interest in pig breeding.

"So, what do you think, Alix? I can't say I'm not curious about the finer details of pig breeding," Callum politely asked while putting his cup down on the table.

"I'd rather cook them," I muttered under my breath. Callum clearly heard and cleared his throat. Aunt Genevieve's eyes narrowed at me, her fingers tightening around her fork, as if ready to strike down any further insolence.

"Oh yes, quite interesting." I turned my attention to our guest with a courtly smile.

"Would you say, Alix," Callum asked, noticing my discomfort, "that you know a thing or two about pigs? I'm sure your knowledge of their... culinary uses is vast?"

I bit back a groan. My reply came out sharper than intended. "I'm far more adept at cooking them than breeding them, Callum."

Aunt Genevieve's foot nudged mine again, harder this time. I held my tongue. One of the neighbouring laird's sons, a tall, broad-faced boy with an air of self-importance, leaned in with a smirk. "Aye, well, some womenfolk are better with the cooking than the... breeding. We know our place, don't we, Miss MacLeod?"

My hand tightened around my wine goblet, but before I could respond, Aunt Genevieve's sharp look had me swallowing my words.

Having provided more than enough entertainment for my brother, I excused myself. "I've forgotten my wrap," I said, already standing. But Aunt Genevieve caught my eye, her hand raised in silent command. A servant was summoned, and my escape was blocked. I could only bow my head in defeat, knowing that my escape would be delayed for just a few more moments.

At some point during the excruciating dinner, my father apologised that my brother Callum would instead take Hector and his sons on a ride tomorrow as both Alexandria and Marcus had to leave at first light to visit their grandmother on the Isles and, due to the impending season, must not delay their travels. I met his eyes and nodded. Taking this as an excuse to leave, I bowed to my father, aunt, and guests, and slowly left the hall. Marcus, having also excused himself, met me in the corridor.

"Well, I guess it's decided then, we apparently leave at first light. No doubt we are the last to know," Marcus said.

"I would give my right arm to be rid of those pig farmers."

Chuckling, Marcus gave a taunting bow and said goodnight.

Knowing Ms Mac would have already packed my bags, I decided I would go for a walk. Reaching the inner yard, I gave a low, smooth whistle, answered soon after with the padding of feet and the big brown eyes of my treasured dog, Cody. Her soft coat, becoming darker with the impending winter, was warm beneath my fingers, and I patted her. We walked the keep grounds following the freshwater stream that flowed from the mountain rivers through the river rocks, under the torrent bridge, then out and under into the sea. At the other end of the keep, another small stream flowed inwards from the sea into a small pool where fish and small sea crabs were kept. The keep surrounded the castle and many of the villagers' crofts, most of whom served in the castle and often ate their meals inside, while others opted to cook by their hearths. Sometimes, I would be invited to eat with them in their homes, often after seeing to sickness. With no money to pay, they would offer small kindnesses: a meal, herbs, a bunch of flowers, or small homemade items. The villagers were always thankful to see a healer, and as reluctant as I was to take any form of payment, their pride and thus whatever small tokens given, were received with gratitude.

The MacLeod family was widely known for its healers over the generations. As bairns, our Da began to teach us, just as we learnt how to use our broadswords and shoot arrows. We were taught to defend ourselves and others, and this involved learning to heal our people. Stories of the MacLeod healers were told around the fire hearths of the villages and castle folk alike. Another tale told was of the fairy princess the laird had married, who taught him the skills of a great healer. These skills were passed on through each generation, blessing and protecting all those in their lands. What magic they thought we did, I do not know, but the old ways of healing were taught to us and had become a part of us and our swords.

Aunt Genevieve also had those healer's hands and often delivered the babies in the castle's grounds. When I was ten, she took me to a small village close by after a terrified young man flew through the keep gates, desperate for help. His wife was in childbirth and he thought she might die. Aunt Genevieve woke me to accompany her, and we rode like the devil until we reached the small croft. A long night and day, she taught me the skills to safely bring the babe into our world—how we must clean, also not forget the mother after the arrival of the babe—then once all was settled, to teach the mother how to feed and look after it. She taught me the herbs for women and women's business. She always had her sword attached to her mare and her dirk on her belt—I had never seen her use it, but Auld Mac would tell us stories of Aunt Genevieve defending the village from raiders when my grandfather had been at war. She alone was left to protect and defend while the men left for war, and that she did.

When I turned sixteen, she gave me my healer's bag. She had made the basket through weaving, an old method passed down through our ancestors in the Isles. Inside were small chambers and pockets for herbs, tools, or bandages, each carefully thought out with some chambers larger than others or closer in reach for urgency. Grandmother and Da taught me other healing knowledge. Da was especially good at what he called war skills—aid required immediately in a battle that could save lives, but allowed the healer to rapidly heal between people without spending too much time on one thing. I knew he was a great warrior, but during the last war, he spent most of it healing others. His brother Brian led the clan to battle, and Alastair battled the wounds and injuries of the men. My granda was the laird and commanded men from all clans, making use of their skills through the war. Grannie commanded the hearths with some of the wives, making sure the men were sufficiently fed. They also provided clean bandages for Alastair's army of healers. The war was won, but still the battle of the healers continued.

Da seldom spoke of that war, but songs and tales of the healer MacLeod were told throughout Caledonia. One song my Da spoke of was the likeness captured in one of a fairy warrior who, with her flaming hair, provided aid to the men, holding their hands at the last breath and riding into the battle to retrieve the wounded on the stretcher attached to her horse. The song was about her bravery in bringing those men to the tent for aid. No man would follow her, but she continued, hundreds saved from both sides by the flaming red-haired and blue-eyed fairy on the white horse.

I could hear a fiddle playing in one of the cottages, an old song about the kelpies. An icy breeze hit me, and we continued to walk. Up and round the eastern torrent, we sat on the edge of the viewpoint. From here, I could see the keep, the courts, grounds, stables, the gate, and the path through the woods.

"*Mo nighean.*" A whisper.

"Aye, Da."

"I canna ride with you tomorrow. It will be just you and Marcus. I need you to travel swiftly to *Dunscaith* to your uncle Brian. I have sent word with a message of your arrival, your grandmother has much to teach you, and you must learn."

"What is it that I must learn that's causing this haste?" I questioned.

"Change, lass, a momentous change is coming. I have not felt the woods unsettled like this since before the last war. I do not ken what exactly, but..." He looked around, then sat next to me, his long legs hanging over the turret wall.

"The wee folk are stirring; the stag and the wolf are the auld gods' warnings. There are secrets and knowledge of our family that you both must learn. Grandmother will show you and teach you their ways... I must stay. I cannot leave young Callum and Genevieve to defend the castle themselves... it may come to nothing, but I would rather be prepared and not worry, than put it all on your brother."

His voice was steady, soft, and a whisper. He stared out beyond the woods.

"Stay by your brother, lass, you will need each other."

I grabbed his hand and leaned my head against his

shoulder. We stayed until the moon rose. Then I left him with Cody watching it set late into the night.

Chapter Two

OUR HORSES WERE SADDLED AND READY to go at sunrise. Ms Mac had packed enough supplies for the journey, enough to last us a few days. Genevieve refilled my healer's bag and attached it to my horse. Da was waiting by the horses. We were to travel just the two of us—though safe in the MacLeod lands, we did not want to raise suspicion in case there was trouble brewing, and it was much easier to hide the two of us rather than a group. It was drizzling slightly, and I wrapped my plaids tight around me, thankful to be wearing pants as much for comfort and warmth but also protection. Sitting on horseback in trousers and wearing a hat, from a distance I would look like a man and reduce trouble. Though, armed as I was, that was likely to also deter harassment. With every trip, long or short, Da would see us off with a prayer of old for the gods to protect and see our journey true. He helped me up onto my horse, checked my sword and bow were secured, then kissed my brow.

"May the road rise up to meet you.
May the wind be always at your back.
May the sunshine warm upon your face;
The rains fall soft upon your fields, and until we meet again,
may God hold you in the palm of His hand."
"Beannachd Dia dhuit"
The blessings of God be with you.

"Don't give Grannie too much grief and try not to get into any trouble with your brother."

"You know me, Da," I grinned, slinging a leg over my horse. "I'll keep Marcus out of trouble with the fairies."

Marcus shot me a look. "Fairies? You're the one I'll need to watch out for, Alix."

"Aye," I shot back, "but I'm far less likely to find trouble than you, brother."

"You'll be fine. You just don't go getting lost in the mist." Da winked, and with a final wave, we were off.

It was always an odd feeling leaving the Caisteal Moar; though we travelled often, something was exciting yet lonely upon leaving our home. Hidden from the view of the trail, it provided only one entry or exit and was narrow enough through the thick woods that only rows of two horses could fit side by side. Strategically placed, it allowed those on watch to see the comings and goings of the keep.

With just the two of us, we would reach the island in four days, then Dunscaith Castle in two more. Travelling through the forest was quite peaceful, and we had not come across anyone. As the Chieftains' children, we would be welcome at any hearth along the way, but we chose to keep the woods and our own company. The Munros we climbed were filled with trees and birds for company. The valleys we rode through were a different feeling of peace with the trickle of creeks and brooks, with trout jumping at the small critters hatching on the surface of the water at twilight. We ate most of the provisions Ms Mac had given us by the third day; thus, we soon sought out the woods as our pantry. The summer provided an abundance of, fresh trout, rabbits, berries, and watercress. At night, we savoured the whisky hidden in our bags. There was no need for fire at night, but the comfort it brought was well received.

We arrived at the small cabin four days into the journey, nestled at the entrance of the sea. Murtagh Bruce, a man of no more than five and thirty, his face weathered by the sea, waved at us as we rode down the hill. His children grabbed our horses and led them to the outcrop.

"The MacLeod sent word of your coming, said I was to take you across to Skye; your uncle kens and brought down horses to meet you when you arrived." Bruce tilted his whisky. "*Slàinte.*"

"*Slàinte,*" we said in unison. Ms Bruce brought us supper and set about filling our bags as we waited for the tides. We would sail at midday if the weather continued. I had always admired the peace and simplicity of the Bruce family; married young and four bairns, their croft was always warming and filled with love. They did not have much, but never complained. Young Murtagh would join us on the water, learning the seas from an early age. This would be his life, as his father's had been, and his before him.

The sea was peaceful at this time of year, cold as ice when the waves splayed, but not rough. The deep blue of the sea surrounded us, dark and mysterious, its creatures hidden from the light. We arrived on the isle late in the evening, and the small croft on the side was only small, but enough to provide shelter. Two horses standing tall were grazing in the nearby field, and an elderly man ran out to meet us, reaching for the ropes to bring us to shore. Marcus jumped out when we met the sand and helped to pull the boat ashore. We then made for our horses and began our travels. It would take us a day or two to reach Dunscaith Castle. We would travel as far as we could until dusk, making camp, then leaving again at first light.

It was slow travels through the island, with no path to guide, and as the mist set in one could easily lose their path and end up lost for days—or, as Granny said, "taken" by the fairies, no doubt. The rocks from the coast later turned into deep green grass. We rode over the small Munros with the sound of the creeks bubbling as we travelled. Crofts and villages were exceedingly rare, and so far, we had not met anyone since arriving. We arrived at the auld forest, a sea of beech trees meeting us. We would find a place to camp and then continue our way west.

The occasional bird sang as we made our way through, and we could hear the creeks clashing with the rocks as it dove down the Munro. Deep inside, we found a small clearing and tethered the horses. The canopy above was a bright green; light broke through, illuminating the leaves and leaving a green shadow below. The forest had taken over the trees knocked down, moss and lichen covering them, and small vines growing above. The smell of wild garlic rose as our feet crushed the fallen leaves. The forest was alive, a world of its own. Peaceful.

I made my way down to the small pool close to the creek while Marcus unsaddled the horses.

A voice then filtered through the beech trees with the wind. A man, speaking Gaelic—or close to it. It was not Marcus or anyone I had known. I crept back to the camp to see that Marcus had also paused to listen. We took our swords and went to look. One voice became many, as we crept closer. There was another clearing. Hidden behind the wild garlic, we could make out three men, all tall and built like warriors. Two had dark red hair tied back, and the other had gold and loose. They were arguing, and it was obvious they were lost. Their voices were odd; they spoke the Gaelic but with tighter lips and in a way that ended at times like the sound of a song. The golden-haired one took charge; they had no horses, but did not look as though they had been travelling long.

Strangers. What could they be doing here?

They all were wearing cloaks; at this distance, I could tell they were not made with wool but leather, dark and worn. These cloaks covered their arms. On the arms and knees was a padding, or armour. They were wearing mostly black, but as the light from the canopy touched them, it looked a deep green. The gold one left and walked towards the creek. The others started to make camp for the night. With a nod to Marcus, he walked into the clearing.

The two redheads turned on him. Surprised and not waiting for a greeting, they had their swords ready and swung. They were clearly skilled fighters, moving together as they circled Marcus. He let them play for a moment, feigning a lunge, and he forced them to shift into defensive positions. He pivoted swiftly, and with the gentle movement of his sword, he disarmed the first man, blade glimmering as it fell to the ground. Immediately, the second one retaliated, swinging fiercely. Marcus sidestepped, bringing his full weight down with a swing, landing the flat edge of his blade on the redhead's wrist, his blade dropping from his hand as he lost grip. Marcus was grinning as both men looked at him in surprise. Before they could say anything, the golden-haired man came running from the creek, sword ready, and pointed at Marcus.

Marcus held his ground, both arms outstretched. "I came across your men and thought to see if they needed some directions." The golden-haired one looked at Marcus, sizing him up, lowering his sword slightly.

"Is that right? Fight first, give directions later. I see they are now disarmed."

"Aye, well, they didn't give me the chance to speak, attacking like marauders before I could open my mouth." Marcus laughed, the sound echoing through the trees.

The golden one lifted his sword with grace, and the dance began. He circled Marcus, eyes calculating and sharp, searching for weakness. The redheads grabbed their knives, rising to jump in. My arrow was already knocked watching, I let two arrows go, stopping just in front of their toes, they gasped.

The golden one cursed. "*Ifrin,* ambush is it, friend, and how many men do ya have, ey?"

"They are lucky they're not dead, but the answer is no, I have no men here," said Marcus.

He cursed again, swinging down hard. I rolled my eyes; of course, he would think only a man would be capable of shooting with such precision. I let them play for some time; they were equally matched, and they were also having too much fun. My stomach grumbled, and I was beginning to get annoyed. I unsheathed my sword and waited. The golden one spun around, knocking Marcus's leg and landing him on one knee. He held the sword out, and Marcus dropped his, grinning like one of the kitchen cats who had found the buttermilk. I snuck behind the redheads; with my broadsword and my dirk, I pulled them out and held the two men's necks.

"Put down the swords, friend, or I'll put your men in the ground," I said, my voice as cold as steel.

"You call me 'friend' while holding my men's lives in your hands. That's not how we do things where I come from," he replied.

"Aye, and where's that? It's not the Isles, I'll wager. You're no fisherman, and you sure as hell don't look like a sheep farmer," I shot back, narrowing my eyes.

He grinned that damn grin again. His men were standing at my mercy, yet he was still smiling like he enjoyed the game.

"Tell me, lass," he said with a mocking bow, "where do you come from then, if you're not one of these Isles folk?"

I was done playing games. "You want your men back alive, you'll drop those swords. I've got no interest in playing nice."

"And what if I don't?" he asked, his sword hovering between us.

Marcus stepped forward, eyes twinkling with amusement. "You really want to see her angry, mate? I wouldn't. She's *terrifying* when she's pissed."

"And when she's hungry," I added, glaring at the man with the sword.

"So, make it quick. Do we fight, or do we talk?" He playfully spun his sword around.

Marcus tensed and tilted his head to the right. "I wouldn't have said that, man, my sister over there would not be too happy about it."

"Sister, ey, well, mistress. You talk a good game for someone holding my men's lives in your hands," he said, his grin widening. "Tell me, are all the women around here this... violent?"

I raised an eyebrow. "Violent? I'm not the one who came at my brother with a sword, am I?"

The golden-haired man laughed, clearly enjoying the banter. "Aye, well, that was a mistake. I admit it. But you're as quick with that blade as I am with mine, so I'd say we're even."

I gave him a sly smile, letting my sword fall into my grip, the weight of it steady in my hand. "You may be quick, but I'm not here for a fair fight. I'm here to win."

Marcus snickered from the sidelines. "I told you."

"Well then, mistress, I'll give you my best. Prepare yourself."

At that, I could feel the anger rising in me. I lowered the sword and dropped the dirk.

"You've done it now, man, I'd yield."

Marcus rolled out of the way of his sword. I strode over, but the idiot stood still laughing. I met his eyes and swung my broadsword in an arch, aiming at his midsection. With instinct, he met me, and a clash like thunder rode out. This time, it was my dance of steel. His eyes met mine. I could see the shock in them. Bright green eyes were wide and glimmering. He met me stroke for stroke, step for step, a dance. All sword fights were a dance Da had taught me; this one was going to be interesting. He was intrigued and began to smile. He did not lessen his strokes and was surprised at how matched we were. But I was angry, I was hungry, and this man was pissing me off.

The other men stood next to Marcus watching, I could see Marcus offering them a drink of whisky—the prick was also enjoying this.

The mist began to roll in, covering our feet. The ground was soft and quiet. He stepped forward to attack, I blocked and stepped back, his movements were calculated and smooth, his sword an extension of his arm. Whomever had been his master had taught him well, almost too well. Marcus and the men were beginning to take bets. I aimed high, the man ducked and swung at my legs, I jumped, stumbled a bit, but caught myself.

Enough, this ends now.

Quick as lightning, I turned and swung high, continuing to turn. He was bracing himself to catch another high swing. Instead, I kicked my left foot into his midsection with the full force of my weight. He flew backwards, his sword left his hand, and he landed on his back. In a swift movement, I was over him, foot on his neck and sword ready.

"I seem to have you at a disadvantage, sir… do you yield?"

All four men had their mouths dropped open like fish, staring at me. The golden-haired man laughed. "Aye, I yield, take your bloody foot off my neck, woman."

I could hear Marcus laughing. "I told you not to piss her off."

I held my hand out, and the golden man grabbed it and stood up. "I apologise for my insults, mistress, and ask for your forgiveness," he said with a glint in his eyes.

Who was this man? He clearly was not from anywhere I had visited; his accent was odd, he was dressed like some sort of warrior or rider, and he had eloquence in his speech and manners that made him higher born. His skill with the sword, not to mention the workmanship of the blade, made him not an ordinary warrior.

"Aye, well, I accept. But who are you and what are you doing in this forest?" I asked.

At this, he bowed, deep and low. "Thomas Mitchell Morrison Patrick, at your service, lass. And may I have the pleasure of your name?"

Marcus stepped forward "Let me introduce my sister Alix, and I am Marcus. We are on our way to visit our kin at Dunscaith."

Thomas, or Tommy, as he liked to be called, explained that he and his men had travelled from across the sea from a place called Éire. They were also bound for Dunscaith; Tommy had kin there who had invited him to attend for a period. He told us that he had been multiple times over the years to visit, but during a storm had gotten lost a few days ago, and thus ended up here. The men he was travelling with were friends and had also visited a few times.

Marcus and one of the redheads, Liam, left to see about some dinner, both leaving with bows. Tommy, Sean, and I gathered our supplies and made our way to where we had unsaddled the horses. As both parties were heading to the same castle, the decision, much to my annoyance, was to travel together. Sean set about making a fire, I tended the horses, and Tommy fetched some water. Marcus and Liam arrived back with some fish, which they had cleaned in the creek. We ate and told stories. We would leave at first light, and if there was minimal mist, we should arrive at Dunscaith before noon.

We left the camp early, and though there was mist, it was no worse than normal this time of year on Skye. I rode and led the second horse while the men swapped tales, gossip, and battle tips between them. Once clear of the beech forest, we were in the glen, surrounded by the red Cuillin mountains. The Cuillins guided us through the valley, and as we reached the final climb, we looked out towards Loch *Eishort*, where, perched along the jagged rocky outlook, stood *Dunscaith Castle*.

Chapter Three

WE STOOD LOOKING OVER THE LOCH at the harsh stone fortress of Dunscaith Castle, standing fierce like a dark shadow against the Cuillin mountains. It was our family castle on Skye, though it was not where Marcus and I had grown up. Our two brothers had spent most of their youth there; Malcolm remained under our uncle's guidance, while Brian trained our fierce warriors and had been training Malcolm to take over. I had spent only a small amount of time at the castle while Malcolm had lived there for the last ten years.

"*Dún Scáith* the shadow fortress," Tommy whispered. "I never get used to seeing it, especially with the mist haunting its feet."

He was right, there was something about Dunscaith that did not seem real. No matter the season, a mist clung to the castle's base, weaving through the cliffs and shrouding the loch below. A single, gnarled tree stood near the parapet, its skeletal branches twisting skyward as though clawing at the heavens.

"Who is it you're visiting, Tommy?" Marcus asked.

"My Aunt Niamh. Her husband Brian MacLeod, is custodian of the castle."

Marcus and I looked at each other. "Oh, to be sure, I expect that's who's waiting up on the torrent then—that or they expect to shoot us." Marcus was laughing, believing himself to be a jester.

We made our way round the loch, arriving on the rocky outcrops. Looking down, there was a steep forty-foot drop. If Dunscaith looked impressive from the other side of the loch, it was almost terrifying from the front. We reached the double stone arches, which held the drawbridge. It was lowered, and we met the guards. Immediately, they recognised us and let us pass. The bridge was a good eight feet high, there was nothing to hold on to, no walls to protect those crossing from the fierce sea winds, and the mist surrounded our feet, making it almost impossible to go forward. The horses were uneasy crossing, though they lived here. There was something eerie about this crossing. We made it through the bridge and into the courtyard.

"Well then, Marcus, Alix, this is where we part. Thank you for your company along the way." Tommy began to walk off with his friends.

"Tommy, for what did you say you were visiting your aunt?" I asked, curious, as Aunt Niamh had never mentioned her nephew.

"Oh, both Niamh and my mother arranged some marriage meeting, no doubt some uptight snot-nosed princess who only talks about needlepoint and gossip. Some Lady… Elizabeth, Mary, or the like. I already told Mother I would not agree to it. I have no plans to take a wife, but I said I would come mostly as an excuse to practice with Brian."

"She's likely not a looker anyhow," Sean piped in.

"Have you met her on your travels? Any warnings or hints to get rid of her?"

"Nah, not met her. Heard of her, real trouble that one," Marcus replied. I stayed quiet.

"Well, see you around then."

Marcus waved then, and the two of us took the horses round to the stables.

***

"Look what the cheaties dragged in today."

A loud, booming voice filled the stables. I turned around to see my brother, Malcolm, hands on his hips, trying to make a face of disgust as he looked at us. I ran over to him, and he engulfed me in his embrace. It had been a year since I last saw him. He had our father's height, towering over me, black hair and dark brown eyes. He must have finished training; he did not have any weapons save a dirk at his side. But I did notice he wore a cloak much like Tommy and his men, although it was a deep blue instead of emerald. Odd, I had never seen him wear it before. "Marcus, good to see you, man. She was not too much trouble, was she?"

"Mal, you have no idea." The two laughed uncontrollably.

Malcolm took us up the stairs to our chambers. I opened my door to find my cousin Claire waiting for me. Claire was a year younger than I, with silky black hair and blue eyes. She was small but strong. Uncle Brian made sure we all knew how to defend ourselves, and Claire was no exception. Claire was delicate like our aunt and mysterious like all the MacLeods. I had not seen her in a year, but we would often send letters to each other.

"I hear you met Tommy then," she said.

"Aye, you never mentioned him, Lady Elizabeth?"

"Aye, that was ma, more proper you ken." And she laughed. "I heard Sean and Liam talking about meeting some wild girl on their travels who landed Tommy on his arse, won't he be in for a shock at dinner?" At this, I joined her in laughter; it was good to be with her again. I only had brothers and, unlike Aunt Genevieve's daughters, Claire was not only like a sister to me, but she also understood me. Margot and Flora were more interested in marriage and bairns than riding and hunting.

"Has Granny arrived yet? Da sent us to see her?"

"Aye, she arrived this morning; she will be down at dinner unless she's shooed everyone out already."

My room looked out onto the loch, where I could see the Cuillin reds looking back. Some of the castle folk would speak of the giants that climbed them, and the creatures in the loch. I found it oddly comforting to know there were magical creatures nearby, even if they were only tales.

We dressed and went to dinner. Claire helped wash and braid my travelled hair, and to please Aunt Niamh we wore dresses and cloaks and looked very respectable indeed. Malcolm and Marcus were waiting for us at the bottom of the stairs. They bowed and led us in.

"What is this I hear of you fighting yon Tommy Patrick in the forest? The story is all through the castle, wild girl indeed. I see you have not changed in the last year. Glad to see you can still knock a lad on his arse in your wild banshee rage," Malcolm whispered before he began laughing down the hall. I whipped my head around to stare at Marcus. A proud, wide grin covered his face. "Aye, I was verra proud of you, sister. I won a new dagger from that match. Do ye think next time you could drag it out a bit? I'd like to get my hands on one of those cloaks."

Both boys became hysterical as we made our way down the hall. It was set similarly to that at Caisteal Moar, the large table at the hall raised slightly above for all to see. My grandmother sat next to Uncle Brian, tall like Da but with dark hair like Marcus—though less shiny and greyer than last time. He waved us over. His other guests were seated at the table. Aunt Niamh sat opposite and stood up.

"Tommy, may I introduce you to my niece, Lady Elizabeth McKenzie MacLeod. This is Thomas Mitchell Morrison Patrick of Ulster, my brother's son, visiting from Eire." Niamh, delicate and small, said it with a glowing smile and eyes. No doubt the She-Devil MacLeod put the idea in her head.

Tommy stood, looked me up and down slowly, his face going red. He bowed low. "My Lady, your servant. However, I believe we recently met under another name."

"Oh, dear *Beira.*" Niamh sat down and slumped her hands on her face. Brian and Grannie's eyes popped up and became interested.

"Tommy, good to see you again." Marcus bowed. "Allow me to introduce my good sister here, you'll remember her from that time recently when she walloped your arse in the forest. Lady Elizabeth *Alexandria Margaret* McKenzie

MacLeod, known as Alix, Lady Alix, or the Wild Banshee of the MacLeods." He winked.

Brian choked on his ale, and Grannie let out a loud cackle, turning the heads of all in the hall.

"I am Marcus Brian Murtagh McKenzie MacLeod of Caisteal Moar, at your service." With an exaggerated bow, Marcus grabbed a jug of ale and proceeded to sit next to our brother. Niamh lowered her head, muttering to herself while Brian and Grannie continued to laugh.

"Well, Tommy, you never did ask my full name, and I hear you owe me your dirk." I walked around and took my place between Malcolm and Claire, smiling at the shocked red-headed lads and their golden-haired friend.

***

The next day, we were summoned to Grannie's rooms: Marcus, Malcolm, Brian, Claire, and Auntie Niamh. We were seated at the round table, candles were burning, and sage was placed delicately around. Odd. There were also no servants to be seen. Granny sat opposite Claire, Marcus, and me, looking serious and suddenly older and wiser than before.

"Something evil has been lurking; the auld folk and the wee folk are stirring." Her voice crackled and sounded distant. A chilling breeze brushed my cheek. "It's time, and you are ready."

I looked around the table. Both Marcus and Claire were as confused as I was, but Malcolm was nodding, and Brian and Niamh were watching us—whatever Grannie was about to say, the three of them had heard it before.

"The three of you will begin your training today. Malcolm and Brian will teach you the way of your ancestor *Scathach*. You will train with the men from Eire. Darkness is coming, aye…. The forests grow quiet, the wee folk and the auld are listening, waiting… They are waiting for the prophecy to be fulfilled." She paused, making eye contact with me. "Niamh will teach ye the songs and the words of the Eire. You will need it. You will travel to Castle Ewen for your lessons with the auld, aye. We will see. Will you be ready? Then we will begin."

She drew a breath in and slowly blew the candles out—all but one in the very centre of the table. It was early morning, but the room was as dark as night.

"The MacLeod has sent you, and it is time. The twin moons are coming, and with that, a great war. The Stag and the Wolf were warnings, your guardians… for both appeared on a moonless night, walking through the old forest. Ye father and mother were in the clearing, the fairy pool, rocks sheltering with a view of the burn. Ye ken the place?"

We nodded, and she continued.

"A moonless night. The stag walked through the clearing, meeting a silver wolf. They faced each other, pausing at a fairy circle, five and twenty toadstools it had, then they made their way towards the west, towards Skye, death—*Donn*. Your parents watched as they walked away, and shortly after you both were born… one dark as night, one gold of starlight, eyes of the deep lochs and moon dust, the fairy heirs had come."

No one spoke; another icy breeze grazed my cheeks. Goosebumps prickled my arms. I could not break her eye contact, I could not speak, and I sat waiting. I had never heard this tale; no one spoke of our birth except it being a moonless night, and no one spoke of our mother or where she was. Why were we here? In Dunscaith, not Caisteal Moar, why was Granny telling us this and not Da? Why was Da not here? And Ma?

"Claire," Grannie spoke softly. "You must go too, the owl watches you, you will guide Alix and Marcus, be their centre."

What the *ifrin* hell did she mean? Be their centre? Claire just stared at Grannie, and Marcus looked sick.

"Come," Malcolm spoke. "Your lessons start now."

Chapter Four

WE FOLLOWED MALCOLM DOWN several stairs, confused and silent. It was cool, the air, my breath, the mist. A large ash door stood in front of us, and Malcolm opened it. More silence; he held his hand up to his shoulders, twisting it slowly towards him. A flame—a flame? It flowed out and glided over to the wall, lighting a torch. It kept gliding around the room until it was completely lit.

Malcolm's hand moved gracefully, gently closing his fingers into his palm and lowering his hand, and he continued to walk, lower into the chamber. The flame danced in mid-air like a living thing, kissing the walls and lighting the torches one by one. I stared, mouth slightly open, my mind trying to catch up with what my eyes were seeing. A flame, moving on its own… no, it wasn't just a flame. It was something more.

"What is this, Malcolm?" Claire whispered, her voice barely above a breath.

Marcus shook his head, his brow furrowed. "Are we dreaming?"

I could feel my heart pounding. No, this wasn't a dream. This was real. But what kind of magic was this?

I looked at Marcus and he shook his head. Claire, wide-eyed, looked around, mouth open, pale as a ghost. I glanced around—the room had been dark, pitch black. A flame, yes, I saw a flame come out of Malcolm's hand and glide around the room, lighting torches; we all saw it. What was happening and where in the name of *Beyla* were we?

Malcolm never turned to check, but he knew we were following, like spirits drifting gently behind. It could not be much further. We must have been travelling into a tunnel of sorts. It was feeling cooler, and the stone walls had drops of water running down them like tears. We reached another door. He opened it and walked in—we drifted in behind. He stood in the centre, hands crossed against his broad chest, a warrior of auld. Silky hair braided back tight, shoulders square and strong, piercing brown eyes, boots to his knees, the long leather deep blue cloak, and our plaid over his right shoulder.

"I suppose you have some questions, but I canna tell you all. I will tell ye what I ken. Know what I speak is true," he said.

The three of us stood still, staring at him.

Marcus spoke and broke the silence. "Brother, what in *Beyla's* name is happening? Are you mad?"

"Why isn't Da here telling us these prophecy stories? Next, you'll be saying there's some fairy flag to win a war?" I piped in, moving closer to Marcus.

"Well, it does not win a war as such, but aye if we were in dire need we'd try."

"WHAT!" the three of us bellowed.

"The fairy flags. How'd you hear about that one? I suppose that's you, Claire, in one of your wee books you read."

"WHAT?" we repeated.

"Our great six times Granda. He married a fairy, and the fairy king Oberon left a flag when his firstborn was born. Heir to the fairies and MacLeods, the flag was for protection—to be used in time of great need, although the magic would only be of use three times.

"Each time, a piece of the flag would disappear. It was hidden, locked in the castle—it was used once when the MacDonalds captured the castle, and the sheep caught plague. We reckon we could use it one more time, but no MacLeod would waste it in case there comes a greater need."

"*Ifrin,* you're telling us that some granda of ours was a fairy—appeared on a bridge, I suppose, or a dune—waving a magic flag, are you daft, man?" Marcus questioned, not angry but confused, a hurt echoed in his voice. "This sounds like a story for wee bairns."

Malcolm's face remained serious. "It's no tale. The flag exists. It was given to us by the fairies for protection, and it can only be used three times before the magic runs dry."

My stomach twisted. "What happens when it's used up?"

"When it's gone, it's gone," Malcolm said with a grim look in his eyes. "And when the need is dire, it must be used."

Malcolm walked further into the chamber to a room with chairs and a table. We followed and sat down. My head felt like it was spinning. Mal handed across his flask. The warm burn of whisky was a comfort.

"The fairy princess came during a time of sickness to help. MacLeod worked with her, wanting to heal his people, working day and night. The princess taught him about herbs, flowers, about their uses to heal. Together they healed many, and then he asked her to be his bride.

"The king—Oberon that is, not MacLeod—allowed them to marry, but she could only stay a year; if she did not make an heir, she would leave, and married no more they would be.

"The fairy princess was true, and the MacLeod had an heir—two. A boy and a girl. The girl would be the heir to Oberon people and the boy the MacLeods. There was magic in their blood, healing magic, and something more.

Creatures, silkies, and the like would find them, speak to them. The people would travel for healing. They taught their heirs to heal and protect. Many converted them, jealous of their power and beauty, and the princess and Oberon's heir was stolen away.

"The MacLeod searched but could not find her. He climbed the Maidens, sought the giant of Storr, and when he could not find them on the island, he rode the silkies to land, searching. When he could go no further, he came home. He sought Oberon, but he would not come, he was angry that his daughter was stolen and could not forgive MacLeod."

I stared at Malcolm, still reeling from what I had just heard. A fairy princess? Stolen away? Did he expect us to believe this?

"Did he find her?" Claire asked, a whisper, but her voice broke the heavy silence.

"No." Malcolm's voice dropped low. "He searched and searched. He carved a throne, a map of his travels, stars, moors, glens, and lochs. A way home, should he need it, and a guide to the fairy flag. He travelled far, where a giant silver wolf appeared. He followed him across the seas and found her. She was sick, from age or time away from the fairies. Their daughter had married and had bairns, she was happy and refused to come home. MacLeod took his fairy princess back across the sea, and he tried to heal her, but could not.

"He searched for Oberon and found him on the bridge holding the silken cloth, beautiful, with flowers and silver. MacLeod begged him to save the princess, his daughter, for he could not. Oberon gave him the flag. The magic would give great peace in war or death, but three times was all before the magic would be gone. MacLeod, being wise with the fairies, knew there would be a price. He offered his life, but Oberon would not take it. For the life of his wife to be saved, she must return to the fairies, and only come back on the fire feast day. MacLeod was distraught, but he accepted this and brought the fairy flag home. His wife was healed, but she would not be able to live in the mortal realm for long and must return to the fairies.

"He explained the deal that broke her heart. They returned to the bridge, and she begged Oberon to allow her to stay, but alas, when a deal with the fairies is made, it cannot be changed, for a life's debt might be asked for. She disappeared only to visit on Sun Fest days, and each year MacLeod would visit—one day is all they would have.

"The MacLeod searched far and wide for a way to break this curse, but couldn't. The fairies are verra clever, you ken, though they don't lie, they do not always tell true. MacLeod sought all creatures and searched until his last breath."

I looked at Marcus. His jaw was clenched, but his eyes were wide. "So, he never freed her?" Claire asked, her eyes still and focused on Malcolm.

"Never," Malcolm replied, his tone hard, as though the loss still pained him.

We stood in silence with many questions, but what to ask first? It felt like an odd dream that suddenly any tale or legend could be true.

"Mal, what exactly is going on? Cause I am a tad confused that I'm going mad or that I hit my head too hard on a branch," I said.

Malcolm's kind eyes looked at me.

"The legends are true. We MacLeods have fairy blood, and at five and twenty it's when we begin to show some sort of magical trait…"

He paused, then twisted his hand. A small, delicate flame floated above his hand, flittering and beautiful. He moved his fingers slowly—like catching trout—the flame licked his fingers delicately, bouncing between each one. He stopped, twisted again, and the flame moved slowly around each of us. As it circled me, I could feel the warmth kiss my cheeks. He moved his hand again, and the flame glided back to him, then disappeared. The three of us went to the stone.

He smiled, eyes twinkling. "Magic… fairy magic. The MacLeod and his bride had borne two children; the daughter who ended up in *Eire* had children, and they were all gifted with magic; they could speak to magical creatures and heal the sick. The son, who would be our Granda of sorts—his line was also blessed, particularly in the healing side. Did you lot think we all were just clever with our herbs? It is because of the first fairy princess that we have that knowledge, but in some, like Da….

"Now remember I said we were all different in our fairy magic? Well, his is much like the fairy princess. Pure healing… ever felt that warm touch, like sunlight when he is healing someone? That is fairy magic you're sensing. Those without the gift canna feel it. Aunt Gen is also a great healer, though not as strong as Da. Now Brian's like me, fire or flame. He has learnt to master it in battle, in the ways of auld with sword and shield. Claire, your mother, Niamh's family is from Eire…"

"Aye, I ken, and Cousin Tommy is her brother's son."

"Aye… well, her line descends from MacLeod's daughter—Fayre. You descend from both Fayre and MacLeod's direct lines and are the last in that line."

"You're telling me somehow I have lived most of my life in between this castle and Eire and haven't seen a thimble of magic yet, both my parents have it?" Claire said.

"Well, you can't expect them to go round showing it—they'd be burnt for devil worship," Marcus piped in.

"He's right, though not so much here, most folk ken it's around just choose not to see it," Malcolm answered. "Now, I ken you're not quite five and twenty but Grannie believes it's time you ken. You two… you are the only other set of twins born to the MacLeod line since the fairy princess and her MacLeod. And the prophecy speaks of a great war on a moonless night. Twin moons born, one light and one dark… a war between fairies and men.

I felt the blood drain from my face. "What does that mean? How do we stop it?"

Malcolm looked at me, his gaze steady. "I don't know yet. But the prophecy says there will be two moons, one light and one dark. And when they rise, the war will begin. A war to stop time and bring darkness. It will awaken the giants and the beasts of the sky and mountains. The flag will be used once more, and Oberon's heir will rise again. The fairy folk shall rise, and the stones will sing. Great bloodlines merge, and a great sacrifice made. Secrets will be spilled, and copper rivers will flow. The ground will sink, and the sky will cry. And the twin moons shall rise."

A drop of water fell from the roof onto the back of my neck, rolling down. Goosebumps prickled my arms.

Marcus was shaking his head, his hands clenching at his sides. "You sound crazy. This all sounds crazy. You expect us to believe this?"

Malcolm's kind eyes looked at each of us. I didn't understand any of this, but I knew it was true. He would not lie, not to us.

"The fairy folk, the auld, and the wee are moving; they are unsettled. Creatures are disappearing and hiding. There are whispers that it's time. The three of you will begin your training here before meeting Grannie, who will teach you more of the fairies. Niamh will begin your lessons today with the language of auld Eire."

Malcolm paused.

"Alix, I suggest you don't cut the head off the Patrick lad, he may come in handy, you ken, with a war coming."

Marcus snorted, and Claire laughed. We turned and followed Malcolm and his flame down another staircase. This time, the chamber we stopped in was filled with clothing, cloaks, boots, and weapons.

"If you are going to train with the *Scathach,* then you must look like the *Scathach Warrior.*" Malcolm lifted both his arms out, and flames lit the torches on the walls. The deep blue leather cloaks covered the walls, along with breaches and tunics of deep, almost black, high, and short boots, and leather corsets with pockets on the ribs. Claire and I were drawn to them. What use could pockets have on the outside?

"You wear it on the outside for *sgian-dubh,* Auntie Gen designed those," Malcolm said.

I pulled my own *sgian-dubh* out of my boot. Its small blade fit perfectly in the leather, held in tight, but would be quick to pull. They did say Auntie Gen defended the keep and village alone—she was more adventurous than the gowns gave her credit. She-Devil MacLeod, Da had called her more than once.

Not that Malcolm gave us a choice, we changed into the *Scathach* warrior clothing. The leather was smooth, not rough like buck or cow. It had a shine like snake scales, but I had never seen its like before.

With the colours of blue and black, I put on a linen shirt. The corset pulled the loose linen tight, allowing air to flow down the sleeve but tight around my chest and waist, not restricting my movement; for once, it was a corset that I could breathe in. The leather breaches were warm and I hoped they were thick enough not to let water in. The boots were much like my own, but once tied came just below my knees. The cloak I liked the most, its top flowed broadly across my shoulders, hugging my arms and flowing down my back, a slit rose from the tail to my lower back, perfect for riding to hang over the saddle, but when walking came together to keep out the weather.

Claire and I braided our hair, hers wrapped in a crown around her head, and mine tailed down my back. Our plaids were waiting, and Malcolm helped pin mine on. Wrapped from waist to chest, the fabric was soft and warm, the MacLeod colours settled into the deep blue leather, and my brooch shone. I popped my *sgian-dubh* into my corset for easy reach.

We turned around the corner, and Malcolm let us pick our weapons. Marcus and I kept our swords; they were a part of us, as much as our arms. As I moved through the room, the weight of the weapons around me felt like a silent invitation. Each one was a promise of battle, of power, of destiny. My fingers traced the sharp edge of a *sgian-dubh* as I added it to my belt. Five more, just in case. In my boots, one more. I couldn't help but think of the old stories about the ancient warriors. Would I be like them? A warrior of legend? Or would I fall like so many before me?

Claire grabbed a new bow and dirk. Though extremely skilled with a sword, Claire much preferred to be further back and attack with a bow. But thanks to her father, being the weapon master, she herself had mastered all.

I looked around at Marcus; his jaw was clenched, and his usual light-heartedness was absent. We were all tied to this prophecy now, whether we wanted to be or not. And in that moment, I could see he was wondering if he could ever live up to what was expected of him. Of us.

Malcolm looked at the three of us, nodded, then turned, this time climbing up a staircase and hopefully into the light. The air felt thicker, and the stone walls began to close in as we climbed higher. With every step I took, a strange sense of dread stuck in my throat. Whatever was coming, there would be no turning back. I had a feeling my world was about to crumble down. Marcus's boots were heavy on the steps ahead of me. I knew he had the same sense of dread. Claire followed behind in silence. We were in this together, but also alone. Burdening something we didn't yet understand. I could see the light shining through another oak door; whatever was waiting, we weren't ready for it.

***

The opening came out across the training yard. *Scathach* warriors were paired up, and we stood watching. Brian had them using both shields and swords, swapping arms. He had always made us learn to use our swords in both hands, take the enemy unawares, and know how to protect ourselves. I could see Tommy duelling with Sean. He was good, skilled with the sword, nimble, strong. As the mist above cleared, the sun rays caught his golden hair. The right side of his mouth was raised; he was clearly enjoying himself. In a dance of steel, he glided around the training yard, taunting Sean, baiting him to become angry and charge, then he would have him in a moment. His eyes caught the sun gleaming like emeralds or perhaps the green of new forest growth. A slight flicker of movement, and he was laughing. Sean had made his move, and Tommy, with the grace of the sword, had disarmed him. The two men clapped each other on their shoulders and walked to the well for water.

He ran both his hands through his hair, and I could see it was damp with sweat. He had been out here for a while; the morning still held on to its cool summer air. He knelt and gathered the cool water in his hands, then proceeded to pour it over his damp golden hair, another splash, and he would have water over his face. Droplets ran down his tanned skin, his eyes were closed, and his shoulders began to relax. They were broad and strong, even beneath the cloak he wore, and I could see the muscles tensed against it. The droplets outlined his jaw, chiselled like the carving of the old warriors. I chased the path of the droplets as they ran down his neck, and a shiver went up my spine. Slowly, he opened his eyes. Emeralds, yes, that was the colour, dark and deep in the centre, then they lightened to a brighter green towards the edges. Long dark lashes framed them. *Beira*, they were beautiful. As they glimmered in the light, I saw a movement in his mouth. His lips were full and inviting; they tilted into a half smile that gave him confidence and a hint of playfulness.

The sunlight filtered in again, highlighting the droplets falling down his body. He stood in a movement of grace and strength. His eyes flickered with a glimmer of mischief and another shiver went down my spine. They met mine and paused. I could feel my mouth open as he began to walk forward. Long, elegant strides closed the gap between us in no time. Suddenly, he was in front of me.

One foot out, he bowed. "My Lady." His deep musical voice began. *My lady,* the way he said it made a shiver run down my spine and lower. He waited for me to speak. My mouth hung open, but I couldn't seem to find the words. He had risen, and those lips widened; that bloody bastard was enjoying this.

"—I um. Lord Ulster, um—Thomas. Please call me Alix."

"Tommy, *my lady Alix.*"

He did it again, that bastard. Why couldn't I form a word? I also had suddenly realised that my party had left me here like a simpleton; who knows how long I had been staring.

"It's good to see you're practising, I wouldn't like to see you on the ground again."

He laughed at that. "Och aye, I'm sure you wouldn't, lass, next time it might be you." He winked.

"I would not get too cocky, seeing as I'll be joining the training tomorrow. It would be a tad embarrassing if I continued to disarm you in front of the other men each day."

"Aye, figured you were with that new outfit of yours. You might look the part, but we shall see. I would do something with that wild hair of yours. It's quite the distraction hanging down your back like that. We don't have enough men as it is; we don't want them dropping swords or cutting themselves." His grin didn't fade, but for a moment something flickered behind his eyes—something deeper I couldn't quite place.

I raised an eyebrow and gave him a half smile. "I don't need your advice on what to do about my hair, Tommy.

Maybe you should focus on your appearance first—how about a bath perhaps?"

Tommy was grinning. "Ah, so we're throwing insults now, are we? Maybe I should teach you how to swing a sword before you start giving me tips, Lady."

I bit my lip, shaking my head.

"And where are you heading, Alix?"

Oh, *Beyla*, how long had I been staring? Worse, how long had he known I was staring?

"I wanted to see what sort of challenge there might be; however, there isn't much of one. I am on my way to a lesson with my aunt if you must know… I um…seem to be lost. We came here through a different entrance."

"Well, *my lady,* it seems we are going to the same place; let me escort you through your castle."

***

We walked across the grounds, making our way to the small internal chamber where we would meet Niamh and the others. The wind carried the scent of salt and seaweed from the coast; it was icy but typical for this time of year.

"Do you like to climb?" Tommy asked.

"Aye, I like a good challenge. I have not explored much of Skye, though, apart from the main castles, glens, and forests. Usually, we come only for a brief time. I spend most of my time on the mainland. We have beautiful Munros and hidden glens. It's beautiful here, but it's different, you ken."

Tommy paused, his gaze flicked towards me. "There is a place I like to climb, not far from here, it's about a day's ride to get there." He seemed to be weighing something in his mind. "If you're not busy with training… maybe you'd prefer that instead of the dirk I owe you."

My heart skipped a beat at his words. Why did that sound like more than just a simple suggestion? My mouth opened, but nothing came out. I shut it quickly, embarrassed by how flustered I felt. I couldn't tell if he was being kind, playful, or—*Beira*—flirting with me. Why was I so flustered suddenly? Was I imagining things? He stopped and looked at me. His hand was on a door handle, but without waiting for an answer, he opened it and walked in. The scent of ink and parchment greeted us as we entered the small chamber.

"Distracted by weapons again, dear sister, we had thought you'd never leave," Marcus teased. His eyes flickered from me to Tommy, and a knowing look passed between them. He then shot Tommy a brief but pointed warning glance. I couldn't tell what the look was about, except that Marcus was watching him carefully. Claire was concentrating on her book, her dark crown bent over reading. She didn't look up, but I could see her lip twitch. "Can we just get on with it?" she muttered under her breath. Niamh was sitting in the chair by the window.

"Come, Alix, we can begin." She smiled kindly at me. I took a seat next to Claire as she walked up to the middle of the room and sat on her desk.

"The language of Eire is like the Gaelic, but older and more powerful. When spoken correctly, it resonates with the natural world—calling to creatures and even healing wounds. You must pronounce it clearly, or the creatures will not understand your meaning."

"What creatures?" I asked.

"It's especially calming for horses, but the magic runs deeper than that, Alix. We use it for rituals and chants, yes, but it's also the tongue of ancient beings—kelpies, fae, and creatures older than time."

Niamh was sensible and knowledgeable; if she was talking about magical creatures and fairies, they must be real. I looked about: Tommy was the only one not confused or bothered by this. Claire knew much of the language and was able to intertwine with the Gaelic, but clearly, she had never used it to speak to a selkie much less a cat. She kept going back to her book, scribbling notes down the side. Ah, that would make sense. She had mentioned a cousin in Eire that would send her books; she must have meant Tommy. Looking at the three of them in the room, they were quite different in appearance, except for the cowlick in their hair, a small curl protruding just above the left ear; all three had it. I knew it drove Claire mad; she would try anything to keep it down, even once resorting to stag grease that only attracted midges with the cowlick sticking out in defiance.

"Ah, kelpies are tricky creatures," Niamh said with a small smile. "Not always as friendly as we'd like them to be. They'll offer to guide you across streams, but they've been known to drag folk down into the depths for a little fun. But if you speak to them in the old tongue, they're more likely to listen."

We practised for hours. Niamh was patient throughout; we would meet each afternoon until it became second nature.

***

We had been training and attending lessons for a couple of weeks now and had just finished with Niamh. Claire and I left the room and walked out to the stables. We often came here; it had the smell of home. The horses were stockier than the ones at Moar. These were bred for the rough terrain of Skye.

"Claire, how often does your cousin visit? You have never spoken much of him, not even in your letters," I asked.

"I'm sure I have Alix, but unless it's got to do with something exciting, you often stop listening. He's met Malcolm plenty; surely he's mentioned him? They spend hours training together and riding. He is wonderful once you get to know him. It doesn't sound like you gave him a chance in the forest." She began laughing; it was kind and sweet.

"Well, he is a cocky, arrogant bastard who thinks too much of himself. He needed to be knocked back to the ground."

I reached down to grab a handful of hay, throwing it across the stable.

"I see he's got your danda's up, ay."

"My dander's are not up, he's an arrogant, know-all, cocky bastard that's all."

We stopped talking, then I turned to her.

"Claire, *mo charaid*, you truly didn't know any of this magic prophecy warrior stuff, did ya?"

"No *mo charaid*, I'm as befuddled as you."

"Do ye want to go for a ride then?"

Suddenly we were saddled and flying out of the stables towards green hills and the meadows beyond. It was a beautifully sunny and cool day, and we rode laughing into the breeze.

***

Our training had moved from the courtyard grounds to a glade nearby, surrounded by towering pine trees, peeking through the canopy like sentries. Sunlight filtered through above, creating a patchwork of light on the glen's floor. A gentle breeze passed me, bringing the scent of wildflowers and mountain air with it.

Right in the heart of the glen was a series of targets all at varying distances and heights. They were weathered but sturdy, seeing many years of use. The glen was covered in soft grass, a comfortable spot for archers waiting. A nearby stream trickled, soothing the sound of arrows hitting their marks.

In the middle was a rack, holding various arrows, bows, and feathers. Extra arm guards and quivers were also there, should one require it.

Tommy walked past, grabbing a quiver filled with arrows and a bow. He had already strapped an arm guard on while Malcolm was instructing. Claire had sat down under a tree, book out and reading, the occasional glance at the archers. Brian sat beside her, writing in his notebook.

Tommy knocked his arrow to his bow, his broad shoulders holding the bow steady. His stand was relaxed and strong; he said something to Malcolm too quiet for me to hear, and the result was laughter. He let the arrow go, and it whistled as it hit its mark, just missing the centre of the target. Not terrible.

The others began to shoot and a variety of targets were hit and missed, and laughter echoed through the glen.

Tommy looked over to me, his face anything but serious. "Reckon you can outshoot me, Alix? I've seen better aim from a drunken bard." He smirked, his confidence glowing. Marcus was laughing across the glen.

"Drunken bards don't have the guts to challenge me, Thomas. Besides, my arrows hit their mark every time. Do ye really want to challenge me?" I lifted my eyebrows, giving him a defiant smile.

His eyes met mine in a playful glare. "Right, *my lady*, the best archer, as determined by Malcolm, will get free range of the hot springs."

"Aye, and when you lose what will you get?"

"When you lose, you mean."

"Has to jump into the freezing loch, naked!" yelled Marcus.

The *Eire* boys joined him, laughing. Tommy and I stood glaring at them.

"Fine," we said in unison. Unable to back down from the challenge.

With a playful wink, Tommy walked to the mark, drew his bow, and let loose his arrow, sending it whistling through the air, striking its target. "Not bad, ey? Your turn."

I rolled my eyes and stepped forward to the mark. In a smooth motion, I released my own arrow. It sailed through the air, striking right down the middle through Tommy's arrow. "Looks like I win again! Maybe you need to take up knitting instead of archery, Thomas?"

"Knitting! I'll have you know I am a master with the bow!" Tommy retorted.

"Right, you two clot heads, that was an easy target. Let's try another. First to hit three pure centre wins, right?" Malcolm piped in, pushing us apart.

Looking at each other, we both grinned. "Deal!"

"Be prepared for a little swim later, Thomas. I hope you're not too scared of cold water." I cackled.

"Oh, lassie, you'll be the one swimming in the cold tonight, not me; I'll be enjoying the view."

A low growl came from behind. Tommy swung his head around to look at Malcolm. "I meant the view from the caves in the spring." He winked at me when he turned his head, then swallowed hard and grimaced. I was too busy laughing.

We made our way over to the next targets, and our bantering continued with the sound of laughter and rivalry echoing across the hills.

With the terms of our challenge set, we stepped into our respective positions, determined to outdo each other. I raised my bow, drawing the string back with practised ease, taking a deep breath, my eyes locked on the centre mark, letting my breath out, I released. The arrow flew straight and true, striking the centre. I turned to Tommy with a smile. "One point to me."

He rolled his eyes. "Just luck, *my lady*, watch and learn, you might pick up some tips."

He adjusted his grip on the bow, drew back, and released the arrow with exact precision, soaring towards the target, hitting it with a satisfying thud directly in the centre. "And one point to me also." With a wink, he walked to the next target.

This one was high up in a tree between two branches, slowly moving in the breeze. I took my stance, slowing my breathing to match the slight breeze I could feel. Letting go, my arrow moved slowly through the air, in between the moving branches, and struck right in the centre. "Two points to one," I said.

Tommy walked up more seriously than before. He stretched his shoulders, then took his stance. Letting go of his arrow, it glided, catching a leaf but hitting the centre target. Damn, he was good. "Two for two."

The boys around us were laughing, joking, and taking their own bets as we followed Malcolm.

The next target was further away; it was difficult to see it, but it was clear, and the breeze had settled. Enough power behind the arrow, if it stayed on its path, and it should hit the target. I walked up to take my stance.

"Hold on, *mo phiuthar my sister*, you didn't think I was going to make it easy?" Malcolm reached out both his hands towards the target, and two rings of fire were circling in the air. If the arrow flew off centre, it would burn before meeting the target.

I turned my head towards him. "Are you serious?"

"Aye, let's see then. You both believe you're the best, it should be easy, no?"

I huffed and stood my ground, thinking about how to approach it. I held the bow still. There was no breeze, well, that was good. I let out my breath and squeezed the line. My arrow was centre flying directly towards the target. As it flew through the first ring, I felt relief. The second ring was smaller, and the flame caught the feather of the arrow, burning it. My arrow landed flat on the ground in front of the target. I lowered my bow and walked towards Tommy. "Your turn."

He looked nervous as he walked up. He concentrated hard and made faces. He pulled up the bow, then lowered it. Finally happy with his position, he let go. The arrow flew through the first flame, then the second flame caught it alight. The flame was burning his arrow, disintegrating it before it could hit the target.

As Tommy walked towards me, an arrow flew past us towards the target. We watched it glide through the air. It cleared the first flame, then the second. I couldn't breathe as it landed silently directly in the centre of the target. Slow clapping began, and I turned to see the archer. A few feet behind us was Claire, smiling widely, Brian next to her, beaming with pride.

"Well, it looks like I won and you two are swimming tonight." She laughed. We both were looking at her in disbelief, our jaws open wide. Malcolm was booming with laughter as he went to collect the arrow.

It was night when we arrived back at the castle. "Have a nice swim, sister." Malcolm laughed as he and Brian walked into the castle gates.

"A bet is a bet." Sean was trying to act serious as he moved his arms towards the loch.

"Oh, I am not going in there! Anyway, we drew," I said.

"Aye, drew last. Claire hit every target," Marcus piped in.

I stood open-mouthed, looking at my brother. We walked towards the loch. The moon was bright and the water was calm. I looked at Claire. "Surely you're not going to make me go in?"

"Aye, well, if it was up to me, then no, but I am a bit outnumbered."

"I'll tell ye what, we won't make ye go in naked, lass," Sean said, Liam giggling behind him.

"You can't be happy about this?" I asked Tommy.

"No, but a bet is a bet," he replied.

"Fine!" I bent down, mumbling to myself and undid my boots, and took off my coat and corset. Tommy had his boots off, shirt and cloak neatly folded on the grass. The moon was shining down, illuminating all the muscles on his body. I turned quickly away to plead with the others. I was only met with four pairs of stubborn eyes and Marcus's hand pointing towards the water. I started to walk slowly towards the loch. I turned back around to stare at them all. Tommy walked up to stand by my side.

"Well, best get it over with, *my lady.*" He winked at me with a mischievous glint in his eyes. "You ken what would make it more fun?"

Before I could react, he scooped me up into his strong, bare arms, lifting me off the ground.

"What are you doing?!" I bellowed.

"Hold on tight!" he shouted back. Laughter was coming from the group behind. He took off running towards the water.

"Tommy, no! You can't—!"

Too late.

He leapt into the loch carrying me with him. The world was spinning for a moment as we soared through the air, the cold water engulfing us as we landed with a splash. As I came up spluttering, I shook the water from my hair. Tommy broke through the water's top, pushing his hair back. "See, it wasn't that bad."

"You're insufferable! What if I'd drowned?"

His laughter echoed in the air as he swam closer. "Not a chance!" He grinned, swimming closer, gently splashing me with water. "I've got you. Besides, I ken you can swim."

I smiled, shaking my head. "Don't flatter yourself." I reached out, pushing him back under. He popped back up, shaking his head like a dog. He let out another laugh I wasn't expecting. My stomach was fluttering. I couldn't help but laugh, too.

We were treading water within arm's reach of each other. The others had finished their entertainment and left, leaving us to the loch. The water's chill was now mixed with the warmth of his presence.

After a moment, Tommy gave me a sidelong glance, his lips quirking in that familiar mischievous way. "Alright, I'll admit it. This isn't as bad as I thought it was going to be."

I raised an eyebrow. "Oh, really?" I teased. "Are you finally admitting you're having fun, Thomas?"

His grin widened. "Fine, maybe I am. Just don't tell anyone."

I bit my lip, pretending to be reluctant. "I suppose… It's not the worst thing."

"Aye, is that right? Are you having a bit of fun, Alix?"

"Fine, it is kind of fun."

"Kind of?" he teased, raising an eyebrow. "I'll take that as a win!" He laughed, his eyes glimmering in the moonlight. Before I could respond, he gently splashed me with water, his hand still lingering on my shoulder. I retaliated with a quick splash of my own, but he was ready this time, catching me by the waist and pulling me closer.

His chest was warm beneath my hands, the heat of him contrasting with the coolness of the loch. I could feel his heart racing. I felt my heart flutter and instinctively pulled back.

Suddenly, I was splashed with water from both sides. I screamed, and he was laughing. I pushed my weight into his shoulders, pushing him back under for a second. "You used magic, that's unfair!" I was laughing and trying to be serious as I yelled at him. All he could do was laugh; it became contagious. We swam in the loch for a while, playing and laughing, the water shimmering under the moonlight, and the world outside the loch faded away. We swung back to the bank, still laughing. We were both dripping as we walked across the shore. I felt a sudden shift in the air as Tommy grabbed my hands, pulling me to a stop. The playful energy between us slowed, and I looked up at him, feeling an unexpected warmth inside me.

"Hold still," he said, grabbing my hands in his. He looked at me with deep concentration. I looked into Tommy's eyes, feeling a rush of warmth that had nothing to do with the cold water of the loch. A warm breeze surrounded us, gently tousling my wet hair, and I couldn't help but smile at him. He let go of my hands, reaching for his shirt and boots, and as he turned to slip them on, he came back to me. "Here," he said, gently wrapping his cloak around my shoulders. "Now tell me, Alix, wherever did you learn to shoot like that?" I smiled, bringing his cloak tighter around me. It was warm and smelled like mountain air and wildflowers.

"Callum, my eldest brother." We began walking back to the castle. "He's at *Moar*, we spend a lot of time in the woods."

As we walked together, I couldn't shake the feeling that this—whatever this was between us—had shifted. The laughter was still in the air, but something quieter, something more real, was there too. And I wasn't sure where it would lead.

***

The rain was drumming against the walls and windows, and a rhythmic patter echoed through the warmly lit room. Outside, the grey clouds were sombre, looming heavily over the castle. The distant rumble of thunder shook the glass. I pulled my plaid tighter around me, feeling the chill sneak through the walls.

The room was lit with candles flickering against the rich tapestries on the stone walls. The hearth cracked as drops of water fell into the coals.

Niamh was standing near the window, looking into the distance. "Ah, *Scathach.*" The glass clouded as she spoke the legendary warrior's name.

"The shadowy one, the auld ones called her. A master of combat, teacher of heroes, and guardian of secrets from long ago. Her fortress of stone and shadows was hidden behind the misty mountains, beyond the giant's home. The air hummed with magic, and the land was alive. Many travelled across lands and seas to seek her out, yearning for her wisdom and skills, but few were able to endure the trials she set before them. She was no ordinary teacher; she taught them the skills and knowledge of their weapons, but also gave them riddles and challenges that would test their very souls within. She forged warriors from the essence of the land itself. Starting with the basics of stance and footwork, she taught them the importance of balance, fluidity of body, mimicking the land, grounding oneself to the soft earth, and bridging the connection to the land.

Her weaponry was an art, her swords gleamed like stars and sunlight, and the steel became alive in her grasp. A true warrior never strikes from anger; instead, they calculate each blow, each movement becoming a dance.

She would set riddles that tested wit and puzzles to prompt quick thinking, believing a warrior's mind must be as sharp as their swords. Honour, loyalty, trust, she reminded them, were never given but earned. She taught them that the burdens of leadership and brute strength aren't everything, learning the ways of strategy and foresight. Each decision made would be a wave of consequences, ever-changing like the roaring seas of Skye.

Her hair and eyes were as dark as the shadows that hid her fortress."

Niamh walked slowly across the room, pushing Claire's dark braid back over her shoulder. As she approached the dark tapestry, her fingers gently traced the ruins and figures woven within.

Her voice softened, drawing us into her story. "*Scathach's* legacy is not only in her battles but the lives she touched; each warrior she trained carried a piece of her spirit within." The rain was getting heavier, almost drowning out her voice.

Marcus leaned closer, captivated by the tale. "What became of those who failed her trials?" His voice was low, as if afraid to disrupt the sacredness of the tale.

The candlelight was flickering, casting shadows that danced along the walls. Niamh paused, her eyes glimmering with mystery. "Some of those who still lived returned home, their hearts and spirits heavy with failure. Others, despite their failure, found their way to greatness inspired by Scathach's legend. She had taught them resilience, the importance of rising after each fall; those who persevered learned to embrace their own weaknesses and turn them into strengths."

Niamh pointed to a particular tapestry in the room. "This one here shows *Cu Chulainn*, Scathach's most known student. He faced unimaginable trials and challenges, yet through her guidance, she transformed him from a boy into a legend. Those descended from her line still to this day teach her ways. What I believe made her remarkable was that she understood that true strength comes from within." She placed her hand across her chest, eyes closed as she nodded her head. "That a warrior's path is not only marked by their victories but by the choices they make along the way and the lives they touch."

"And did Scathach have no fear?" Claire asked, her voice an eerie whisper through the room. Niamh smiled as she opened her eyes.

"Even the strongest warrior has fears, *mo nighean*. It is how we face that fear that is important. Scathach faced the many shadows of her past. It is said that she once stood on the edge of a cliff overlooking the sea, contemplating whether the sacrifices she had made and the lives she had taken had been worth it. But she embraced those fears and used them to fuel her strength."

Niamh gazed out the window, the rain blurring the mountains in the distance. "Just as Scathach did long ago, Brian teaches his students that fear can be a guide rather than a hindrance. To harness this fear, to let it flow through them, becoming a strength. This is part of the journey to become a true Scathach Warrior."

I looked at the tapestries, warriors and battles woven through the walls, each telling a tale.

"This is why we continue to tell her story, to remember even in the darkest shadows, there is always light. We must embrace our weaknesses and fears, overcome challenges, and become the legendary warriors of our own tales."

"What was it like, training under her?" I asked softly, wanting to know more about the woman behind the legend.

Thunder rumbled again, shaking the castle walls. Goosebumps covered my skin, and the door creaked open. The icy breeze blew out the candles. A tall, dark figure stood in the doorway, water plastering dark hair to his face, dripping from his cloak, pooling on the floor. His face was obscured by shadows in the doorway.

The sound of glass smashed onto the stone floor below, and a small squeak came from Claire. I reached for my dagger, feeling the warm comfort from the cool handle.

A flash of lightning illuminated his face; sharp features and piercing blue eyes stared back at us.

"*Ifrin,* really, Brian, did ye have to scare me half to death?" Niamh called across the room.

"Sorry, lass, I came to see if you lot were coming to dinner. I was hoping you could sing or tell a ghost story or two. By the look on your faces, you have started without me." Brian began to laugh, deep and warm. Niamh grabbed her papers and slapped them across his shoulders. He kissed her hand, then walked out of the room.

"Aye, well. Off with ye lot before all the warm food is eaten. We will continue in the daylight, I think."

***

As I walked into the courtyard, I could see Mal and Brian standing in the middle by the well. The six of us made our way over. "We thought we'd give ye a challenge today, a bit of fun," Malcolm said, grinning as he pushed his dark hair out of his eyes.

"In pairs, you will be given clues to unravel. Each challenge you complete, you will find an item. If someone has been there before and found it, it will not be there. So be precise, clever, and quick," Brian said. "Right, Marcus and Sean, you will be first, make your way over to the stables and begin."

"You lot needn't bother, we'll be finished before you start." The two boys walked away laughing.

"Liam and Claire, you're next."

Great, that left me stuck with Tommy.

Claire walked away, looking at me with sorry eyes. Malcolm looked at me with a big grin, holding back laughter. Clearly, I was making an amusing face.

"Well, I guess that leaves us, *my lady.*" Tommy pushed past, grabbing a pack and flask.

"Ye have the whole day, if it's too late to make your way back, make camp, there is some food and water in your packs," Brian said.

The stables were a short walk from the castle, and the smell of horses and hay filled my nose as we walked inside. Both of our horses were saddled and ready; a scroll lay on the rafter. Written in Auld Eire.

"Find the bridge where the Red and Black meet."

"Easy, MacLeod's bridge, the Cuillin ranges are on both sides," I said. Climbing atop my mare. I kicked off, not waiting for my partner. As I rode, he caught up.

"Ye know we're meant to work together," I called, but he only laughed, his golden hair whipped by the wind as he kicked his horse into a gallop. "Aye, a race it is."

The wind was whipping through my hair as I urged my mare to catch him. "You will need more than that to beat me!" I yelled. The thrill of the race ignited within and I was laughing as I rode. My horse's powerful legs pounded against the earth, and we rolled through the lush landscape, wildflowers swaying in the breeze. I could see the distant peaks of the Cuillin ranges rising majestically above the greens of the glens. We rode through the glen, twisting around the loch, water shimmering and reflecting the bright sky above. My heart was racing with exhilaration as I could see the bridge ahead.

"Over there!" he was yelling out. "Aye, I see."

The ancient stones arched gracefully across the stream running from the loch. He reached the bridge seconds before me. As we ran to the top of the bridge, he grabbed the scroll jammed into the stone crevice.

Standing on top of the bridge, the Red Cuillins were clear, standing out against the green glens; distantly, the Black Cuillins towered over them; they looked to be joined, though in truth they were very far apart, close but never meeting. But, in this spot, they seemingly crossed paths for just a moment.

"What does it say?" I asked impatiently as he read.

"If you give me more than a bee's arse to look I'd tell ye."

"A bee's arse, really?" I was bursting with laughter. He was trying to be serious as he read, holding back a smile.

"They have hidden something up high, in the tallest of the beech—I reckon we're going to the beech woods, there is a small opening with a verra tall tree."

Our horses were drinking in the creek, so we took a moment to fill our flasks before heading off. We rode fast through the meadows deep into the island, and pine woods began surrounding us.

"Are ye sure this is the way?" I asked.

"Aye, possibly, I cannot remember exactly."

He stopped turning his horse around.

"Possibly, Tommy, you *eejit*, we've been riding for hours."

"Yeah, well, it looks a bit different from down here, alright."

"What's that supposed to mean?"

"Nothing, it just looks different, alright."

I shook my head. "Right, there is a loch over there, let's go back towards it. If it's the old beech wood, I remember it being not far from a loch—maybe that's it."

We rode in silence to the loch. We followed its creek as it headed to the small gap between two rock faces. As we made our way through, the beech trees began to branch out.

"See, I was taking us the right way. If we follow the creek, we'll end up in the clearing." He turned his head behind and winked. He had no idea where we were and got lucky. I shook my head, rolling my eyes and followed him.

The beech wood was dense; there was only enough room to file through in a line, and the birds were loud over our heads, whistling to one another. I saw a rabbit run through the bushes below. The canopy above let the warm light through. As we went further in, the light became brighter, the canopy thinner, before the trees spread out into an opening—circling around, tall and wide. One was left in the middle of the opening, higher than the others. We left the horses to forage and made our way to the centre.

Up high above in the tree was a dagger, its end catching the sun's light. The lowest branch was at least twice my height. How were we meant to reach it? Surely they didn't expect us to get it out.

"Ok, if I run, I could stab my dirk in and lift myself," Tommy said, head looking up at the tree. "Give me a boost up from here instead—I think I can reach," Tommy said, his eyes fixed on the branch high above.

"I can't lift you, have you seen you? You're huge!" I squinted up. "Anyway, you won't swing far enough to grab it. We could build a ladder, but it'll take too long."

"Then it's you that'll have to climb."

"Me?"

"Aye." He walked over to the tree, knees down and arms up. "Climb away."

I reluctantly walked towards him "Well, it can't be too difficult if Mal and Brian climbed."

He chuckled. "Right, up ye get."

I put my foot on his thigh, and he leaned his back against the tree. I tried to grab hold of the bark, but there was nothing. I was on my toes, reaching above. His hands grabbed my legs. "Higher, Alix." He lifted me, moving away from the trunk so I could lean out. I grabbed a small broken branch and, losing my grip, I fell forward. He had a grip of my legs, my body bent over his shoulder.

"*Ifrin*, stand still, will ye, pull me back!" I shouted, half laughing, half embarrassed. My heart was racing as I stared at the ground below.

"I just stopped ye fat arse from falling and that's the thanks I get?" He was teasing, his laughter ringing in my ears.

"Fat arse! Fat arse!" I was wiggling, trying to pull myself up and back over. I used my hands to grip his back and climb backwards, pushing myself up. I could feel his muscles tense, strong through his shirt. His fingers dug into my calves as he held on.

"Stop wiggling!" Tommy growled through gritted teeth. "You're going to make me drop us!"

"Then pull me up!" I shot back, nearly losing my grip. His hand slipped, but then he reached again, this time with more care, and grabbed my thigh, lifting me higher. I could feel the warmth of his hand through the material of my pants, and I steadied myself against him. He released one hand, and his other grasped my thigh, pulling me closer. As I slid down his body, his grip tightened around my waist, the heat of his touch making me feel more aware of the closeness. "Oi," I said playfully, whacking him on the head as I regained my balance. He let go, and I slid down the rest of the way, shaking my head. "Next time, a heads-up before a lift would be great."

He released me, and I took a step back, shaking my head with a smile. Our eyes met, and for a moment, the world around us faded, the evening light casting a soft glow around us. "You need to get higher," he said, a playful challenge in his tone.

"Fine! Just don't drop me!" I retorted, a mix of excitement and nervousness rushing through me. "One more go, but this time, be ready to catch me if I fall!"

With a deep breath, I stepped up into his cuffed hands, and I held onto his shoulders. He nodded. "Ready."

"Aye."

He lifted me as high as he could, and I reached out my fingers, able to touch the lowest branch. I got a grip, and I pulled myself up; his hands held my feet as they were moving.

"Get them on my shoulders."

I tried to look down without letting go, and I moved them with his hands guiding. Found them. His hands gripped my calves, tender but tight. I wasn't going anywhere. I felt him breathe out.

"I've got a good grip. Can you give me a push?"

His hands moved down, grabbing my ankles.

"Ready, three, two, one!" He lifted me, and I pulled my body up and on top of the branch. My heart was pounding.

Puffing, I looked down. Tommy's hair was damp with sweat. He brushed his hands through it, looking up at me. "Easy." I winked. He shook his head, smiling.

I wiggled towards the centre and stood up. The trunk was easier to grab here. "One step at a time, MacLeod," I whispered to myself. With each careful movement, I made myself higher, reaching out to pull myself up each branch, testing the weight. The afternoon breeze was cool, brushing through the branches as I climbed. There was a sense of magic in the air, as though it was steadying me as I climbed.

I reached the branch where the dagger was stabbing into the trunk. Looking out, it was beautiful. I could see the rolling hills, the shimmering lochs, and the green glens. "It's breathtaking up here!"

"Aye, how about you keep ye eyes and your hands on the tree instead?" he yelled.

I turned to grip the dagger. It was old, almost ancient. The sap of the tree had coated the blade, holding it in place. I gripped it with both hands, but it would not budge. I was pushing, pulling with all my strength.

"Will ye be careful!"

"I can't. Get. It!" I was grinding my teeth as I yelled.

I pulled out my smaller knife and chiselled at the dried sap. Breaking it off slowly. The breeze was cooling me as sweat dripped down my face. At last, I had removed it all. I dug deeper around the site, flicking bark away. Both my hands gripped the handle. "COME ON!" I pulled it out, losing balance. I dropped to the branch below, catching myself. The dagger went flying.

"ALIX!"

It felt like a gust of wind had caught me as I fell. Holding me tight as I pulled myself up. "I'm alright, I'm coming down."

I took each branch down carefully and slowly, and it suddenly felt a lot higher than climbing up. It was beginning to drizzle. I got to the last branch. "Well, here goes nothing."

"Alix, wait!" Tommy called out, beginning to brace himself for what he could see I was about to do.

I swung my legs over, ready to drop down gently, but as I let go, my foot slipped on the bark, now damp with rain. Instead of the smooth descent I had planned, I tumbled down, arms swinging as I fell straight towards Tommy. Just as I was about to crash, he lunged forward, catching me by the waist, pulling me tight against him. His grip was firm, almost too firm, like he was afraid I would slip between his fingers. In the chaos of impact, we lost our balance, and with a thud, we crashed into a heap on the ground. We were a tangled mess, breath knocked out of both of us. My heart was hammering in my chest, and it wasn't just from the fall. He had caught me, and I now lay on top of him, wrapped tightly in his arms. The warmth of his body pressed against mine, making everything feel sharper, more vivid. His fingers dug into my sides, steadying me, but there was a hesitation in his touch—as if he didn't quite know whether to let go or hold on longer.

"Alix," he said, his voice low, a little strained. His breath was warm against my ear, and I could hear his heart racing as fast as mine. "Are you alright?"

I blinked, trying to shake the moment from my head, trying to ignore the way his hands lingered a fraction too long on my waist. The dampness of the rain and sweat mixed, and the feeling of his body against mine was unsettling in a way I hadn't expected.

"Yeah, I'm fine," I muttered, though I wasn't sure if I was talking about the fall or something else entirely. I finally pushed myself away from him, the weight of the moment fading slightly as I steadied myself on the ground. He let go slowly, as if unwilling to fully release the tension that had built between us.

"Next time," I said, forcing a light tone, "maybe a little heads-up before the lift would be nice." Tommy grinned, but there was a flicker of something in his eyes that made me pause.

"Aye, I'll work on that." His voice was quieter now, but there was still that teasing edge, even if it wasn't as sharp as before. He turned his attention back to the tree, but I caught the way his gaze lingered on me for a heartbeat too long. I could feel the weight of it—like the rain had stopped for a moment, and the world around us held its breath. I swallowed hard, hoping I hadn't said too much, or worse, that he hadn't noticed the change in my voice.

"Maybe I'll leave the tree-climbing to you next time."

Tommy smirked, but there was a softness behind it now, something a little more vulnerable beneath the teasing. It made the air feel warmer, even though the rain was still falling.

We lay there, both looking up at the tree. I began laughing.

"What is so funny?" he asked, still winded.

"We scared the horses, and I lost the bloody dagger."

"*Iffrin.*" He was laughing too now, deep and beautiful. Facing the sky, the sun was poking out, and the rain was falling onto our faces. I turned my head to look at him. Emerald eyes were sparkling in the light, his hair was soaked, and he pushed it out of his face, one arm resting above his head. Droplets were landing on his face, glittering in the sunlight. He turned his head to face mine, and he smiled, reaching out. "You've got half the tree in your hair." He grabbed some leaves out of my hair, throwing them away, and we both laughed.

I sat up, brushing the dirt off my hands, and scanned the clearing. The horses were long gone. "Well, we'll need to find shelter soon. At least we've got our swords," I said, trying to sound more practical than I felt.

Tommy grinned. "Aye, come on, then." He picked up both our cloaks and draped them over his arm. The evening air had already turned cool, and the promise of rain loomed heavy. We walked deeper into the beech woods, the creek babbling nearby. My thoughts were still on the fall when something caught my eye—something glimmering in the grass. I bent down, chuckling. "Bloody dagger."

**

We made camp under a rocky overhang, sheltered on either side by trees and ferns. We set about making a small fire as it was getting dark and cold. I turned the dagger over in my hand, its ancient metal gleaming faintly in the firelight. It had been preserved within the tree for centuries, its markings barely visible beneath layers of time.

Tommy reached into his coat. He pulled out a flask, and after taking a sip, he threw it over. I passed him the blade as I drank. Whisky, warm and bold, wouldn't fill our bellies, but it would make us forget them for a while. "Have ye ever seen anything like it before?" I asked, my voice quiet against the soft crackle of the fire.

Tommy turned the dagger slowly in the flickering firelight, shadows dancing across his face, deepening the lines of concentration. "No, I haven't," he muttered, his brow furrowing. "It's very old... too old. But I don't think this is what we were supposed to find. We might have gone to the wrong spot, or maybe someone's already been here."

The night closed in around us, the woods quietened with only the occasional hoot from an owl.

"Try and sleep, I'll take the first watch," Tommy said.

"Thanks."

I lay down beside the fire, the warmth of it soothing my tired limbs. But as my eyes drifted shut, the image of a golden warrior flashed before my mind, lingering even in my dreams.

***

I woke to the warmth of an extra cloak draped over me, the chill of the morning air brushing against my skin. Tommy lay nearby, his back leaning against the rocky wall, still fast asleep. The sky was drizzling, but the sun was beginning to break through the canopy. There was no sign of the horses nearby.

We decided to follow the creek further west, hoping it would lead us closer to Dunscaith. Without the horses, the journey back would take much longer, but it was our only option. We found a pass through the woods, opening before a loch. The water was sweet and cool. Continuing, we headed towards the trees for shade, making our way through ferns, wildflowers, and trees. We climbed the rolling hills and hoped they were the ones close to the castle. Looking out into the distance, I could see two horses grazing in the clearing ahead. "Look." I pointed at them.

"Quick, run, we can't let them get away," Tommy said.

I darted forward, Tommy right behind me, his footsteps pounding the earth as we raced through the underbrush, the sound of our feet crashing through the leaves and twigs echoing in the quiet morning. I turned around the bend, and the ground gave way. I felt my feet slipping as I tumbled down the hill. "Tommy!" I screamed, my voice high with panic as I felt myself helplessly sliding faster.

"Al—" Before he could finish my name, I heard crashing behind me. He had lost his balance too and was sliding down the slope behind me. We slid and tumbled in wild abandon, limbs flailing in every direction, our laughter mingling with cries of surprise. The world spun as we collided with the cold, sticky mud below, the splatter of it filling the air. I lay there covered in mud, laughing and gasping for air when I saw a large mass coming towards me, covered in mud and plants. Tommy fell into the mud pool next to me. His face was covered, his emerald eyes shining through, his hair matted with sticks and leaves, and his clothes were filthy.

I pushed myself upright, my knees sinking back into the mud as I squelched toward him. The wet earth was cold and sticky, but I couldn't stop laughing. "You've got half the forest in ye hair, lad!"

His eyes bulged and his face beamed into a white smile. In an instant, he grabbed my arms and pulled me back toward him, throwing me into the mud pool with a grin of triumph on his face. We were laughing hysterically like pigs in actual mud, covered head to toe, looking like something out of a farmer's field.

We eventually managed to squelch our way out, making our way into the open meadow. The horses had run away again. I reached into my pocket, pulling out a somewhat clean kerchief, wiping my face as much as possible. I then reached out, gently wiping the mud free from Tommy's face. His skin felt warm beneath my touch, and for a moment, the world seemed to slow. He smiled, eyes lighting up. "Thank you, *my lady,*" he said, his voice soft, but with a hint of something deeper beneath the teasing.

***

We walked into Dunscaith late in the afternoon, the courtyard filled with people, including the family. The courtyard fell silent for a moment. Eyes turned toward us, some widening in disbelief, others holding back smiles. I caught Claire's gaze, her eyes growing wide, as she clapped a hand over her mouth to stifle a laugh. Malcolm's sharp eyes recognised us first as he burst out in laughter. Everyone was laughing as we made our way towards the well.

"Ooooh no, I don't think so. Both of ye round to the stables. Get that mud off before you come traipsing through my halls." Niamh was standing hands on her hips at the top of the stairs, but she was trying very hard not to laugh.

As we walked past Malcolm and Brian, I shoved the mud-caked dagger into Malcolm's hand. "Yeah, yeah, laugh it up, brother. Be a good laddie and clean this up for me." I kept walking, boots squelching as I continued to the stable well.

The stable lads looked as though they saw banshees coming through the gates; they were as pale as snow as we walked towards the well. One of them nervously scratched the back of his neck. "Uh, do ye need help with... that?" he asked, glancing at the mud caked all over us. The two of us burst into laughter.

After what felt like hours of scrubbing the mud off, we finally managed to get ourselves somewhat presentable. My boots still squelched with every step, but I couldn't help but chuckle at the absurdity of it all. Tommy, on the other hand, had taken the 'muddy warrior' look to a whole new level. We were a far cry from the proud adventurers we had been earlier, but at least we weren't dripping anymore. We'd cleaned most of our boots and clothes before walking to the top of the stairs for Niamh's inspections.

"Right, I suppose that will do. Straight to yer chambers, I've got hot baths and a lot of soap waiting for you both. Do not come down to dinner until you're all clean, or it's you who will be cleaning the floors."

"Thank you," I smiled.

Tommy grabbed Niamh in his arms, spinning her around with the force of a gust of wind. "Thank ye, Auntie!" he said, planting a kiss on her cheek before running off. Niamh, caught by surprise, let out a startled laugh.

"Thomas Patrick, you better run, lad!" she called after him, trying—and failing—to hide the smile tugging at her lips.

Tommy shot me a grin as he raced up the steps, and I couldn't help but laugh. Niamh, now wiping mud off her dress, chuckled softly under her breath. "If ye don't hurry, lad, I'll put ye to work cleaning the kitchens next!"

***

Over the following days, I continued to wash mud from my hair, wondering if I ever would be rid of it. Claire and I managed to sneak away after morning training for a ride out to the caves. There were hot springs nestled deep within. The ride out was peaceful, not far from Dunscaith. As we walked through the entrance, the ceiling came alive with light worms and fireflies, casting a magical shimmer across the cavern.

Stepping into the spring, the warm water greeted me, easing the tension of my aching muscles. Cool drops of water fell from the ceiling, sending chills down my spine. It felt easy here, peaceful and calm, a stark contrast from the last few weeks. Claire and I talked about everything and nothing.

I rested my head along the pool's edge, the stone cool against my neck, closing my eyes. For the first time in days, I felt truly relaxed. The scent of the earth and mineral-rich water filled the air, making me forget about the world outside the rock walls.

***

We returned later in the afternoon and got ready for dinner. The array of food was abundant and delicious, and the flowing ale was well needed. Brian had his favourite whisky out, and everything seemed normal again. The fiddle was playing, and Malcolm asked Claire to dance. With such excitement, Claire jumped up, knocking a plate to the ground—a bit of chaos helpfully cleaned up by Brian's dogs lounging beside his chair. Claire and Malcolm joined others as they danced to the bard's music. They were a beautiful pair as they danced together effortlessly. Malcolm came to live here permanently at eighteen after he had been fostered here at fourteen. Claire was ten and became a little sister to him. He cared for her as he did for me, and it was a comfort to both when he stayed.

The hall came alive with the sounds of fiddles and the singing that seemed to gallop through the air. Many were dancing, Marcus had grabbed Niamh and was turning her around the room, Brian was laughing and reached a hand for Grannie. I was sitting next to Liam, who provided some interesting conversation about hunting on his family's lands. I noticed as he watched Claire with admiring interest. She was quite beautiful, her hair still in a crown. She had placed some flowers we had found near the stables in her hair; her humble dress floated around her—a fairy princess indeed. A long arm reached between me and Liam, placing a glass of whisky down, making a deep noise in his throat. I looked up. Those beautiful emerald eyes met mine.

"My Lady Alix, would you like to dance?"

His voice carried a playful note, teasing me as always, but there was something softer underneath, a hint of something deeper.

"Only if you do not tread on my new boots."

"How you got boots under your dress without my auntie noticing is beyond me." His smile was warm, eyes glimmering in the firelight.

I shook my head and laughed. "Aye, and if you bring them to her attention, I shall enlighten her that it was you who took her whisky."

His hand was held out with a low bow. "A dance would be my honour," he said.

I placed my hand in his, and a spark jumped. Our eyes met. He secured my hand before I could let go and took me to the dance floor. The music was loud and wonderful. The melody took me over hills of heather and out to sea, it quickened and slowed, and occasionally the bard would sing in Gaelic, or now what I learnt was Auld Eire.

He was elegant in his tunic, embroidered with a silver thread along the edge, his golden hair pushed out of his eyes. It was shorter than most, neat and to his ears. The dark of the tunic complemented his eyes. My dress, though more than fine, made me feel underdressed; my hair flowed long down my back, copper and silver catching the firelight. Of course, Tommy could dance well. I had seen him with a sword, like our dance of steel in the forest; we were also evenly matched when it came to this unfamiliar dance. He turned us around and I realised I had let him lead. The music bounced off the ancient walls, walls that had seen so many tales, both old and new. It held our clans' secrets and future. How many of my line had danced in this hall? The lifting melody enchanted the dance, and I could not help but smile as we turned and flowed through the floor for hours. Tommy was smiling; mischief twinkled in those eyes.

"I thought I asked you to do something with that wild hair of yours; it's very distracting."

"You said at training, I am currently at dinner. Well, dancing but not training. If you have the focus of a butterfly, then that is your problem and not mine."

I smiled and he laughed. "Aye, I guess it is, *my lady*— it is quite distracting, like a *Sidhe Draroi* whispering through a forest."

"Aye, and what's that, some kind of demon in Eire?"

"I guess, what you call a tree nymph here, a fairy spirit with flowing hair in the winds."

I quickly turned my head to hide my smile. "Away with your nonsense, that Eire trickery will not work on me."

"Now, *my lady*, you're the one running round with the distracting hair, not I."

The music swirled around us, and with every turn, my thoughts became a little clearer, a little less distracted by the crowd, the laughter, and the noise. Tommy's grip on my hand was steady, confident now, and though his words were still light-hearted, I noticed the way he looked at me—the way he said "my lady" with more weight than he had before.

It wasn't teasing anymore. It wasn't an offhand remark. The way he said it now—it felt like a term of endearment, one that he didn't even realise he was giving me. Every time he called me "my lady," it held a little more care, a little more affection, and I wasn't sure if he knew that, or if he was aware of how the simple words made my heart flutter, just a little.

We continued to dance, the rhythm of the music filling the space between us, and the more we moved, the more I felt it—his presence next to me, his hand on mine, guiding me effortlessly. I wasn't sure when it had happened, but somewhere between the twirls and the laughter, Tommy's teasing had melted away, leaving something tender in its place.

The melody slowed again to a song I did not know. A beautiful voice sang: Claire and Niamh were seated at the dais, Niamh playing the lute. It was beautiful and old, they were singing in auld Eire, I could not gasp all the words. We stopped dancing to listen, but Tommy's hand was still interlaced with mine. He leaned down and, with a whisper, interpreted the song for me.

He said the song was called *"Eleanór a Rún."*

It began gently and the melody drifted like the wind through heather, they were singing with such emotion in their voices; beautiful was not enough to describe it.

Mo ghrá den chéad fhéachaint thú,
'Eleanóir, a rún,
Is ortsa a bhím a' smaoineamh,
tráth a mbím ar mo shuaimh,
Mo ghrá den tsaol thú,
ó mo chéad searc,
is tú is deise ná ban Éireann,
'S a bhruinnillín deas óg,

Is tú is deise, is milse póg,
Ach chúns a mhairfeadsa beo,
beidh gean a'm ort,
Mar is deas mar a sheolfainn
na gamhna leat,
'Eleanóir, a rún.
'S bhí bua aici go meallfadh
sí na héanlaith ón gcrann,
'S bhí bua eile aici go dtóigfeadh
sí an corp fuar ón mbás,
'S bhí bua eile aici nach ndéarfaidh mé mar
'sí grá mo chroí is ó mo chéad searc,
'S a bhruinnillín deas óg,
Is tú is deise, is milse póg,
Ach chúns a mhairfeadsa beo,
beidh gean a'm ort,
Mar is deas mar a sheolfainn na gamhna leat,
'Eleanóir, a rún.

Tommy's voice was barely a whisper in my ear, his breath warm against my cold skin.

"Eleanor, a Run, my darling Eleanor,

They sing of a forbidden love.

He whispers her name, *Eleanor,* like a prayer. They were separated, and with each beat of his heart and every breath, he feels her, longs for her.

He hopes she will come back, that the deep love they have for one another will be strong enough to stand time. Like the ever-flowing rivers, and the stars shining bright in the night sky.

Their love will endure all and live through all those who hear their tale."

I watched as Brian reached out a hand to Niamh and kissed it. And as the fiddle began again, Claire sang a song of joy and happiness. The music continued to swirl around us, the dance floor became a blur of revolving bodies, and happiness and laughter filled the air. I stood still watching the shadows. The song that had just played—the haunting melody of "Eleanór a Rún"—had stirred something deep inside me, a sorrow I had not expected to feel. The moment the last note lingered in the air, Tommy glanced at me, his expression softening.

"Alix, I feel I've had a turn. Will you accompany me out for some air?"

I nodded, blinking away the tears that threatened to fall, my heart heavy with the weight of unspoken thoughts. The song had reminded me too much of my parents—separated, longing for each other. The soft glow of the hall felt too bright now, too full of life. I turned slowly, careful not to meet Tommy's gaze, and noticed then that I hadn't let go of his hand. And nor had he let go of mine.

We stepped outside the hall, and a cool breeze wrapped around us, a welcome contrast to the warmth inside. We walked the corridor, the sounds of laughter and music dulling behind us as we made our way towards the parapet. I could feel the weight of the moment—of everything unspoken—settling between us. We ascended a narrow staircase that led to a sheltered parapet, and the icy wind from the loch greeted us. The dark outline of the Cuillins stood tall against the night, their peaks kissed by the stars, which shone bright and endless, offering a strange kind of peace.

Tommy must have grabbed his cloak when we left the hall. He let go of my hand, wrapping the warm cloak around me. He gently adjusted the clasp, his fingers lingering on the fabric before gently cupping my face, wiping away the stray tears that had fallen in silence. His touch was warm, unexpected, yet soothing and safe. I found myself leaning into his touch, grateful for the comfort he offered.

"Are you alright, *my lady*?" he said in a gentle, kind tone, like one you would use to speak to a startled horse.

I nodded. "Aye, thank ye for your kindness."

"It's no trouble, lass. Here, let's sit a while, shall we? Until you are ready to go back down, ey."

We sat with our backs against the stone of the turret, looking out across the loch, the stars so bright they seemed to be holding the world together. The silence between us was peaceful, but my heart felt heavy. It was cold, though the cloak was warm; a shiver ran through me. Tommy placed his arm around me, drawing me closer. "Lay your head, lass, it's alright."

I let myself lean against him, my head resting against his chest. The rhythm of his heartbeat was steady, like a quiet drum keeping time with mine. As I looked up at the stars bright in the sky, silent tears came, quiet and unexpected. I cried for those whose love survived but could not be together, for all the secrets I had just learnt, but most of all, I cried for my mother. And as I cried, Tommy held me close, one hand softly patting my hair.

He whispered, looking out to the sky, my head resting in his chest, held tight, heart beating in time to mine.

"You are alive,

You are safe,

You are whole,

a chuisle mo chroi, my lady."

Chapter Five

WE SPENT THE NEXT THREE WEEKS regimentally waking at dawn to train in the yard, with broad swords, knives, arrows, strength, and hand-to-hand. The afternoons we spent with Niamh. She taught us histories of the land, tales of the fairy folk, those from her homeland and of ours. She sang the songs of auld, taught us how to read and write the auld languages. It was exhausting and some nights I would bypass the main hall, wanting solitude, grabbing something from the kitchen and heading to my chambers or the parapet. There were so many thoughts running through my head: betrayal, lies, secrets, trust, understanding, magic, joy, warmth, pain, sorrow, loss, completeness, and a sense that everything was going to come crashing down around me.

We were in the training yard. I had been partnered with Sean, who, although strong, was not very quick, and if I kept my speed up, then he couldn't catch me. It became easier to overcome. Claire was sparing with Marcus, but her mind was in her books. She had her face screwed up—something must have been bothering her and she was trying to figure it out. Brian noticed and halted everyone.

"Time for a break, ey, Marcus, I want you to spar against Malcolm, give him everything you've got. Everyone else, take notes."

Marcus grabbed his double swords and headed to the ring. Malcolm also had his swords strapped against his back in a cross. He did not unsheathe them. I had not seen my brothers spar against one another in years; Marcus idolised Malcolm, hence the double swords, and spent as much time as he could travelling to Skye to spend time with him. They had a similar sense of humour and rebellion that our eldest brother, Callum, did not have. Marcus, cocky, had his swords ready. Both brothers were tall, well over six feet and strongly built. Folks would not want to meet either one in a brawl.

Malcolm unsheathed his swords, and they began. The clanging of steel on steel rang through the court. Malcolm didn't hold back, but Marcus was becoming stronger; he was matching Malcolm move for move. He'd spent years watching and following Malcolm, and this was his chance to shine. But there was a reason Malcolm was training to be a weapons master; he became the blades; he was the weapon. Within a few minutes of having fun with Marcus, he had him disarmed and lying face down in the dirt without barely breaking a sweat.

"Right, who's next? Alix and Tommy, keep your sniping remarks to yourselves. I want a battle of strength, pick your weapons, let's go," Brian said.

I grabbed my sword from Claire and sheathed my dirk in my thigh. I had all my *sgian-dubh;* I was ready. Tommy had his sword. We hadn't spoken since that night—the night I danced with him, only to fall apart. A nod here, a glance there, but no words. I had stained his shirt with my weakness, let him see the cracks in my armour. I had shown him too much, and now he kept his distance. He was cold, detached. Perhaps it was because I had revealed the parts of myself I'd fought so hard to hide—the vulnerability, the uncertainty. The kindness he once offered felt like a cruel joke now. I wasn't worthy of it. I wasn't worthy of *him*. But I would show him otherwise today.

Well, Tommy, I think it is time once again to kick your arse into the ground.

I took my stance and he took his. Though taller than most women, I was still not close to his height; I met his shoulders and had to look up. But I refused to look into those eyes; I couldn't bear the embarrassment.

"On three, two, one!" Malcolm called.

It began, steel on steel, with grace and precision. The steel echoed like thunder across the court with each blow. I turned, meeting his blade with mine, and sparks flew out on each meet. Odd, it must be the sunlight. Without time to contemplate this, we continued. He came above with a powerful strike. I met it and deflected. The dance in the forest was naught to this. We were serious, and there was unfinished business.

Our breathing became one, synchronised with each swing of the blade. Our feet mirrored each other. His heart beat loudly in my ears, a steady drum, and for a moment, I could almost feel it in my chest—matching the pounding of my own heart. Each move was calculated, testing for weaknesses—physical and emotional. He knew me too well, and I knew him just as much. This wasn't just a fight; it was a test of everything we hid from each other. The yard was silent, the only sound was the occasional grunt or clang of steel.

He pushed me back across the yard, driving me toward the well. I climbed onto it, seizing the opportunity. I sprang off the stone edge, my muscles burning with the effort. The air rushed past me, cold against my skin as I flipped through the air, sword raised high. I felt the weight of the blade in my hand, coming down with full force, aimed for his chest. But Tommy was ready. His eyes locked onto mine, calculating.

With a practised move, he parried my strike, the blades locking together in a violent clang. Sparks flew from the force of it, the sound ringing through the yard, and the hot sting of the impact numbed my hands.

I knew I couldn't win with swords—not against Tommy's speed and strength. In one fluid motion, I tossed my sword to Marcus, the blade catching the sunlight as it spun through the air. I drew my dirk from its sheath, feeling the weight of the small, deadly blade in my hand. Tommy's eyes flickered toward his own weapons—he'd sheathed his sword and now held a knife of his own. Sweat stung my eyes, and I could taste the salt on my lips, the effort of the fight burning through every muscle. This was it. Close combat. No more distance, no more games.

I reached for one of my sgian-dubh, feeling the coolness of the steel against my palm. My movements were swift, precise. But Tommy was faster. He disarmed me with a flick of his wrist, sending my dirk skidding across the ground.

I wasn't going to stop though, not now.

He threw his dirk aside, his hands ready, waiting. He wasn't attacking anymore. No, now he was playing defence—blocking, dodging, disarming me one knife at a time. Every time I lost a weapon, a knot twisted tighter in my chest. He was too good, too quick. But I wasn't done. Not yet. I still had five knives, maybe three now, but each one was as sharp as my resolve.

We kept going, and the crowd was quiet. I could feel the eyes of those watching. Claire would take a deep breath each moment one of us should have been harmed. Amazingly, we had not drawn blood. Malcolm and Brian were watching with interest, finding ways to critique and improve, no doubt.

We continued, and I was down to one knife. I kicked up and got my leg between his, but he twisted, blocking my knife and grabbing my leg. We landed on the ground, me on top. I had a knife to his throat. He smiled, that stupid, wide grin. His legs lifted and wrapped around my waist. He flipped me, and I was pinned. His weight and height completely stopped me from moving. I was breathing heavily, and so was he, my arms above my head, trapped under his; he had flicked away my last knife.

I closed my eyes, the weight of his body pressing me into the dirt, his chest heaving against mine with each laboured breath. His strength was a crushing force, unrelenting, but it wasn't the weight of his body that held me down—it was the weight of his presence. His hands were firm on my wrists, his body pressing into me, and I couldn't escape. Yet I could feel the softness in his voice, almost like a whisper just for me.

"Look at me," he said, his words slipping through the chaos of my thoughts. "*My lady*, open your eyes and look at me." I clenched my jaw, refusing to give in. But his voice, his presence—it broke something inside me. "*A chuisle mo chroi,* please."

I felt something shift inside me, something I had buried deep, and slowly, against my will, my eyelids fluttered open. There, so close, was his gaze—emerald eyes, flickering with sadness, regret, and something else I couldn't quite name. I felt something twist in my chest, something I had been ignoring for too long.

He lifted some weight, adjusting himself so as not to hurt me. I got my knee free and kneed him in the bollocks. I shoved him off me, breathing hard, every muscle screaming. My heart was racing, but it wasn't just from the fight. It was everything I had tried to bury and everything I had been running from. I looked at Malcolm and Brian, their eyes watching me intently. I threw my last *sgian-dubh* to the ground with a force that made it clatter across the stone.

"Seen enough?" I spat, my voice trembling with the weight of everything unsaid. Without waiting for an answer, I turned and stormed off, my boots slamming against the ground as I disappeared into the trees. Every step I took felt like I was leaving behind a part of myself. Maybe it was the part that had cared too much. Maybe it was the part that had trusted him. Either way, it was gone now.

No one followed me, and I was glad. Claire would have tried, but both Marcus and Malcolm would have pulled her back. I needed time alone. I started to run and run, paying no heed to where I was running, only that I needed to go. Tears ran down my face, my chest hurt, but I kept going. I could hear a stream trickling in the trees. I followed the noise.

The woods became thicker with beech trees, and ancient rocks covered in moss. It was peaceful, it was green, shades and shades of green. Birds sang and butterflies flew; it was beautiful. I slowed down, making it to the flowing stream. I splashed my face and drank deeply. I continued walking.

It was getting late. I could feel the summer air become cooler, and the mist began to flow in, covering my feet. I would have to camp; I was not sure where I was, and would not be able to make it back before dark. I looked around, suddenly having the feeling of being watched. I knelt at another fresh stream, listening. Something was stalking me; I could hear it even in the deep leaf matter, and it was large. *Ifrin*, the wind changed. I could smell it.

Bear.

I realised suddenly how reckless I had been. I had left the training grounds, throwing my last knife at my brother. I had no weapons. I reached into the water, grabbing at anything that I could use, a sharp stick or rock. I grabbed it, a thick stick, hopefully not too softened with age, not that I had much choice. I could hear the bear bend and begin to charge. I turned quickly, holding my stick ready to strike.

Unexpectedly, an arrow flew behind my left ear, a small gust of wind blowing my braid. The arrow hit the bear in his shoulder. He raised himself on two legs and roared.

Suddenly, a flash of gold. *"Fag bear agus imigh abhail!"* Leave and go home, bear.

Tommy's voice was calm as he stood tall as the bear, his arms out wide, right hand extended with his blade. *"Laithreach."* Immediately, the bear walked back into the trees and disappeared.

I slumped to my knees, feeling sick. Tommy waited for the bear to go before sheathing his blade. I noticed his bow was already on his back. He turned slowly.

"What the hell were you thinking! You're crazy, Alix! What were ya thinking? That's right, you weren't, you never think, you just do!" Tommy yelled.

He was angry. Well, so was I.

"Me, crazy! You're the fool who followed me. You absolute idiot, you arrogant, self-thinking, numpty bastard!" I shouted.

"Numpty? Numpty?"

"Yes, you bloody numpty bastard!" I stood, walking closer and punched him hard in the chest. "What bloody self-righteous arrogant bastard walks up to a bear for a chat! It could have killed you! Then what? Then what!"

"You're the one who came blazing like a banshee into the forest with no weapons here, Alix. No plan like a mad woman. Were you planning on getting eaten before or after the sun went down?" He was speaking through his teeth, shoulders clenched. Raging.

"I was doing fine without you. Go, leave, I don't want to look at you or talk to you, for that matter!"

He stared at me, emerald eyes glowing. Anger? I could see he was pissed, and so was I. Why was he here? He began to shake his head.

"Aye, you've made that clear this last week, lass, you can't stand to be in the same room as me. I dinna ken why, Alix?"

"Why? You tell me. You haven't spoken to me since that night when I was weak, helpless. I guess I'm some needle-pointed, spoilt princess just like you expected, ey, or is it that I'm not and I can knock you on your arse, which one? Because I can't keep up with you."

"Me? You're the one training all hours and turning the opposite way from me in the hall. I've been trying to catch you on your own for days."

The birds had gone silent. If the bear was around, all our noise would have scared him off, any wee folk or auld would have scatted too. Crazy, I'm not sure we are not.

"Alix." Tommy's voice caught in his throat, my name trembling as it left his lips. For a moment, he stood there, eyes locked on me. He opened his mouth as if to say something more, but the words wouldn't come. Instead, he stumbled a step forward, his expression cracking, like something he'd been holding back for so long was finally breaking free. I opened my mouth to speak, but he held his hand up, the slight gesture silencing me. He was trembling, I could see a rawness in his eyes—eyes that had always been so guarded, so composed. Now, they were wide with something else: pain, frustration, and helplessness.

"A chuisle mo chroi," he whispered. He took another step forward, but his legs gave way, and he dropped to his knees, his hand clutching at his chest. His face twisted with emotion, and a tremor ran through his body. "You're tearing my heart out, Alix. You don't even see it, do you? I've tried, I've tried so damn hard to be there for you... to make things easier. But you just keep pushing me away, and every time you do…"

His voice faltered, the words becoming harder to speak, his breath catching as he blinked rapidly, trying to fight back the tears that welled in his eyes.

"I don't know how much longer I can stand it, Alix," he continued, his voice barely above a whisper, but it carried the weight of everything he had been holding back. "You don't let me in. You don't let anyone in. And I…" His words trailed off, his breath shallow, like the air was too thick to breathe. Tommy's eyes searched mine—pleading, desperate, but also filled with so much hurt. "I can't fix this. I don't know how to fix this. *You're* tearing my heart out, Alix."

He sat there on the ground. The weight of his words hung between us, and suddenly the distance between us felt impossibly large. I watched his chest rise and fall with each breath, the sharp edges of his words still cutting through the silence. He wasn't looking at me now. His gaze was fixed on the ground, his hands trembling at his sides, as if even touching anything was too much.

I wanted to say something—anything—but the lump in my throat made it impossible to speak.

I took a step closer, unsure of what to do, feeling the undeniable pull to reach out. I could see how much he was hurting; my own heart was aching. Tommy—always so strong, so sure of himself—was breaking in front of me. All I could do was stare at him, my chest tightening with each shaky breath he took. He wasn't angry anymore; he was broken.

God, I was the one who'd broken him.

My heart clenched, my vision blurring as tears began to fall.

"I didn't mean to hurt you," I whispered. But the words felt hollow, weak, and I hated how powerless they sounded.

I moved forward slowly, dropping to my knees in front of him. I reached for him, unsure of what to do, but my body seemed to know what my heart couldn't express. I lowered myself until I was right there, with him, where the silence between us felt unbearably thick. *I'm sorry,* I thought, though I wasn't sure those words could ever be enough.

"I'm sorry, *a leannan*," I managed to say, my voice breaking. I felt the wetness of my tears. It wasn't just for him, but for everything I had been running from. For everything I'd pushed away.

Tommy reached up, his fingers trembling, and wiped my tears away. His touch felt like an anchor, even though he was trembling as much as I was.

"God, Alix," he muttered, his voice filled with desperation and concern. "What were you thinking? You ken how dangerous it is, and you just left… with nothing."

"I wasn't… thinking. I just needed to leave."

His head dropped to my shoulder, his body shaking as the weight of his emotions pressed him down. He was still so broken, and I didn't know what to say to fix him. But I held him close anyway.

God, I couldn't fix it. Maybe nothing could be fixed.

We were both kneeling now, the cold of the evening creeping in as the last of the daylight began to slip away. The air felt thicker somehow, growing darker, quieter.

I held him close and whispered, "Tommy."

He inhaled deeply, lifted his head, and finally looked me in the eyes. His gaze softened, though the ache was still there.

"Aye."

"I think we should leave in case the bear comes back."

"Aye," he said, voice steadying, but there was a trace of something softer, too. "No running, aye?"

I smiled weakly, the heaviness in my chest still there, but lighter now. "I can do that, aye."

He rubbed his face and then stood. "I have a pack just around here. I dropped it when I saw the bear." I followed him as we climbed over a fallen log. We grabbed the pack and kept walking; we were not going back and seemed to be going forward. I kept quiet. We walked to a clearing, and I inhaled: horses. He had followed me with a horse. He climbed onto its saddle, reaching out his hand towards me "Come, we have a little bit to ride."

We rode until we reached a small clearing, we tethered the horse and took off its saddle, neither one of us speaking. Both were silent with our own thoughts. Apart from a small bag, there wasn't much on the horse. Clearly, he'd run after me as soon as I had left the gates, grabbing the first horse and bag he saw. "We'll be safe here; it will be dark soon." His voice was quiet, soft as he walked around an old croft, hand resting on his sword hilt.

I gathered what dry kindling I could to build a fire, since it was beginning to get cooler. The spot he had found was an old ruin, a croft of some sort, old, and only a corner section of the croft remained. I built the fire close, with our backs to the corner, so we would be sheltered from the wind. There was no roof, but I did not think we would have rain tonight.

I rummaged through the bag and found an apple: dinner. To my delight, there was a small flask of whisky too. Tommy had come back with a fish, he had gutted and cleaned it, and had it hanging on a stick. He placed it over the fire to cook. We ate our fish and apple in silence, and the water from the stream was fresh and delicious.

"Thank you for before." My words caught in my throat. I didn't know what to say or where to begin. The emotions from earlier overwhelmed my mind.

He took a deep breath and slowly exhaled.

"Did I hurt ye, Alix? Is that why you ran?" his voice was barely a whisper; he was staring at the fire as he asked, avoiding my eyes.

"Aye... no. I think it was me, Tommy."

He stared at me, emerald eyes wide with confusion and hurt. He had thought he had hurt me, in the sparring or earlier, he had said he tried to find me and get me alone, and I had avoided him, ignored him. But he came anyway. Dropped everything and ran.

"I was embarrassed, Tommy. I've never cried in front of anyone. My world... It's upside down. My family has this incredible history... magic, but they kept it from us. Now there's this prophecy, this training, and I... what if I fail? What if I'm meant to do something, and I can't? What if something bad happens because of me? I don't even know what I'm doing anymore. I don't even know who I am."

I looked up at the stars shining down, pushing back the tears that welled in my eyes. Then, I looked back across the fire at Tommy. "Then you came along, and oh god, you were so kind, you made me laugh and hope, and I didn't know how to face you, and then I was so angry, and you wouldn't fight back, so I ran." I rubbed my hands over my face, then through my hair.

He stood up slowly and moved across the fire. He knelt in front of me. "Ye could have told me, ye ken? I would've listened."

"Aye, I see that… and that scares me too."

He smiled softly, his hand brushing my cheek as he wiped away my tears. "Get some rest, lass. We've got a long journey ahead."

I watched as he walked to the horse and grabbed his cloak. He sat next to me, back against the ruin, and pulled me closer, wrapping the cloak around us. It was warm and soft against my skin. It smelt of him, wildflowers, and mountain air. I looked to the edge of the forest, flittering in the night with little green lights: fireflies. They were beautiful. We sat together in silence, the only sound was the singing of crickets and the occasional hoot.

"Were ye talking to that bear?" I asked.

"Ah, ye noticed, did ye? Aye, I was. Haven't you been paying attention in class? Or were ye too busy planning my slow and painful torture instead?"

"I have not!"

"Aye." He chuckled. "I spoke to it in Auld Eire, I speak to many a creature like that. Some do not ken it or choose not to, but some do. It's the auld language the Auld and the Wee speak, it has changed through the years, but some remember—the bear did and should stay away."

I leaned in closer, and he wrapped his arms around me, pulling me tight against him, warm and safe. His sword was at his right side, if he needed it. I knew he would not sleep tonight. I watched the fireflies dance and began to close my eyes. I could feel his heart again in time with mine, his breathing solid against me, arms around, safe, nothing would hurt tonight.

"Goodnight, *a chuisle mo chroi*... my lady," he whispered.

It was silent. I felt him lean his head back against the wall to look out at the stars.

He breathed slowly out.

"Alix, ye really are rippin' my heart out."

Chapter Six

I WOKE UP AS THE SUN WAS RISING. Tommy had his head back against the wall, his eyes closed, but he wasn't asleep. The fire was almost ash, mist was floating above the stream, and the sun was filtering through the branches of the trees across the clearing. Fireflies had long left, and the bees and butterflies had risen. A small bird sang behind us. I saw movement in the trees, a small flicker, no more. I stayed still, feeling the rise and fall of Tommy's chest as he breathed, arms still wrapped tight around me. He hadn't moved or slept. I, whether from exhaustion or the feeling of safety, had slept well, my mind clear. I was ready for whatever this new world would throw at me. I stayed still and watched the sun rise.

***

I felt a gentle hand brush my cheeks.

"My lady, it's time to go," Tommy whispered. I must have fallen back to sleep, curled up against the wall with the cloak wrapped tightly around me. I looked at the rock across the fire, and a ring of flowers had popped up. I didn't remember seeing them earlier. I was staring and walked over to it. "The wee folk," Tommy said. As I got closer to the centre, there were some berries. "A gift—they must have come when I was with the horse."

I knelt and picked them up. "Thank you," I whispered. We shared the berries and made our way to the horse, which was saddled and ready to go. It was a warrior horse, proud and tall—larger than those at home. Malcolm's for sure.

Its beautiful black mane was braided tight, ready for battle. Tommy reached out his arm, and I climbed on in front. We set out. Looking at the clearing, I realised I had no idea where we were, there were no landmarks, the forest was thick, I couldn't see the Cuillins red or black, moss was growing on all sides of the trees, and it sounded like streams, burns and falls were scattered around us. I wouldn't have found my way back alone, but the horse or Tommy knew where we were going, so I relaxed and leaned back.

We rode for hours before the forest began to thin. The sun was high, and the breeze was fresh. I could smell the salt water before I could see it. I could now see Dunscaith ahead, perched on its rock. Suddenly, the rock face seemed deeper.

The chambers were deep below, hidden to the naked eye. We crossed the bridge and nodded to the guards, making our way to the stable. Niamh was waiting at the gates.

"The others have left, *a lennon*, you are both to follow. Tommy, take Alix to *Ewen*. Grab what you need and make haste. Margaret will be waiting; go by Storr. Malcolm's horse will find his way home." She smiled and nodded. "I'll leave you now, I'm journeying to Moar in the morning for the gathering." She turned and walked up the stairs, a smile on her face. I could hear her softly humming to herself as she went.

"I'll get my things." I ran up the stairs and to my chamber. Niamh had packed my bag, and my sword was polished and lay on top alongside my daggers. I got changed, noticing a blue flower on top of my pillow. There was a small note, and something wrapped up inside. I sat on the bed and opened it.

Alix,

Your mother left this in my possession to give to you when you were ready, and you are a lennon. There is much you dinna ken yet, in time you will. Remember your lessons and the tales of auld, they will guide you.

Know that when you do discover it all, ken how much she loved you.

Open your heart; it is strong enough to survive.

Auntie Niamh.

Inside, carefully wrapped, was a ring. It was delicate—tiny leaves carved from a dark copper created a band, interlaced and meeting into the centre, which held a stone. This was a deep dark indigo, with flecks of light—like the night sky and its stars reflecting in water. It was beautiful and magical. I tried it on, and it fit the third finger on my right hand perfectly. I tucked the note inside my breast pocket. It felt like more than just a piece of jewellery—it was a piece of her, my mother, someone I barely knew, but whose love and secrets were now wrapped around my hand. I wondered why Auntie Niamh had left this note instead of telling me in person. There was more to it, I could feel it. I braided my hair, pulling leaves and twigs out. Grabbing my pack, I sheathed my sword. I was ready.

I descended the stairs and walked to the stable. Pausing, I watched. Tommy's head was bent against the horse as he spoke softly to it, his hand brushing its face and neck. He was deep in thought, pouring his soul out to the creature. I turned to walk back to the castle. I didn't want to interrupt. I sat on the grass watching.

After a while, he turned around. Noticing me, the right side of his lip was lifted. "Ready, *my lady?*" His eyes were eager, glowing in the sun's reflection.

"Aye, I am."

He took my pack and sword, securing them on the horse. He climbed up and grabbed the reins in his left hand. His right reached mine, and he turned it. "I've never seen a stone like that before. It's like the stars are trapped inside."

"Auntie Niamh left it for me... with a note."

Tommy leaned in slightly, a grin tugging at the corners of his lips. "Aye, it's beautiful." He took my arm and lifted me in front. With his arm adjusted around me, he kicked, and we were off.

We left the rugged weather stones of Dunscaith, travelling across Loch *Eishort*. The sleet crunched under hooves, and the glittering waters reflected the Cuillin reds. We moved inland, shifting to the green hills, and the cool, salty breeze followed as we found a narrow trail leading through the heath and moorland. Stopping to water the horse, I could see in the far distance the rugged tops of the red Cuillins peeking out from the mist, leaving *Dunscaith* far behind. As we rode, Tommy told stories of travelling through Skye in his youth with Brian and Malcolm; they'd camp and ride for days, mapping the mountains, old crofts, and lochs. He compared it to his homeland and told tales of the auld, the selkies who could take you to the mainland, the silkies who would shed their furs and walk on land. The water horses would appear in deep lochs to find a bride, stealing her down to the water below.

He was a born storyteller, describing the isles, their secrets, and tales.

As we crossed further inland, the path became more rugged, the horse was sure-footed, and I could see rock figures twisting and turning into ancient shapes. *Giants*. We rounded the mountainscape; overlooking the loch, the sun setting in the distance was reflecting in the water, deep colours of yellows and purples lit the sky. We stopped and made camp in a small alcove of rocks. The mist rolled in, covering the rock formations in the distance. I unstrapped the horse and tethered it near the heather. We built a fire and sat down.

I had stopped here long ago with Da and my brothers on our way to see Malcolm. Giants covered the land of Skye long ago, fighting between the mountain tops, the clashing of their swords heard throughout the land—crashes loud as thunder. During one of these battles, a massive giant was slain, and he fell upon the mountainside. The other giants left him, taking his mountain. Eventually, the land reclaimed him, swallowing him up, leaving only his thumb in defiance. From where we camped, I couldn't see him, hidden by the mist. I'd never been closer than we were. I looked up and a flash of lightning lit up the sky showing a silhouette of rock which then disappeared again. Goosebumps prickled my arms. I shivered.

"Are you cold?" Tommy asked.

"No, just remembering the tales of the Giants, the Old Man Storr, you ken the tale?"

"Aye, Malcolm took me here and showed me. I didn't sleep well that night."

"Where is Castle *Ewen*? I don't ever remember Da or Grannie for that matter, speaking of it?"

"It's a fair ride from here. You must travel through the fairy pools, over the black Cuillins, then through the fairy glen. The path is hidden and few ken the way. Your Grannie Margaret lives there mostly, but officially she is at Dunscaith. I have only been there a handful of times on visits with Niamh or Malcolm. Niamh said Malcolm took the others, Claire likely will stay there, I think; there is a great library, it will be hard to take her away." He laughed, a big smile across his face.

"Why do you think they didn't tell Marcus, Claire, and me?"

"I don't know, I have known since I was six and ten. My mother sent me here to train with Brian and learn from Auntie Niamh. I have spent time here often since. I am sure they had a reason, Alix."

I looked at the ring on my finger, so many secrets. I nodded.

***

I woke in the morning to see Tommy speaking again to the horse; he had left only the saddle and reins on. It was making its way down the cliff path.

Where then were we going with no horse?

"Do you remember I asked if you liked to climb?" He had that cheeky grin on his face.

"Now? I thought we were riding to Ewen?"

"Well, we are in a way, but we need to go on a bit of a climb... there's something I want to show you."

He passed me my flask and pack, and, grabbing my sword, I followed. It was beginning to drizzle, and rain splashed my face; it was fresh and cool. There was no path, but he seemed to know his way. We passed heather slopes and rocky outcrops; he paused now and then for me to catch up. The mist was thicker the higher we climbed; the air became thinner, making it harder to breathe. I could smell the wildflowers and the salt of the sea on the breeze. It was beautiful up here, long flowers with stuff that looked like white fur swayed in the breeze. Bees buzzed around the heather, still green and beginning its winter rest. We reached a path of sorts; I looked up to find multiple rocks of all sizes making a staircase. Some steps raised to my knees, others to my heels; this was going to be tough. I followed him up slowly. At the large ones, he waited to offer a hand to steady me. I was looking at my feet when a large shadow flew over, quickly. It must have been a cloud, although the wind had stopped. I checked my footing and climbed higher.

Tommy was waiting for me, sipping his water. His hair was damp with sweat and rain, and it was beginning to curl on the edges as it dried. As I drank my water, I looked out. The view was impressive, the green hills rolled in the distance, the loch like a mirror reflected the sky and the mountains above. The sky opened and I could see the rugged landscape of the red Cuillins in the distance. It was bewitching. As I turned to face our heading, I saw him.

The Old Man of Storr.

I took in a deep breath: the legend, the rock formation of the swallowed giant, stood before me. It was jarred and rugged, surprisingly intimate and imposing. It towered easily over one hundred feet above me. I bent back to see its top. The mist covered it, making dark shadows. He was weathered from centuries of wind and rain. The picture of endurance and wisdom watching all below.

"Impressive, no?" Tommy grinned.

"Aye, I've no words."

"Right, well, we still have a while to go, come *a chuisle mo chroi."* He continued around the Man of Storr and up further into to mountain tops. We curved around the different rock formations, the drop below was deadly, but the view as the mist cleared was breathtaking. We reached a large rock formation rounder than the old man but just as high. When I looked behind me, I could see the old man standing tall and proud. Waiting just ahead, I could see Tommy.

"Sit."

I sat on the smooth step under my feet. He was standing, and for the first time, he looked unsure.

"I was not sure I should bring ye here, you ken. Auntie had said it was ok, but it was up to me; it's my secret and my people's."

I was unsure what he could have to tell me, taking me to the top of a mountainside to do so seemed extreme, and if he had changed his mind, who was I to know it wasn't just the view he wanted to share. I waited and watched; he was running his hands through his hair. He turned and sat. He held my hands in his tightly and looked into my eyes.

"I know now…. They are the silver of Skye. Aye… that's what colour they are."

Was he talking to me or himself? "What is?"

"Your eyes, *a chuisle mo chroi*." Tommy's voice softened, the playful teasing replaced with something more reverential. "They're like the silver of Skye, the mist that rolls across the hills, always changing—like lightning waiting to strike when you're challenged. Or like a storm that never quite settles. They shift, Alix. Shift with the weather, with your thoughts, with your moods. Like a storm waiting to break."

I held his gaze, unsure of whether he was speaking of my eyes or something deeper. He seemed to find some secret in them, something I couldn't yet see.

"I'm going to show you the secret of my people—our language, like yours, is auld, auld as time. The creatures some ken it still. Remember the stories in Niamh's songs, they are real, as real as you and me… Come, it's not far." He stood and helped me up. We walked around the rock formation and stopped near the cliff. It was thick with mist. "Are you ready?"

"Aye."

Tommy's hand trembled slightly as he gripped mine. The mist hung thick around us, pressing in as though it too awaited his words. "There's something I need to show you, Alix. A part of me I've kept hidden, a gift, or a burden, I suppose." He turned and looked at me. "This… this isn't something I take lightly, Alix. It's not just about magic. It's my people, my past. And if I show you, things will change. I need you to understand that.

"You asked me once how I came to the forest that day with no horse, well… this is how I came"

As he turned, he stretched his hand before me, and the mist began to part. The sensation was otherworldly, as though the world itself had shifted for us. My heart raced as the air grew thick with power.

"What is this, Tommy?" I whispered, barely able to catch my breath. The mist cleared.

My pulse quickened as if the mountain itself was holding its breath. I could feel the weight of Tommy's words pressing down on me, and the world seemed to hum with an energy I couldn't understand.

And I dropped down to my knees.

Chapter Seven

HE HELD THE FLASK OF WHISKY OUT TO me; I drank deeply, then rubbed my eyes. I couldn't be seeing this; it had to be in a dream. Dragons.

There were dragons of every shape, colour, and size—some covered in deep browns, others silver and blue, with one dark green dragon so striking it shimmered with onyx and emeralds when the sun hit it. They were miraculous. Their bodies were large and powerful, but differed from each other. My god, they were beautiful.

I could see their four legs; some were climbing the rock faces, others dangling as they flew, and the green one had its wings tucked in. I could see long claws black and shining on the one closest. The strength it must have had in its legs to be able to climb. They all had long tails stretched behind them, each different—one had a large spike, skinnier than a broad sword, but I'm sure it would be sharper; one had an end like a mace; another like a club.

I wanted a closer look at their eyes. I imagined they would be gold and wise, or would their eyes change with their colouring, allowing their personalities to shine through. The wingspans were impressive, like their tails; each was different. They soared through the sky with such elegance and ease; they were the kings of the sky. There was no doubt about it.

My heart was racing. I could not believe what I was seeing, yet for the first time, it wasn't surprising, like a part of me knew they existed. I could feel Tommy behind me, standing still, not speaking, clutching the flask tightly, unsure whether to move or speak. I slowly stood up and turned towards him.

"Dragons... You have dragons?" I could see my smile and excitement reflecting in his emerald eyes. I tried to contain my excitement in my voice, like a kid on Hogmanay; I was exhilarated.

"Aye."

"Tommy! Dragons! These are dragons, they're real?" I held his face in my hands.

"Aye." He nodded, a smile broadening his face. His eyes lit and gleamed like the green onyx dragon.

Dragon...

Dragons...

There were dragons in Skye.

"So, you're not going to scream, punch me, or run like a wild banshee cause I kept it from ye?" he asked.

"No, how could you even explain this even if you had wanted to?"

"I wanted to, but couldn't. Few ken about them. They live in peace, some here and some in Eire. That's how we can travel so often. Niamh taught Brian to ride when they married, and he's helped to develop battle strategies. The riders of Skye had mostly vanished, but in Eire there are still many. Niamh has taught others, and Margaret's people also rode. Over the years, we have been improving how we do it. Most riders are very traditional, but Malcolm has been changing a few things. Places to put swords or bows, even food. This is why you were taught our language—the magical creatures of auld speak it, and it helps us talk to them, ye ken"

"Could we… go closer?"

He nodded, his face was bright, and his body relaxed. He grabbed my hand and went closer to the edge. He looked around. Who was he looking for? Then he turned, looking at me. "Do you trust me?" he asked.

"Aye, Tommy." Before I could say anything else, he held me close to him and learned backwards over the edge of the cliff. We were falling. I screamed and held tight to him. His head tilted back, his body relaxed, and he was bloody smiling. We were about to die, and he was smiling. My heart pounded in my chest as we plummeted, the world around me spinning, and for a second, I thought I might pass out from the rush. Tommy's calmness only made me more frantic. How could he be so relaxed? It was a weightless and terrifying feeling, we were falling and all around was slowing, I began to see the details of the rocks and they moved past us, mist clearing showing the cliff face from where we had started. I could see the dragons around us, colour bright and disappearing, and we dropped. We were slowing somehow. I held tighter to Tommy: either my voice was gone, or I had stopped screaming.

Suddenly, we stopped, and my feet fell on something solid. I could no longer feel the wind in my face; his arms were still strong around me. I looked up and he was smiling. I turned my head. We were in the air, miles away from the cliff face, but not on the ground. I looked down, the deep onyx green scales under my feet. *Beyla*, I couldn't be. Tommy slowly turned me, keeping hold of *Beyla,* yes, I was. Giant wings spread before me, strong and pulsing up and down, keeping us still. The wings were transparent leather; I could see the light filtering through them. They were huge. My eyes drifted up and along a thick neck, following the scales reflecting the sun, up and over. I moved my eyes. Turning slightly towards me a head, a giant, beautiful. Long and elongated, proud, it had two horns pushed back and curled; these were onyx and glimmered as though polished. Its long nose breathed out, and a mist drifted. Its eyes, large and intelligent, were slitted in the middle and a brilliant green of emeralds.

"Lady Alexandria, we have been waiting."

Chapter Eight

A PROFOUND, ECHOING VOICE SPOKE, A deep growl rolling behind like thunder. Warm mist blew into my face, another thunder growl. Giant emerald eyes saw straight into my soul.

"Lady Alexandria, we have been waiting."

I swallowed.

It knew my name. Tommy held me steady, but I wouldn't let myself faint—not in front of this creature. Strong. Fierce. Unafraid. I gathered myself, standing tall. I moved Tommy's hands from my waist and nodded. I could do this. I took a step forward on the dragon, yes, the dragon's back. In a swift and steady movement, I extended my leg and arm, bowing low, head down.

"It is my deepest honour, auld one," I spoke to the dragon in Auld Eire. I remained low, waiting.

"Lady Alexandria, we've awaited your arrival. Heir of the Mackenzie MacLeods, rise."

I rose slowly. The dragon's eyes met mine, mesmerising and intense, as ancient as gemstones. He tilted his head.

"We ken who you are, and whence you came; your people have protected us for centuries; they are our friends.

You will also learn our ways and protect the lands and the creatures of auld.

Come, we ride."

The dragon turned his head forward and lowered it. Tommy guided me closer to its wings. There were rows of spikes all the way to its head. Right in the middle, there was a gap. I sat down. Tommy sat behind me, reaching around my waist to grab the spikes in front of me.

"Hold on, *A chuisle mo chroi.*"

I grabbed the spikes on either side of me as we dropped. We were diving down into the ground so fast I could hardly keep my eyes open. We reached the green grass below and flattened out. The dragon leaned to one side, and I could see the trees deep green as we flew past them.

I had never travelled so fast—faster than the fall from the cliff just moments before. We kept going until I could see the side of the mountain. The stone face loomed closer, every jagged rock clear as day. Just as I braced for impact, the dragon shot upward. The wind howled, and I slipped— my arms ripped from the spikes. Strong hands grabbed me tightly before I could fall completely from the beast. We plummeted toward the earth, too fast for my eyes to stay open. Strands of hair whipped across my face. Then the dragon turned sharply and flew towards the loch. From the sky, the island was magnificent, greens, blues, greys, the Grahams and Munros were small, and the water shone silver.

He flew lower and lower as we came towards the water of Loch Fada. We were not far above it when the dragon tilted to the left, his wing tip slightly touching the water, and a ripple followed us the distance of the loch. We slowed as we reached the bank, and the dragon descended, landing on the stony banks of Loch *Fada*.

He lowered its head and neck, tilting his body and wing to one side, dropping one leg like a bow. Tommy stood up and walked along the thick of the wing, sliding down the foreleg, landing elegantly on the bank. I paused, rubbed my eyes. With legs like seaweed, I followed the same path he did, slipping as I attempted to climb down the dragon's leg, sliding down un-elegantly. Thankfully, before I could break a leg, Tommy had caught me. It took a few minutes to steady myself back to walking on the ground. Once right, we walked towards the grass and sat down. Tommy pulled a flask from his pack and drank. I took my share and sat marvelling at the creature in front of me.

"I came here by the dragons, my aunt also. They fly often between Eire and Skye. Many live on the island, hidden in the mist. There aren't many clans that remember the auld ones.

"Like my family, yours has protected them. Your grandmother's kin have guarded them for centuries. She doesn't ride, but she knows their ways, their secrets. Your father and Callum learned healing from them—but they're not riders.

"Brian and Malcolm learnt to ride from Auntie Niamh, and we have been able to adjust our battle skills to flying in case we have the need."

He paused and looked up. Through the openings in the sky, I could see multiple dragons flying through the mist, diving between clouds. How had I missed them all these years? Their scales caught the sun's light, sparking assorted colours, reds, blues, purples and green. I turned to look at the dragon we had ridden. He was stretched elegantly like a cat across the grass, mist breathing out his snout. I looked at Tommy, who nodded his head. Standing, I walked cautiously towards the dragon.

"You seek answers and wisdom, lass, our world has always been here; it has only been hidden behind the mist until you were ready....

It was the wish of your parents and the elders that you should be protected, hidden from our world," his deep voice answered before I could ask.

"Why hide this? Did they not trust Marcus or me? Did my brothers know all along?"

"Oh, they visited when they were ready. Callum, brawly and red. He knows our secrets, but no rider is he.

Malcolm is a warrior and rider. He has spent much time with our kind, Marcus we shall meet soon. But know we have always watched those in your line. The twin moons especially, guiding and waiting."

"Twin moons? You do not mean Marcus and me?" I said with a snort.

"Aye. The Twin Moons must rise. A storm approaches. Your path is before you, Lady Alexandria, and time does not wait."

He lowered his right leg to create a ramp, and Tommy was already moving towards it.

"Wait… auld one, what is your name?"

The dragon snorted mist and growled in a deep, echoing laugh. *"You may call me Cian; it is the closest to your language."*

"At your service, *Cian*, auld one. I am Elizabeth Alexandria Margaret Mackenzie MacLeod of Caisteal Moar, but Alix is what I prefer." I bowed again and attempted to climb up his leg. Tommy had already climbed with our bags and was waiting on his back. With a slight leap, I managed halfway before I reached for a large spike to balance myself. Eventually, I straightened and reached his centre.

I gave a wink and a wicked smile to Tommy, and I made myself comfortable between the spikes of Cian's back.

Tommy laughed, shook his head, and tucked himself behind me. Before I could prepare myself, Cian had pushed his powerful legs off the ground, and the impact had us airborne. I held with all my strength to the spikes in front and squeezed my calves into the tough skin of his body. I could feel Tommy behind me, relaxed as though riding a horse, his left hand resting on my thigh. We rose through the clouds and circled the Loch. Cian turned back towards Storr and, with precision, flew close enough to the rocks that I could touch them if I wanted. We passed the other dragons who looked on with interest. And headed towards the Black Cuillin mountains, through mist and drizzle, the sun was setting behind us.

It was peaceful and yet terrifying as we flew high above the ground. At times, I could see nothing but the scales in front of me as the mist cleared. Cian dropped lower, twisting and turning around rocks and cliff faces. He spread his wings as wide as possible, then, without warning, brought them tight against him and dove through narrow passes. He slowed down as we reached two of the Cuillins, twin peaks close together; he adjusted himself and flew low between them. As we lowered, I could see lush green hills, winding stone formations circling down them, and I could see moss growing over their tops, creating a circle through the hills. From above, each hill looked to be created with multiple rings trailing down. A small stream also wound its way through the hills before leading towards a flowing brook into a small loch. Wildflowers and reeds lined the stream opening towards the loch. As we glided further down, I could see perched atop the highest hills what must be Castle Ewen.

The fortress was tall, made from rock; it was an incredibly imposing structure sitting upon a tall hill. As harsh as the stone was, cascading down it were multiple green vines, and from one of the tall windows, a plant had crept out, spreading its violet flowers down the wall. Around the rocky base, white flowers rose, swaying in the wind. It was situated in a spot to not only look over the loch but also into the only entrances between the Cuillin mountains.

We circled the castle, and I could see a large area of meadow, green and lush, but it had no trees or rocks, just open grass with wildflowers spread throughout. The hills with their rings circled the area. Cian slowed and dove towards the meadow. I braced myself for landing. I could see people walking down from the castle. Long black hair swinging down, and once again a crown of flowers— Claire—she looked like she belonged here among the fairies. Grannie leaned on Malcolm as she descended the rocks. Marcus came running, laughing.

"Alix, about time!" He stopped, bowing low. Cian snorted, puffing mist, then lifted his head. *'Arch dark one, we are not late, but right on time.'*

Marcus was beaming but was not at all shocked by the extremely large dragon talking to him. Malcolm and Grannie must have told him. Tommy jumped down and walked towards Grannie, lowering his head in respect, and kissed her hand. She giggled like a child and shooed him away.

"Grannie." I embraced my grandmother. "I believe you have much to teach me, your real home is magical."

"Och, lass… come along then, a strong glass of whisky is in order."

Claire grabbed my arm and linked it through as we walked along the path. She was smiling and looked beautiful—no leather today, just a long dress, although she did have a belt, and a dirk attached. I also noticed boots. Her blue eyes were sparkling. "Oh, Alix, dragons and fairies are just the beginning! Wait until you see the library." She was smiling like a cat with cream. Linked together, we climbed the path and entered Castle Ewen.

***

The courtyard was a living dream. Trees towered over us, their leaves a rich blend of green, red, amber, and purple. Flowers bloomed from every crack in the rock, while bright vines with white blossoms cascaded down the inner walls. Benches woven from strong branches were tucked beneath the trees, and a well stood at the heart of the yard. The space felt timeless, as if it had always been here, untouched by the world beyond. We walked through the courtyard and up a set of stairs into a large chamber. A small hearth crackled softly in the corner, warming the room. Flowers and vines cascaded from the ceiling like something alive, and candles flickered in the dim light, though the large windows, open to the courtyard, brought in a golden warmth. The air smelled of flowers, fresh and sweet, and small birds fluttered in and out, landing on vines or the trees tucked in the corners of the room. We sat along the long bench, and someone brought out food and whisky. It was just the four of us; Tommy had disappeared. He'd been here before, and his friends must have been somewhere in the castle.

"Well, I suppose you have some questions," Grannie said, settling back in her seat.

"Questions? Nah," Marcus scoffed, though his voice trembled just a little. "I think I'm still trying to process the part where I find out my family's been hiding a flock of dragons in their mountain pass and has some fairy magic running through their veins." He leaned back, running a hand through his hair. "Does this even seem real to anyone else?"

"How about you start at the beginning, Grannie?" I said, my voice softer now. There was still too much I didn't understand. My heart was a storm of questions I couldn't yet voice.

Grannie gave me a long, knowing look before answering. She settled back in her chair, the weight of the moment settling over us. "It's going to be a long night, my dears," she said softly. "You'd best eat up. There's much to explain"

Chapter Nine

THERE WAS A LOUD BANGING ON THE doors to my chambers. I jumped out of my bed, grabbing the stone pitcher from its table. I swung open the door, holding the pitcher high. *"Ifrinn, Mac na galla! Thalla gu h-lot."* Hell, son of a bitch, to saint Kilda with ye! Two large males stood back laughing.

"Ey, the wild banshee of the MacLeods is awake." Malcolm threw me a bannock as he spoke. "Alix, hurry yourself self we have training."

My two pigheaded bastard brothers strolled away laughing and pushing each other. By the look of it, Marcus had lost some kind of bet. I threw one of the bannocks at them, hitting Marcus in the head. *"Ifrin,"* he said, and Malcolm pushed him into a wall.

I turned back into my chambers; it was dark, barely dawn. I washed myself and got changed. Making my way downstairs, I saw my brothers walking to the meadows with

Sean and Liam, swords strapped to their backs. At least I'd be able to take out my frustration at being woken. I walked into the courtyard to see Claire sitting on a bench reading a book. "Claire, are you coming?"

"Nay, I have much to read. Grannie has given me a pile to get through. I'll catch up later." She let out a yawn. By the look on her she had been up most of the night. I nodded with a smile and continued across the courtyard. The trees were swaying, the reds, purples and orange leaves were a deep contrast to the stone walls surrounding them. At the end, I could see him—Tommy was leaning against the wall, one leg bent against it. Arms crossed against his chest and his head back, he was dressed in his *Scathach* warrior clothes, both of his swords crossed on his back, a knife strapped to his thigh, golden hair was damp and pushed back. He looked every bit a warrior ready for battle. He'd heard my footsteps and opened those emerald eyes to meet mine.

"*A chuisle mo chroi,* your brothers said they'd woken a banshee this morn, barely escaped alive, throwing pitchers I hear." He was laughing but not taunting. "Here, *mo chridhe.*" He passed me a folded-up cloth. I opened it to reveal two warm scones, slathered in jam.

"Thank you, Tommy." They smelled delicious. I was salivating. I leaned against the wall and ate. They were as good as they smelled; it was heaven. I hadn't realised how starving I was.

I finished and he passed me a cup; it too was warm. Tea. He must have been in the kitchens waiting. I couldn't help but smile.

I could see Claire watching from her bench, a large smile on her face too.

"We had better go before they start without us," he said.

We made our way down the back of the Castle and out into the meadow. The cool morning air felt like a slap against my face, ridding me of any lingering sleepiness. I felt the weight of the sword strapped to my back, the cold metal against my skin like a reminder of the challenge ahead. Malcolm would be tough on me; he always was. I was ready, but I wasn't sure if I was ready enough. I could see four dragons today with Cian. The boys were taunting each other.

"Aye, Sister, I see for our safety you have left the pitcher behind," Malcolm said, and the crowd roared in laughter, even Cian blew mist from his nose.

"Aye, well, no point having you all knocked out before breakfast, is there?" I said, and I saw one of the smaller dragons roll onto its back, making chuckling noises.

"Right, today you will pair up, Alix, you're with me. I want you all to work on trying to draw your powers with your weapons. I'll show you." Malcolm instructed me to spar him as normal. He pulled both his swords out, and I drew mine. As he sprang to meet me, I saw a flicker of fire travel up his swords. The more he pushed me back, the more flame covered the steel. I'd never seen anything like it. I could feel the heat of the flame touch my face, stinging it. The flames became the swords, and we sparred. I proceeded faster, trying to avoid getting burned; he didn't look to be breaking a sweat while I was drenched. The flames were creating a wheel of fire, and he was using one sword as a shield to block me and the other to attack me. "*Ifrinn!*" I yelled. He disarmed me, and I yielded.

"Now, focus. Let's see what happens, ey. Draw your magic from within and become your weapon." My fingers tightened around the hilt, the cool steel a grounding sensation against my clammy skin. I closed my eyes, blocking out everything except for the beat of my heart and the blood rushing in my ears. Was I supposed to feel it— magic, some crackling force deep inside me? Or was it something subtler? A whispering pulse that I had yet to find. I couldn't even remember the last time I felt anything resembling magic. Maybe it wasn't there. Maybe I didn't have it at all.

"That would be easy if you told me if I had any magic, Malcolm, for I'm yet to discover it." I was leaning over, panting, wiping sweat from my face. I looked over, and the others were paired up. Liam and Marcus were sparring. I could see Marcus squeezing his brows in concentration, and while he was doing just that, Liam moved an arm towards the creek. I could see water travelling across the meadow. He spun his sword and body, and the water flew into Marcus's chest, knocking him to the ground. He stood up, brushing the water from his face, and charged. Tommy and Sean were further back, Sean pushing his sword at Tommy with as much strength as he could manage. He was trying to focus on something, but kept getting frustrated too early, making him an easy opponent. Tommy was playing, like it was a daily exercise for him.

"Right, come on, Alix, show me what ye got, ey?"

I stretched my neck and smiled at my brother. Tall, strong, fierce, the weapons master who I now knew could wield fire as an extension of himself. His swords were beautiful, forged long ago. I noticed their runes up close. I couldn't read them, but it was clear that what I had thought when younger, the twirls and loops were flames, dancing through the blades. It wasn't old Eire or Caledonian runes, though. I couldn't remember where the swords had come from, only he'd got them when he was sixteen after a trip north with Da. His dark eyes were sharp and calculating; he'd spent years teaching Marcus and me. But I had also spent much more time with our brother Callum, who was by no means ordinary with a blade. He was twirling his swords around, playing with me, egging me on. I could feel the heat he was generating, though there was no flame. Yet. The air was pulsating a heat towards me. *Ifrin*, it was frustrating. Faster, I had to be faster, patient, wear him down, and take him unguarded. I could do it. Callum and I had practised; he was the fastest wielder I had met, and I had spent countless hours with him at Moar.

I moved forward, blade ready. An extension of my arm. Bring him closer, make him work. With any luck, his fire would burn out. We burst into action, clashing steel on steel. He pushed out heat with each impact, and the swords began to ignite. Like lightning, I danced around it. Turning my body with each movement of the sword.

He was smiling. "Aye, you're quick, but are ya quicker than me, sister?" The ground around us was beginning to singe. I could smell it as the flames of his sword licked the grass. He was using his right sword as a shield, forcing me to adjust my position. Each move was calculated, and he was pushing me to defend. I met each attack with precision. As we continued, I could see him channelling more power within; the flames grew stronger and hotter. I was dripping sweat from my face, and Malcolm was cool and smiling. I had no idea if the others were still sparing or if they had stopped to watch. I couldn't take my eyes off Malcolm, not even to check my footing. His strikes were becoming more forceful as I jumped in and out of reach, striking at any opening I could find. The singed ground must have begun to light. I heard a small rumble and a cool mist blow down from where the dragons were watching. It circled our feet, putting out any flames. Cooling me down.

My arms ached, sweat dripped into my eyes, and my chest was burning with each breath. But I couldn't stop now. I could see it—Malcolm's foot had shifted just slightly, his guard weakened for the barest second. I took a breath, steeling myself. The ground beneath us seemed to hum with tension, the heat of his fire pressing against me like a physical thing. And then, it happened. I spun faster than I thought I could, and in that moment, everything slowed. I wielded my sword around and behind, it caught him off guard, he met the blow and twisted it, disarming me with a vengeful force. My blade flew to the meadow. As it flew, I dropped low into the mist, kicking my leg out in a spin and catching his. Malcolm dropped to the ground, landing on his back.

For a heartbeat, everything stopped. Malcolm, the older brother who had always been untouchable, lay prone beneath me. The weight of his fire was gone. I had done it. I had... disarmed him. But it wasn't over. Not yet. I had to move. Quick. I grabbed his blade and jumped, holding the sword with both arms, and swung downwards. He immediately grabbed his other with both hands, a shield of fire met my blade, and there was a binding light. Heat pulsated and threw me backwards into the sky.

***

It felt like time had stopped as I landed.

I hit the ground hard, but without the full force I had been thrown with. I was lying still, I could feel I was winded, I began to breathe in deep. It hurt. I was sure I had, if not broken, then bruised at least three ribs from the impact. The ground was cold beneath me, and my breath came in shallow gasps. The air felt too thin, as if I couldn't quite catch it, and the pain in my ribs was sharp with each intake. I blinked hard, trying to focus on the blue sky above me. Dragons wheeled through the air far above, their wings catching the sunlight in long stretches. I couldn't remember how I'd gotten here, but the pain in my side was all too real.

Suddenly, a gush of water flew on top of me, winding me more but cooling me down. Turning my head, I noticed the ground was black, scorched. *Ifrinn,* had I been on fire?

"Alix, Alix!" Malcolm's voice was frantic, his hand trembling as he reached mine.

"Alix, ye wee banshee, are you alright, lass?" His words felt distant, like they were coming from somewhere far away, as I struggled to breathe. Marcus, I closed my eyes and slowly opened them again. Indigo – yes, Marcus, they were his eyes looking at me.

"Give me a moment, brother, to catch my breath, and we'll go again," I pushed out.

Malcolm's hand grabbed mine. "You're done for the day, lass. Who taught ye to fight like that? Callum? You were as quick as lightning. I was starting to get worried."

"Three older brothers, did you all think I wasn't paying attention?"

"Ouch, aye, you sure you're alright, lass, I was worried I'd set you on fire. Thank *Beira* Liam put it out," Malcolm said.

"Yeah, at least you don't have to worry about braiding your hair anymore," Marcus piped in.

"*Ifrin!!*" I lifted my hands and touched my hair, pulling my braid forward. Thank *Beyla. Only* the very end was singed.

Marcus was laughing. Real *eejit* there.

"Right, let's get you up, lass." Malcolm helped sit me up. I felt my head swirl and began to fall back. Something stopped me, the same rush that I'd felt as I had landed, bracing me from impact. Malcolm held me tighter, his hand bracing my back. My eyes glanced around those in the meadow. Six dragons watching, Malcolm at my side, Marcus close by, Sean and Liam. "I should thank you, Liam. I might have no hair left if it wasn't for you."

Liam winked at me. "Och, no worries Alix. We like having such a bonnie lassie around, couldn't have yon Marcus being the pretty one, could we?" Everyone but Marcus was laughing then. Almost everyone. I could see

Tommy standing near Cian; he was running his hands through his hair with frustration. He looked to be arguing for some sort, but it was too far for me to hear. No one else noticed and was too busy laughing. Cian puffed large mist through his nose, stood up, and flew away. Tommy turned and met my eyes. He brushed his hands through his hair and tilted his head. He started to walk closer. Malcolm noticed him.

"Well, lads, let's continue. Alix, you're sitting out this afternoon."

"*Ifrinn*, I'm fine, Mal, just give me a moment, ey." I was grinding my teeth together as I tried to get up.

"Tommy, I trust you'll watch my sister, get her checked out with the healers."

"I am a healer, Malcolm, a bloody good one, so if I say I'm fine, I'm FINE!"

"Aye, well, Elizabeth, I'll be taking your swords, *sgian dubh,* and what you got in your boots… aye, I'm taking that too. You are leaving now, even if I must make Tommy carry you myself." He grabbed all my weapons, throwing them to Marcus.

"Don't. Call. Me. ELIZABETH!"

Malcolm wasn't smiling. "*Mo phiuthair,* you wild banshee… You were a flaming arrow across the field. I will not be explaining to Da that I set you on fire for a second time, ey. You are leaving now. Without. Another. Word. Tommy, help me get her up."

Tommy held me up. Malcolm grabbed my face between his hands and looked me up and down, his dark brown eyes held back tears. "Alix, please. You scared me, you're the only sister I've got, and somehow you went flying across the *ifrin* sky in flames when I blocked yer. I've never seen or heard of it. If it wasn't for Tommy..." He was shaking his head. "Go *A ghraidh, my love.*"

I nodded. Tommy steadied me, and I was able to walk. We got close to the castle walls when I stopped. "I… need a minute."

"Aye, here, " he passed me his flask, and the whisky was warm and sweet.

"Could ye, maybe stop moving for a minute, unless there are two of yer, you're making me a tad dizzy." I leaned forward onto my knees.

He bent down and lifted me into his arms. "Ney, *my lady*, we are getting you checked."

'Och, aye… I think that may be best."

He carried me up to the castle. My head cradled against his chest. He was clammy. I could smell mountain air and wildflowers. I closed my eyes, leaning in as much as I could into the solid warmth of his chest. Tommy's arms were firm around me, his strength a quiet reassurance. I felt his breath against my hair as he carried me, and there was something so comforting about the way he held me. It was more than just the physical support; it was the quiet care in the way he moved, making sure I was secure in his grasp.

"Alix! Alix! Tommy, is she alright!" Claire—I could hear her panicked voice as she ran down the side. Without waiting for an answer, I could hear her running back. "I'll get Grannie. Get her inside, to Grannie's rooms."

Tommy continued up the slope, and we crossed the courtyard. I could smell the trees as we walked past them. Eventually, we arrived in Grannie's rooms.

"What's the fuss, lass? Claire, will ye calm down? I cannot even understand what language ye are fretting in." Grannie was walking through the room, her stick clinking on the stone floor. Her rooms smelt of sage, lavender, and fresh biscuits.

"*Nighean-ighne, granddaughter,* what's happened… come, Tommy, lie her down. Claire, stop flapping like a bird, water, bandages, get my medicines, lass."

"Grannie, I am fine, I think it's just my ribs, maybe, and my head is a bit sore. I just need a moment, and I'll be able to go back."

Grannie's hands were warm and steady as she ran them over me, feeling for injuries I couldn't remember. Her eyes were sharp, though, glinting in a way that told me she'd seen more than I could guess. "You've been through worse, *nighean-ighne,*" she muttered, her voice a soothing constant as Claire fussed beside her.

"Tommy, sit the lass up, we'll need to take her cloak off and that corset my daughter made, no wonder she can't breathe."

Claire gave me a tea to drink. The tea was bitter, the taste of juniper and willow bark sharp on my tongue, but the warmth settled into my bones. Grannie's room smelled of dried herbs, sage mingling with the scent of freshly baked biscuits. Grannie's hands were running over me, slowly touching each section. I must have hit my head harder than I thought. I could see a faint blue light covering her hands. She was smiling at me when she met my eyes. At some point, Malcolm came in, and I could hear his deep voice speaking with Grannie, explaining what had happened. A flicker of light from the hearth caught my eye, its flames casting shadows across the stone walls as I drifted in and out of sleep.

***

When I opened my eyes, I found myself in my chambers at Ewen. I could see Claire curled up on the window seat, book clutched to her chest; she was asleep. Through the window, the sun was going down. I wondered how long I had been asleep. My hair had been washed and braided loosely, and I was in my nightgown. Touching my hair, I could feel flowers: Claire.

Two large legs were draped across my bed, and I followed them up. I should have known he was here. I dreamed of Storr and could smell the mountain air. Tommy was asleep in the chair pushed against my bed, his legs stretched out and leaning on it. Looking closely, his face looked exhausted, his golden hair sticking at odd ends; he must have been running his hands through it. His face still had dust on it, and I could see a track clean from his eyes to his chin. Had he been crying, I wondered. I stared at him for a long while.

"He hasn't left your side, Al," Malcolm said, leaning against the doorframe. He, too, looked like he hadn't slept. "Three days. Grannie was the only one who wasn't overly concerned... Alix, if he hadn't stopped you, I don't know if you'd still be here."

"What are you talking about, Mal? We were sparring. I knew the risks."

"Alix, I've never seen anything like it. Grannie thinks it was a clash of our powers. The force of it—when you were thrown—pushed me into the ground. There was a huge hole where you landed... and you were covered in flames. I could hardly believe it. Thank *Beyla* for Auntie Gen's clothes, and Tommy..."

Malcolm looked over at Tommy.

"He was so close to burning out, Alix… He threw a wall of freezing air at you to encase you. Marcus said Tommy's feet were pushing into the ground with the force it was taking to concentrate. He couldn't stop you completely, but he managed to slow you down and cool you off.

He stopped you from smashing into the ground. Then Liam directed water to put out the flames, and Tommy had to pull the air around you to cut it off… That's why you were struggling to breathe, you ken.

When we draw too much magic, it's… Grannie says it's like a well, you ken. We all got one and if you draw too much it goes out, ye burn out, is what we call it. Sometimes you cannot survive….

He was so close, by the time you were on the ground, Marcus said he was on his knees, he was shaking, but he kept going. I owe him everything, Alix. He almost died saving you. Cian was so angry, ye ken. I haven't seen him back."

He breathed out slowly.

"I don't know how he did it, Al, and to still be here…."

Malcolm stepped closer, his hand gently cupping my face. He looked at me with something like awe in his eyes. "You know he loves you, Alix?" His voice was soft, but the weight behind it made my chest tighten. He wasn't just asking about love—he was asking if I truly understood the depth of Tommy's sacrifice and feelings for me.

It was then that I realised my left hand had been holding Tommy's. I smiled, looking down then at my brother, tears in both our eyes, I nodded. "Aye, I do."

Chapter Ten

A FEW DAYS LATER, GRANNIE TOOK ME to the castle gardens. Enclosed within another courtyard, protecting us from the wind, I heard the faint sound of singing. Looking around, I saw them—the wee folk. Dozens of fairies flitted about the gardens, about a hundred, some tending herbs, others sweeping leaves, some dancing, and others picking flowers. They ranged in size, from as high as my knees to small enough to fit in my hands. Their pointed ears and glittering golden and brown skin caught the light. Some wore flowing hair, others had it short and spiked. Their clothes were made from all sorts of natural materials—leaves, grasses, fur, bark... and was that spider silk? I looked at Grannie, who was smiling. "Who do you think keeps this castle running, lass? Surely you don't think I was doing the cooking." She laughed and pointed towards a bench.

"You see them now because you've come of age. But the wee folk have always been here and…. everywhere." She waved her hands around.

"Grannie." I paused, unsure how to begin. She raised a hand, signalling for me to wait.

"It's called an Awakening, lass. Those with fairy blood—like you—are marked by it. When you reach five and twenty, your full power awakens. Some show signs earlier, though. Claire, for example, started seeing the wee folk when she was younger. She even had visions of them last year, but as she grew older, they faded away. She kept searching, though, sure they were real."

Callum, you ken, is incredibly wise; he's what we auld ones call a wise one—calculating, patient. He seeks knowledge and speaks many languages. He's a great healer, too.

Malcolm, as you know, has fire magic—it's quite powerful, and he's spent years mastering it. He's got the patience of a hawk. As for Marcus... I see fire in him as well. His magic is starting to manifest, but it's still young. Malcolm will guide him, help him control it.

There are all kinds of magic. Your grandfather's line of MacLeods is intertwined with Oberon's—the king of the fairies. My mother's line follows the Fairy folk of Skye, see the small point of my ears, lass?" She bent her head to the side to show me.

"Now, you'll ken I'm a healer, yes?"

"Aye, Grannie, I've always ken that."

"Och, aye, well, there are healers like yon brother and Auntie Genevieve with their knowledge of herbs and mending and then… There are healers like your Da and me… You saw the light, didn't ye, lass?"

I nodded, remembering the blue light when she was running her hands over me.

"It's our magic, it comes from my line, ye ken. Fairy healing magic. We can see what's going on inside, and we can imagine how it should be and make it so. When we do that, those with fairy blood can see or feel our light, but like all magic, if we use too much, we will burn out. That's why we also must have knowledge of all healing herbs, tonics, and mending. If ye Da used all his magic to heal during the last battles, he wouldn't have saved as many, and likely wouldn't have come back himself."

She stood up and held out her hand. "Come." We walked through the wee folk in the garden, their heads bowing slightly as we walked by. Grannie stopped by a small pool, which was flat and dark. She sprinkled some herbs from her pouch, then with her staff she tapped the pool, ripples spreading across the surface.

"Aye… yes, Marcus will ride and bring fire. Claire will fly also, but see from a distance, like an owl, ye see." Grannie was pointing her finger at different spots on the pool. I couldn't see anything. "You," she said softly, "your future... It's clouded, lost in a thick mist. But I can see a large standing stone, and beyond that... a journey. A journey to unlock your true magic. The vision is hazy, but I see twin moons rising, casting their light over a world on the brink of war and darkness. And there—starlight, distant but clear. She will return."

Grannie paused, her eyes locked on the pool. Tears welled in her eyes, but she shook her head, as if trying to shake the vision away. And with a soft tap of her staff, the ripples in the pool smoothed out.

Her gaze softened as she met my eyes.

"No need to worry, lass," she said gently, her voice a comfort. "Come now, let's begin."

***

We were in her chambers, which were bright and airy. Large windows along the western wall opened to the hills beyond. Small birds flitted in and out, and a white owl perched in the far corner. She had flowers and herbs drying from the ceiling; the breeze would rustle them as it blew in. I sat down on one of the chairs and listened to what she was saying.

"Now, we cannot raise the dead, before you ask, and we do not harm. That is particularly important, lass."

I nodded, a tight feeling settling in my chest. I'd never seen her so serious before.

"There are places where magic is more powerful, fairy rings—made with rocks like here, mushrooms, or flowers. If you heal in these spots, your power is stronger. They allow you to draw deeper but also stabilise you. There are also sacred groves or glens. You ken you're in one, there is a feeling of peace and stillness, protection.

Some healers have an item of some sort to help channel or centre their magic." She tapped her staff. "Notice the amulet around ye Da's neck? Aye, you don't need one, but at some point one may come along, it will be natural but filled with magic, it will help guide yeh true.

Unlike your brothers, you won't channel just one element—you'll work with all four. Fire, water, air, and earth. It will come to you as light or energy. Blue light or a warmth ey. It allows us to heal." She paused, her eyes narrowing as she gauged my reaction. "To heal, you must channel them all. It's a delicate balance. Now, this light, you will see it as you heal.

To heal with magic, you must imagine it, see what ails the person, the damage, and visualise what it should look and feel like. Your hands will channel the elements into healing them. They will feel a warmth, a light. You will see it, like a vision in your mind, bones knitting together, wounds closing, soothing of pain.

The greater the injury, the more magic will be needed; the more magic you draw before it has time to replenish, the more likely you'll burn out. This will risk your life.

This is why we must know our herbs and other ways of healing.

Now. *Nighean-ighne*, lie down. Close your eyes, and I want you to feel. Feel what the blood running through ye feels like, what your heart feels to beat, start from your toes and work your way up. Visualise it in your mind."

I lay on the lounge trying to visualise my insides. What was it meant to feel or look like, I wondered. Surprisingly, it didn't feel odd at all.

I wasn't sure how long I had been lying there when I felt something odd. "Wake up, sister!" a loud voice directly above me shouted. Instantly, I swung my fist up and crushed it into a long nose.

"*Iffrin*! Alix!" Marcus was holding his head back, hands clamped against his nose, blood dribbling down his chin onto his shirt.

"Sorry. Hold up, what idiot sneaks up and yells at someone? It's your own fault. Come here."

Grannie woke up from her chair, snorting. "Sit him down, lass. Let's see if ye've got the touch, then."

I sat Marcus on the chair I'd been on. He was still clenching his nose and leaning his head back. "Take a good look, feel around… visualise."

I put my hands on his nose, gently feeling my way. I closed my eyes. It was swollen, and I could feel that one of the small bones was broken.

Right, visualise what it should look like.

I could feel warmth under my hands, or was that just his blood?

Concentrate, Alix.

I could see the blue light in my mind, could feel it getting bigger, like a small star growing in the night. Ok, I knew what Marcus's nose looked like; I could see the broken bone and the blood running out.

Focus.

The light grew bigger. I wanted to see it fixed. My mind was knitting the bone together, the light brighter, and I could feel warmth coming from my hands. The blood was slowing. I kept my hands there for a few minutes more. The bone knitted together beneath my hands, the warmth of the magic pulsating like a heartbeat. The swelling eased, and the blood slowed to a stop. My light was dulling and tucking back inside. I slowly opened my eyes, meeting a pair of deep indigo eyes wide open staring at me.

"Wonderful, I ken you had it, lass." Grannie came over, taking the cloth away and dipping a new one into some warm water. She gave it to me to clean his nose. It was straight, the blood had stopped. Marcus sat there staring at me.

"Iffrin! Did you just *do* magic? Grannie, is my nose alright, she didn't put it on backwards? There was a blue glow all around it; it was hot too, and I thought it was going to fall off."

It was perfect. Once cleaned up, you couldn't even tell it had been broken.

"Now what did you want?" I demanded from my brother.

"Och, aye, I came to tell ye I lit a candle—finally! Grannie should've seen it; I'm practically a fire mage now." He was grinning wildly.

Grannie began to laugh. "That'd be right, you both finding it at the same time. Off ye go, Alix, no breaking any more noses to practice, ey." She was laughing and waving her hand at us as we walked out.

***

"Did you see all the fairies in the gardens?" I asked Marcus, still surprised by the sight. "I hadn't until today."

"Fairies, eh?" Marcus scratched his head. "I thought they were just some odd-looking relatives of Grannie's. Though some were a bit small for my liking." He laughed, and I joined in.

"Speaking of Grannie," I said with a grin, "she told me you'd be a rider with fire magic."

"Is that right? I'd love to ride the dark blue one," Marcus said. "She's a bonnie dragon, though she looks a bit dangerous."

Malcolm appeared at the end of the corridor, walking toward us with a raised brow. "What happened to you two?" He glanced between Marcus and me. We exchanged a look and burst out laughing.

"Aye, looks like Grannie was right," Malcolm said. "You're a healer, like Da—a fairy healer, eh?"

"It would seem so."

"Well, at least we won't have to worry about Marcus falling off a dragon," Malcolm added with a smirk. "You'll be there to put him back together. Speaking of which, Marcus," Malcolm said, "I was thinking of taking you for a ride. Alix, if you're up for it, Sean's waiting for us. He wouldn't mind if you joined us, but I know Claire was looking for you. She said she'd be in the library."

"Aye, well, I'd better go find her then," I said. "I'll join the next ride."

I watched as my brothers shrugged their shoulders, snorted, and walked off. With a sigh, I turned toward the library.

***

The library was tucked away in one of the torrents, at the very top. Shelves of books stretched from floor to ceiling, and large windows let in the bright sunlight during the day. At night, the space offered the perfect view of the star-filled sky. A central staircase led down through multiple levels, all crammed with books and scrolls. Claire often moved between them, but I knew she favoured the topmost level best. It was a large open area with views of the meadows; she could look out and see the glen and the mountains below. I now noticed there were wee folk flying around, lifting books and placing them back where they belonged. One was rearranging flowers on a large table, and another had carried a small tray of biscuits and tea to a lounge area where I assumed Claire was. I could see boots high in the air, wiggling around. She often changed positions on the lounges depending on what she was reading; to see her upside down normally meant a truly fascinating tale, especially if her legs were wiggling.

Looking around, I could see another area around the hearth; Liam and Tommy were sitting there reading and talking. Liam looked up and smiled. I nodded my head. I walked over to Claire, who lay with her legs up, her hair spilled out onto the floor. A tiny fairy was weaving white flowers into it, their pale petals standing out against Claire's onyx hair. "*A lennon,* you were looking for me?"

Claire jumped up. The little fairy flew away, not bothered by the sudden interruption. "Alix, yes," Claire said, "I found a book on healing magic I thought you'd like. It's very old, beautiful, and filled with drawings and sketches." She rummaged through her pile and pulled it out. The cover was a deep-sea green linen, its pages worn with age.

"Thanks."

I sat down next to her and opened the book. It really was beautiful, I'd never seen colours like it, they were dancing on the page, gold and silver lines became alive linking words to the sketches below. I was intrigued and sat across the lounge, Claire had now moved completely to the floor, spread out, hidden in a circle of books. She was jumping from one to the another. The wee folk would take the ones in the pile she discarded and put them back.

I munched on a biscuit while reading, starting to wonder if it was getting late. Yet the room remained bright, with the wee folk lighting candles as the sun began to set. Out of the corner of my eye, I saw the flowers on the table shuffle as though a breeze had blown through. Then, I felt a cool wind brush my cheeks, soft as fingers grazing my skin.

I looked around. Liam was now asleep in the armchair next to the fire, and Claire was immersed in her books, eating the never-ending plate of biscuits close by. I closed my book and sat up. "Claire, I think I am going to go for a walk."

"Mmhmm, ok," she answered.

I walked towards one of the windows where vines slowly moved in a breeze. I stopped and looked out. Nothing. Then I felt it again on my left cheek and turned. *There you are.* Leaning on the balcony of the floor above. I smiled and made my way up the stairs.

I reached the top of the stairs, and a lightly tanned hand was held out. I placed my hand on it.

"*My Lady.*" Tommy's soft lips kissed my hand, his golden head bowed. As he lifted his head, his emerald eyes met mine, shining in the dimming light. I smiled.

He brought me into the light of the hearth, both hands gently cupping my face, turning it side to side, brushing my cheeks before slowly running his hands down my hair, eventually resting them on my shoulders. Goosebumps prickled down my spine, and my legs felt weak.

"How are you feeling, Alix?"

"I'm fine, really. Just needed a moment."

He looked down his nose at me, emeralds dulling, and I could see concern in his eyes.

"A bit tired, but physically I'm fine, I really am. Grannie has cleared me for training."

He nodded. "Right, well. I thought maybe that is… well, I heard the dragons speaking of falling stars tonight, I thought maybe you'd like to watch. There is a perfect viewpoint at the top of the torrent, unless you have other plans?"

"That sounds wonderful."

The emeralds lit up, and he smiled at me. "Alright."

Tommy grabbed my hand tight and we ran up the stairs; there were three flights, and I was puffed. He opened the large oak door onto the rooftop. The rooftop was flat and circular, except for the small entrance way we had just come through. The stone floor glimmered under the moonlight, and a small wall ran around the edges, providing safety but also an uninterrupted view of the night sky. In the centre was a small platform, underneath small lights shimmered like starlight under the step to make it look as though it was floating. There was a semi-circle of luscious cushions on top, shades of deep purples and greens. Small candles were hovering above the rooftop, lining the way from the entrance. I could see glasses and a small table of food. As I looked closely, I could see small white flowers also lining the path. I laughed. I knew why I needed to retrieve the book from the library this evening.

"What would you have done if I'd said I'd rather read my book than look at the stars?"

"Aye, well, I suppose I could have invited Liam to join me for dinner instead."

I shook my head, smiling. "It's truly lovely."

"Aye, you are, *mo chridhe*," he said, and I felt the soft breeze brush my face.

We sat for hours, sharing stories of our hopes and dreams, discussing the coming war and what it might bring. Softly spoken with occasional laughs, we sat there picking at the food and drinking wine. It was a cool night, but the candles provided warmth. There was also a fur blanket close by. I snuggled into it as the night grew cooler. Tommy leaned back on the cushions, one arm holding his head, emerald eyes glittering in the candlelight. He had a lovely smile, and when he laughed, his whole face glowed. The stars above were twinkling like fairy dust. Now and then, we would catch a shooting star flying across the sky and stop to view it.

As we were talking, I began to hear a melody coming through the breeze. It was distant and delicate, played on a harp and flute. It was enchanting, its notes blending seamlessly into the backdrop of the night sky, with stars twinkling in time. We had both paused to listen. I met Tommy's eyes with surprise; he'd been watching me as I listened. We both smiled as the music seemed to lift into the torrent and out into the sky.

As the music floated in the air, a subtle smile tugged at Tommy's lips. He stood, bowing low with a playful glint in his emerald eyes. "Would you like to dance, *my lady*?" The words were soft, yet charged with something deeper. I took his hand and rose from my comfortable cushions.

"Only if you promise not to step on my new boots." We both laughed, remembering the first time he had asked me to dance. Was it only a couple of months ago? We walked away from the crescent, with a slight sweep of his hand, and the candles had moved, spreading out into a circle. He lifted his arm, spinning me around and meeting me at the end. Our bodies gave way to the harmony of the music, twirling and swaying close together. Both the moon and starlight glowed deeper, and the stars became floating orbs of light surrounding us.

The melodies were beautiful, and I began to wonder where such music was coming from; it must have been the wee or the auld folk, celebrating the change of the season with the falling stars. As though it were summoned, I saw one fly across the sky. I turned my head to see it when I realised I couldn't see the turret wall. I twisted my head round and looked down.

We weren't on the ground anymore. I grabbed Tommy tighter, and he looked down, then back at me, eyes wide with disbelief. Smiling, he shrugged and spun me around. We were floating—just a few meters off the ground—but it felt like we were weightless, suspended in the night. Our steps were light, and it was an odd sensation; we truly were dancing in the night sky.

He was looking at me, deep in thought. I tilted my head and smiled. "Didn't I tell you to do something about your hair, *A ghràidh*, my love? It's distracting," he said, his voice soft and serious, though his eyes danced with laughter.

He brushed the loose strands behind my ear, his fingers lingering in my hair. I'd worn it out, with small braids to keep it from falling into my face, but now I was grateful for the softness of it around us. I looked at him as seriously as I could, holding my nose high. "It is not my problem that you have the concentration of a butterfly."

I lost it laughing, and so did he.

He brushed my face with the gentleness of the soft breeze in the library, tenderly bringing my body closer to his with his other hand on my lower back. His movements were slow and unhurried, looking into my eyes, and his top lip rose in the corner. His forehead touched mine, and I closed my eyes. I could feel the warmth of his breath, the beat of his heart, slow and steady. His lips were a whisper away. My heart began to race. Both of his hands touched my face, bringing it slowly and gently up higher, and his fingers brushed my hair behind my ears.

Our lips finally met in a soft, tender kiss.

It was gentle at first, delicately exploring for a moment, then moving into a sweet, unspoken intensity. It was filled with affection, warmth, and magic. Goosebumps ran down my spine. The kiss lingered, slow and tender, as though time itself had paused. I felt weightless, suspended between his lips and the stars. My heart raced, every beat in sync with the soft, melodic rhythm of the music that surrounded us. The world faded away, leaving only the warmth of his breath and the taste of magic on my lips.

As he pulled away, his face remained close, his soft breath was still on my face, his eyes looked into mine with affection, love, and joy. I could feel my cheeks flushing, and I smiled. He touched my face again gently and whispered, "*A chuisle mo chroi.*"

I rested my head against his chest, listening to the soft, magical melody that swirled around us. The stars, like tiny lanterns, drifted lazily through the sky, as though they, too, were part of the dance.

Chapter Eleven

I MET THE OTHERS IN THE MEADOW EARLY that morning. Malcolm had left a note, instructing us to pack our weapons because we would be riding today.

Claire and I left the castle excited. I discovered that dragons were quite inquisitive; they would spend most days watching us train, flying in and out, never interacting more than a huff, grunt, or puff of mist. But there were ten dragons watching today.

Cian's deep green scales glinted in the sunlight. Beside him, a smaller but equally striking silver dragon stood. Its scales shimmered silver as the sun's rays caught them. I could see the dragons Sean and Liam rode, both brown ones with yellow eyes and the other rich mud.

A large dragon swooped down into the meadow, landing gracefully. Its rider jumped off and rolled into a smooth stand. Malcolm. It always surprised me how little attention he seemed to get from the girls. Perhaps it was because he spent so much time training, never giving them a chance to notice him. He was what I imagined a great warrior to look like, solid as stone, face tan and worn from being outside, while he also had broad shoulders and muscles that I could see through his clothing. His dark hair was pushed back from his eyes, also dark and mysterious. Claire and I had always said he looked like a selkie warrior who had shredded his fur and came to land.

"Right, today we will be making sure you can all ride, draw weapons, and not fall off ey. Claire and Alix, you haven't bonded yet, so you can pair up. Sean, Liam, show them how it's done."

The two redheads ran towards their dragons, already beginning to lift off. As they got closer, Liam jumped onto his dragon's front right leg, then leapt, grabbing a horn and swinging up onto his dragon's back, landing in the centre and immediately holding on. Sean leapt onto the front leg and ran up it as though it were a ramp. The dragons didn't stop their launch while the boys climbed. They were in the air before they had sat down. Once they were flying above us, I saw Liam pull his bow. While his dragon was flying in a circle, banking tightly, he shot his arrows perfectly centred on the targets set in the meadow. Sean drew his sword and stood up. He ran across one wing and leapt onto Liam's dragon. In an instant, Liam was up, and the two were sparring on dragon back high above us.

Malcolm let out a whistle and waved them down. Sean ran across the dragon's back down towards the tail and jumped; his dragon below caught his landing. They flew towards the ground, and both boys jumped from a height and rolled, landing in a fighting position. It was remarkable. I knew they had had years of practice, but I was not expecting the skills they had just shown. I'd thought of the dragons as a form of transport, not as a tool for war. The skills and trust the riders had with their dragons were incredible; one mistake and they were dead.

"Och, now I don't expect you lot to be at that level, the boys have been riding for years. But I'd appreciate it if you do not get yourselves killed, ey?

"Marcus, you're up, now take it at a run, the faster the better, ey, once you're up, I want ye to unsheathe your swords and still retain balance, you'll need to trust your dragon to fly without your direction.

"On three, two, one... run, Marcus!"

Marcus just bonded with his dragon Ignor about two weeks ago, a medium-sized dragon and according to Sean, one of the elder ones. He was a dragon from Skye. Deep indigo with matching eyes, and had a temperament, he also blew fire.

Marcus took off, running at full speed toward Ignor. Ignor began to move in sync with him, anticipating the leap. Marcus's gaze locked onto the dragon's right front leg, his focus intense. The terrain ahead was steep, but Marcus pushed forward, every muscle straining. He was making it— almost there. Then, the slope grew too high, and for a split second, he faltered. He paused, took a breath, and leapt.

Ignor's keen instincts kicked in. As Marcus flew through the air, the dragon adjusted his flight just enough to lower himself, giving Marcus a chance to grab hold. With a burst of strength, Marcus pulled himself up, his hands finding a grip on the dragon's scales. He was on. A close call, but he made it.

As Marcus steadied himself, I couldn't help but glance at Claire. Her face was full of concern, and I felt my own stomach tighten. Once airborne, I noticed Sean and Liam had taken to the skies as well, circling just in case we fell. They were ready, but I couldn't help wondering how much I'd screw this up.

With a slight grunt, Marcus began to balance, reaching for his sword. He tightened his grip on Ignor's scales, focusing on staying steady. But as he reached for his second sword, he lost his balance. The first sword slipped from his grasp, falling toward the ground.

No, I thought, watching it plummet. But before Marcus could follow, I saw a flash of green—Liam. He leapt from his dragon, landing behind Marcus, his hand grabbing Marcus's waist before he could fall.

"Got you," Liam said, his voice calm but sharp.

Marcus blinked, momentarily stunned, but quickly regained his focus. Once steady, he reached for the second sword. Liam hovered nearby, offering advice. The sword was stubborn, but Marcus didn't give up. After a tense moment, he freed it from its sheath, his laughter reaching us below.

"Right, sister, you're up."

"I don't have a dragon." I tried to steady my voice as I said it.

"You are with me, Storm Rider." A deep rattle echoed across the meadow. Cian was walking and nodded his head. He started to adjust himself for flight, waiting for me.

I looked at Malcolm, who nodded. Taking a deep breath, I looked up at Cian. He was massive—much larger than the other dragons, and I was far smaller than my brother. Think, think... I wouldn't be able to scale the front; it was too steep. The tail? No, that was impossible, especially at a run. Looks like it was to be the back legs.

I glanced at my brother, then took off, running faster than I ever thought possible. My heart pounded as I darted past Cian's massive head and legs. Nearing the last hurdle—his back leg, angled downward—I pushed off with all my strength. The scales there were larger, rougher, and I gripped them, pulling myself up with a gasp. "Thank, *Beyla*," I whispered under my breath as I scrambled to his back. I was on. The wind rushed around me as I steadied myself, my feet finding balance on his enormous body. Cian's muscles rippled beneath me, and I could feel the steady rise and fall of his breath.

Carefully, I moved toward the middle of his wing joints, my body tense with focus. I turned to look behind me— Tommy was running with effortless grace toward Cian's tail. With a single leap, he landed there, his feet steady.

As he made his way toward me, Cian adjusted his wings, gliding effortlessly through the air as if I weren't even there. Tommy reached me with a grin, his golden hair shimmering like sunlight on water.

"Back legs, *my lady*. Clever move," he said with a wink. He gestured toward my swords. "Now, draw your weapons."

I felt my eyes widen.

Ok, Alix, you climbed a moving dragon; you can surely manage to not fall off now.

I let go of the large spike I was holding and tried to steady myself to stand.

"Have you stood on a horse before?" Tommy asked.

I nodded, my heart pounding. I didn't dare let go of Cian's spike. The wind whipped against my face, threatening to knock me off balance.

"It's much the same, just a little bigger, I won't let ye fall, lass."

"Just a little bigger? A bloody dragon, Tommy. A giant dragon. You think I'm not noticing?"

Cian was laughing. Did dragons laugh? He was making odd noises, and I could feel his chest jiggle. Tommy was trying very hard not to laugh and only gave a kind smile.

"Aye, you are. But focus now… Keep your eyes on mine. Cian will fly steadily, just trust him. Push your feet down into his scales, anchor yourself, and use a bit of magic to hold him. You've got this. Aye, that's it… breathe… Keep looking at me, now."

He was speaking gently, and I was concentrating like I did when healing. I envisioned a glowing rope in my mind, linking me to Cian. I held onto it tightly, my only anchor in the chaos. If I could maintain the connection, I was safe.

"Alix, my eyes, that's it, look at me." He gave a gentle smile, the one he used around horses. I realised he was speaking in the same way he spoke to creatures.

"Look at ye, you're standing now. Slowly, arms back, pull yer swords free like I ken you've done on a horse many times… Keep pushing your feet down… look at me. That's it. Now throw me one, ey."

I threw one to him. Tommy grabbed it and swung it around, turning into a fighting stance.

"What do you reckon? A duel for old times' sake?" He winked.

Without hesitation, I stepped forward, meeting him sword for sword, shifting with ease as he circled me. And then it hit me—I was doing the same! My movements were becoming second nature, almost like we had been practising this for years. In the heat of the moment, I lost focus on the rope I had tied in my mind and felt my feet slip from Cian's back. My sword slipped from my grip, tumbling toward the ground, and I prayed it wouldn't strike anyone—or worse, a dragon. Then, suddenly, I wasn't falling down—I was falling up?

Cian dove beneath me, his massive wings pushing him upward. I had lost the connection, but instinct kicked in. "Think," I told myself. "He won't let you fall. He believes in you." Cian was faster than I had anticipated, and I reached for him, knowing this was my moment.

Got it!

I forced myself to steady my breathing as Cian soared vertically to catch me. Twisting my body, I dove to meet him. As he closed in, I reached for the massive horns above his head—my targets. I could feel him slowing as he came closer—he knew where I was going. I reached quickly, grabbed hold and held on. Cian dove again and spun. I retied the rope in my mind. I would not fall. As he straightened out, I let go, falling into his mid back between the wings. I landed in a crouched position and looked up into bright emerald eyes.

"Aye, *a lennon*, exceptionally good, next time don't let go, ey. Your brother looks like he's about to vomit."

As we flew to the ground, I looked at Tommy.

"Ok, as we get closer, you will feel Cian level out. That's when you need to run… You want to run across a wing, away from his legs, then jump into a roll. Like jumping from a height. He's slowing. Let's go."

I ran fast and leapt from his wing into a roll.

I landed in a fighting stance. I saw Claire running towards me and Malcolm, red, shaking his head. Apparently, I had attempted a bit more than he had asked for. I laughed and turned my head. Tommy had landed just beside me, and I could see Cian close by; he looked at me, bowing his head. I followed.

"Here's your sword, Alix," Claire said with a grin. "You know, I've never heard Malcolm curse so much. I thought he might pass out, he was so mad!"

Tommy came closer and handed me my second one. He smiled and whispered in my ear. "I ken you could do it, *my lady*."

He walked away a sliver of breeze lightly brushed my face. Claire giggled as Malcolm stormed toward Tommy, his face red with fury. He was cursing in every language he knew. Tommy raised his arms in mock surrender, and I couldn't help but laugh with Claire.

"Maybe we should see about some food, ey?" We turned and walked towards the castle.

***

Claire and I rode up to the fairy pools, we could only take the horses halfway before the rocks became too slippery for them. We tethered them and hiked the rest of the way. It was still early, and there was mist rising from the Bern. We took our time climbing and talking.

"Have any of the dragons taken a shine to ye, cousin?" I asked.

"No, but I'm not too worried. Sean said it took him a few years of training before he bonded with his dragon. He still rode and trained with others, but one day, his dragon found him, and they bonded. He says you have to wait for the right moment."

"Mmhmm, dragons really do things on their own terms, don't they? I suppose they haven't lived as long as they have without testing all the options."

"Grannie says you're a natural with the healing, said ye remind her of herself."

"Aye, that's kind of her. Sometimes I feel I'm not doing enough. The herbs and mending that's simple, it's the magic side that's hard—some days I'm very exhausted."

"Oh, so nothing to do with dancing all hours of the night with handsome princes, ey?" Claire began to laugh.

"It wasn't all night, and it was once! You know too much for someone who was meant to be reading."

"Och, well, I just helped with a few of the details, making sure it all came together, though I felt it was about time. I've never seen Tommy so happy afore. You bring out the good in him."

She stopped walking and turned. "Please, don't break his heart, Alix," Claire said softly, her eyes full of worry. "You've seen how much he cares for you—just be gentle with him, aye?"

"I'm worried it's mine that will break," I said, my voice quieter than I meant. We continued our climb in silence, the weight of her words hanging between us.

Then, breaking the quiet, Claire spoke again. "How much farther did Grannie say we have to go? We've been climbing half the day."

"It can't be much more. I can see the white thorn tree up ahead," I replied.

The creek had disappeared into a large rock formation. We climbed through the gap and could see the top of a waterfall. It fell softly into a large, clear pool. As we went closer, the hidden cabin was above us, the sky visible through the mist. Small flowers grew through the rocks' crevasse—white and silver against the dark stone. Butterflies and small birds were flying around.

"Well, I think it's perfect," I said to Claire.

We stripped off our leathers, then dove into the water together. The cold hit me like a shock, but as I swam, the warmth of the springs began to wrap around me, soothing my muscles. It was clear, fresh, and tasted sweet. The waterfall cascaded from the rugged mountain streams of the Cuillin Range, its waters cool and clear as they tumbled over the rocks, feeding the smaller creeks and burns that ran through the island.

"Alix, look," Claire whispered and pointed.

I could see small fairies peering their way around the rocks. "It's alright, we won't harm you," I said in a quiet, hopefully less terrifying voice. They stayed still, then slowly flew out. The fairies were ethereal creatures, their delicate, glittering faces framed by flowing hair in hues of lavender, silver, and gold. Their wings, as transparent as a spider web, shimmered in the soft, dappled light. A soft breeze carried the faint scent of wildflowers as they fluttered around us, their laughter ringing like chimes, filling the air with a sweet, melodic tune.

***

We left the pools late in the evening, a cool breeze sweeping over us as we made our way back to the horses. Along the way, we picked herbs and flowers, the growing darkness painting the landscape in hues of purple and gold. By the time we reached the glen, the light had nearly faded. Marcus was sitting on the steps as we arrived, sharpening his knives on a whetstone. Claire said goodnight as she made her way to the library. I sat with Marcus watching the moon rise in silence for a good while.

"Aye, well, my sister, ye ken Malcolm says we must leave in a few days for the gathering at Moar. Da wants us all there. We can get there quickly by dragon, but Grannie left with the horses this morning. She said you were to bring your medicines—and practise."

"She doesn't expect me to sleep these days, all the extra training I do."

Marcus shrugged his shoulders and stood. He reached out a hand to me and tilted his head to the path. A walk it was. We set off into the dark, only the moonlight to guide us. It was bright, the small stone rocks reflecting moonlight and lighting the path around the glen. We were far beyond the castle, and turning to face it we saw the mythical high fairy castle covered in vines and flowers peeking out through the stone. Its walls stood out in the moonlight.

There was a fallen tree, and we sat down, fireflies surrounding us, dancing to their own music. I could see large dark shadows flying past the castle and the moon, heading out—dragons. It still was hard to believe they were real, although now suddenly every magical creature in the tales were real, so why not dragons?

Immensely large, they were elegant in flight, weightless as they glided across the sky.

I walked out into the open glen. A whispering breeze swept through, surrounding me with a smell of the wildflowers from the meadow. I smiled—he was flying then. I turned to face Marcus, drawing my sword, and bowed low. "What do you say, *bhràthair , brother,* a moonlight duel before we head in?"

My sword felt like an extension of my very will, and the night seemed to come alive around me. I could sense the rustling of fair folk, the subtle sway of flowers, and the creatures of the dark—everything in the glen seemed to pulse with life. I adjusted my stance, feeling the thrill that always came when we sparred. We had fought countless times against one another, but each time felt unique, like a new chapter in our shared history.

Marcus laughed and drew his own sword. "Aye, but I will not go easy on ye this time. Mal's not here to stop us, ey."

We both laughed at that. My sword cut through the air with grace as it met Marcus's broader sword. A silver sheen of moonlight reflected off his sword, lighting the powerful figure before me. Indigo eyes fierce, glimmering with starlight. His dark blue armour blended with the night, and his sword—broader and sturdier than mine—sent tremors through the ground with each powerful swing. Each stroke was with the purpose to win, to test my strength and deep down, I knew to protect myself. Twins, we fought to protect each other. *"He is your right hand, your strength. Do not forget that,"* Da had said when he handed me my first broadsword.

Our blades clashed with a ringing echo that reverberated through the glen, sparks of gold and silver flickering in the moonlight. Each strike was met with the soft rustling of the enchanted glen, as though the very forest were watching. I ducked beneath Marcus's powerful swing, rolling to the side and coming up in a fluid motion, bringing me close. I could feel the warmth of his breath as I thrust my sword forward, aiming for the gap in his armour. Anticipating this, Marcus pivoted on his heel, deflecting my thrust with a quick parry; the force of the blow rippled up both our arms like lightning. It was a reminder of his strength and skill. Marcus had always been stronger, but it was his precision and experience that I respected the most.

"Nice move," he said, his voice a deep rumble that cut through the night air. There was a hint of approval there, a rare acknowledgment that made my heart race with pride.

"Thanks," I replied, my voice steady despite the adrenaline coursing through me. "I've been working on that one."

We continued our dance of steel, the rhythm of our fight perfectly synchronised. Each clash and parry felt like a conversation between us, a silent exchange of unspoken words and mutual respect. The moonlight caught our movements, casting fleeting shadows and creating a mesmerising play of light and dark. I could see the glint in Marcus's eyes, a mixture of concentration and something softer, something that spoke of the bond we shared.

We continued our dance. I twirled, finding my mark and striking. Marcus was forced to take a step back, and a rare smile formed on his face amidst the intensity of our spar. He was acknowledging my skills, knowing the endless training I had put in was paying off.

"Not bad, you've been holding back on me." His voice was warm despite the competitive edge to it.

Now I was grinning. "Well, I ken how you'd appreciate a challenge."

Our blades continued to meet, silver and gold sparking between the blades and our dancing feet. Sparks landed on the grass, fizzling out in the coolness of the night. Then the duel came to an end and the glen around us quietened. We paused, facing each other, our breaths like mist in the cool night air.

"I've been practising too." He began to spin his sword in a circular motion, faster and faster, than a flame appeared, a shield of fire. He slowed again, swinging steady, side to side, his sword flaming bright amber and gold against the night sky. I could feel the heat; it was beautiful. He brought it out slowly, holding it with both hands drawn to a point in front of his face, then stabbed high into the sky, like a mythical warrior leading his clan to war. With a twist of his wrist, it was out, and suddenly the night drew dark and cold. "Impressive, no?"

"Aye, aye it is." And boy, it was. He suddenly seemed older, wiser than the playful Marcus who travelled here. More focus; fine-tuning himself to be the warrior he was destined to be.

"Those sparks, the gold and silver, has that happened before?" he asked. I paused, thinking, had it happened, or was it the sun?

"I think maybe once, back at Dunscaith, but I thought it was just the sunlight."

"It's not sunlight, it's the colours of your hair. The stars, Alix. I ken you're a healer, I have no doubt after my nose. I saw the light then, too. Like stars, Alix, there is more magic than I reckon you ken. Speak with the auld ones, I reckon."

We sheathed our swords and walked back to the castle in silence, the night closing around us. A profound sense of connection lingered, the weight of our shared moment settling between us. With Marcus at my side, I knew I was invincible—not just in battle, but in the unspoken promise of our unbreakable twin bond.

***

I spent the next days working with Malcolm while the bonded riders practised in the air. He asked me over and over to describe the sparks, what Marcus had called starlight, what exactly I was doing or thinking when they appeared. From dawn to dusk, only stopping to eat, we sparred. Sometimes Marcus would take over, and we continued. The dragons would stop and watch. The silver one spent hours on the grass watching, never speaking, just quietly still in the close distance, its silver eyes intent on the swords. I was becoming frustrated; nothing was working. We were done for the day, and I was splashing water on my face at the stream when I saw them fly in, Tommy, Liam, and Sean. I hadn't seen them for days, which wasn't unusual. They were scouts, always flying out, sometimes at night, but usually spent a few hours—those they could spare—to help Claire and Marcus on their dragons.

I still hadn't bonded; I could ride, and Cian was always happy to train me, but the others had their own dragons. I'd listen to their stories as I fixed their scrapes and breaks. Claire was always kind enough not to say much and would rather speak about her books or the fairies. As I looked up, I saw Cian land near the silver dragon, and Tommy jumped down. He lifted his hand in a wave. I ignored it and threw water on my face, stood, and walked towards the castle. I stormed my way up the path and into the courtyard. I could hear him call out my name. He ran behind me. I could hear the soft landing of his boots on the rocks.

"Alix! Alix, will ye stop for a minute, *a lennon?*"

I stopped, swinging around, my face fierce and eyes blazing, "What!"

He stopped, taken aback, his eyebrows raised, and a smile on his face. His stupid, beautiful golden face with stupid emerald eyes stared back. He brushed his hands through his hair. "Ye alright, *mo chridhe?*"

"Delightful, excuse me." I turned in a fury towards the stairs to my chambers. I saw Marcus and Malcolm come down the stairs. They took one look at me, paused, then walked past. I heard them slap their hands on Tommy's shoulder, "*adh more mo charaid.*" Good luck, my friend. "*Cracicailte banshee.*" Crazy banshee.

Both my brothers were laughing as they left the courtyard.

"Alix!"

I stormed up the steps towards my room. As I reached the top floor, the open door slammed shut. I turned around to find two emerald eyes looking at me with golden eyebrows raised. "Ye going to talk to me now, *mo chridhe*? I've all the time in the world." His arms were wide open in a gesture.

"*Ifrin,* I don't want to talk. I want to go to my room, open it." I slammed my hand on the wooden door.

"No, not until you tell me what's wrong, you're storming across the glen like you're about to raid a village, hair flying behind ye in the wind."

I took a deep breath and drew myself to my full height, looking down at him as much as possible for someone a foot taller than me. "You don't get it! It's all about dragons and magic, and I can't—"

My voice faltered. I turned away, fighting the heat in my face. My breath was quick, but I couldn't stop myself. "I can't bond, I can't wield magic! I can't ride a dragon, and I—" shouting now, my fists clenched. "I'm just a healer! That's it! Nothing more!"

"You're a great healer, Alix, with or without magic, and you're only just starting with the magic. They have had years." Tommy was calm, voice soft. The door wouldn't budge, but I kept shaking it, pushing on it. Bloody bastard, stupid magical bastard.

"Let go of the bloody door!"

"No."

"Yes, you bastard, open it."

"No."

"Do you ken who I am? These are my lands, leave, leave me alone."

"Aye, I do, better than ye think, lass. No, I will not leave until ye mean it. I ken ye don't." He was trying to stay calm.

"I do mean it, leave or don't, I do not care! I'm leaving, so it doesn't matter." I pounded on the door. "Let it go!"

He did, and I fell into the room. Regaining my balance, I turned quickly to slam the door in his face. I was too slow; he was already in the room. The door slowly closed behind him. His hands were on his hips. Ready for a fight, then; well, he was going to get one.

"Get out! Get on your dragon and go back to Eire! To wherever you belong, just go." I turned away. I wouldn't cry.

"Lass, I'm not going anywhere, so you'll tell me what's actually the matter and I ken it's got nothing to do with dragons."

"Yeah, well, I don't have a dragon, do I? So, get on yours and leave!"

"Aye, you might never bond with a dragon, but it doesn't mean you're not a rider."

"Oh, so you suggest I just start climbing on all the dragons I see, hopefully I don't get eaten or burnt up, aye. I'll get right on it."

"You ken very well what I mean, *a lennon.*"

We were silent. I turned away from him, the rawness of our argument still ringing in my ears. I walked to the window, my fingers brushing the cool stone, feeling the weight of the silence that followed. Outside, the twilight deepened, matching the heaviness building in my chest. Tommy didn't speak, and neither did I. The quiet was unbearable, but neither of us could break it.

"I can't go back, Tommy. Not after everything I've seen. Not pretending this world doesn't exist anymore."

"This world is not only here, Alix, it's just a bit freer, aye. There are more fae, auld folk, and those who protect them here. Those who were scared left the islands long ago, and those who stayed accepted them. They're everywhere in our lands and so is their magic, and yours… it's not going anywhere *mo nighean*."

"I don't want to go."

"It's not like ye won't come back. After the gathering, Brian, Niamh, Mal, Claire, and your grannie—they'll all be back. Just come back with them."

"Aye, well." I continued to look through the window. "Things change." My voice was almost a whisper.

"What do you fear, *a lennon*?" I heard him sit on my desk. He had taken his swords off and placed them against the door.

"I fear being locked away in a tower, Tommy, where all I am is a title, a responsibility, a duty. Not Alix. Not me. I fear the weight of what I'm expected to become, what I'm expected to do... And I can't—"

I shook my head, looking out at the fading sky. "I just want to be free. To choose. To fly without being tied down to something that isn't me."

"*A chuisle mo chroi,*" he walked over, placing a hand on my cheek. I hadn't realised I was crying, as he wiped away a tear. "You are strong and fierce. I do not think anyone could put you in a cage, even dragons who choose to bond are not bound. They are free, free to fly to be themselves. They choose to stay." He kissed the top of my head, soft and gentle. "I also choose to stay *a chuisle mo chroi.*"

The sun dipped lower, casting a soft, golden light over the room. The stone walls seemed to glow, the tapestries deepening in colour with the fading light. Outside, the sky shifted from brilliant yellows and reds to the rich purples of night, the last embers of daylight burning out, just as my own heart seemed to burn with all that had passed between us. Tommy stood next to me, looking out. He was a comforting warmth against the coolness of the twilight breeze. The soft glow of twilight illuminated his features, his eyes glimmering bright in the light.

"Alix," his voice was soft, almost a whisper. I turned to face him, my heart beating rapidly against my chest. "Marry me, *a chuisle mo chroi.*" His words were hesitant, but there was no doubt in his eyes. "Not because of tradition. Not because of duty. But because, from the moment I met you...

From the moment you knocked me on my arse in the forest, I knew this was it. You're everything I never thought I needed.

"What I feel… It's god, I love you, but it's more. I feel it in every beat of my heart. It didn't matter then whether you were Alix from the woods, Lady Alix, or some princess. It doesn't matter now.

"Alix, I know you don't want to be married. I never planned to either; I've been fighting it for years.

"Until you. You, you're stubborn, infuriating, fierce, beautiful, and when you smile, my heart skips a beat. It's like I was drowning for air, but you pulled me out.

"So, marry me, but not if it means putting you into a cage for a life you do not want. But Alix, I like to think we could be different, break the tradition you ken? We could be free together, happy."

I couldn't speak; the words hung between us. He took a deep breath, his hands reaching out to hold mine. His touch sent a shiver up my arms, and I looked up at him. The question hung heavy in the air between us, resonating with the weight of every emotion I was feeling. Was this really happening? His words were both a promise and a plea, a declaration and a request, the question wrapped in the tenderness of his emerald gaze. As his words sank in, the moment I had been avoiding my entire life was suddenly in front of me. My heart was a storm of joy, disbelief, happiness, and overwhelming love. Every moment we had shared, each challenge, argument, every glance, every smile, every stolen moment, each touch was flashing through my mind, reinforcing the depth of what we had together. This wouldn't be for convenience, alliance, or gain. This wouldn't be a cage, this wouldn't be for someone else. This would be for us.

"Yes," I whispered, my voice trembling with emotion. "Yes, Tommy, I will marry you."

I had barely gotten the words out before Tommy's face lit up with a radiant smile. His shoulders dropped in relief; he was nervous. He was laughing with joy, and I couldn't help but laugh also. He pulled me into an embrace, wrapping his arms around me and spinning me around the room. His arms embraced me in a way that made me feel both safe and excited. I could feel the steady beat of his heart in time with mine.

In that moment, as I looked out the window into the deepening twilight, the fairy glen below shone in the magical light of twilight, and I was surrounded by the love and promise of a future, whatever it held, and that moment felt perfect. The prophecies, the upcoming wars, the unknown future, and truths, they didn't matter. I could be me, I could be happy, and I could be free. Because whatever was coming, we would face it together.

A strange shiver in the air made my skin prickle, a crackling energy like static before a storm. Suddenly, the castle shook, and a bright explosion of light tore through the room. Dust filled the air, and the world seemed to splinter into chaos. We dove under the table, my hands on my head, Tommy's body pressed against mine as he shielded me with his own. The weight of the debris rained down, but he didn't move, didn't flinch. His eyes met mine, concern etched in every line of his face, his arms tightly wrapped around me. "You're alright, Alix. Stay with me," he whispered, though the trembling in his voice betrayed his fear.

"What is happening?" I asked.

"I think we have been attacked, *mo grá*, that was a magical explosion, are ye alright?" He lifted himself off me; he was covered in ceiling dust, and I wasn't much better. The right top corner of my ceiling was caved in. The room above, the staircase.

"Claire—she's likely in the library!" I stood up, running to the door. Tommy grabbed his swords, throwing mine as we ran to the door. It took the two of us to push it open. The landing was only just there, but the staircase above was missing.

"Ifrin."

We would have to go down and across. I began to run, jumping across the missing stairs, and fire lights were appearing around the courtyard. Malcolm—he was ok.

"I'll meet your brother, try and get access to the library. Chances are she wasn't alone, I ken Liam was heading that way to see her," Tommy said, and nodded as he pointed to Marcus. "Stay with Marcus, be careful." He jumped down into the lower courtyard, all happiness from the last hour missing and pure warrior focus on his face.

Right, Marcus. I could see him not far from me. I called out, and suddenly he drew his sword. I could see a large dark figure, draped in a cloak with a hood covering its head. It had a long staff swinging to match Marcus's drawn sword. It was only a few metres jump from here; if I could get a run, I could make it. I turned, running backwards, checking to make sure my weapons were secure, then ran as fast as I could. I jumped, leaping with all my speed and strength to the other side, landing in a crouch position.

I heard the soft patter of small rocks tumbling down as the air above me shifted. I looked up, just in time to see a cloaked figure descending, a staff raised high. Its dark silhouette loomed above, casting a long shadow over me. Panic surged as I realised it was about to land directly on top of me. Without thinking, I rolled to the side, the ground rough against my shoulder as I hit the dirt, scrambling to my feet just as the figure landed with a heavy thud, its staff swaying dangerously. My heart raced—two of them now. We couldn't afford to let our guard down.

Marcus and I were back-to-back, swords out, each other's right hand. My sword met a staff, and a loud clang echoed across the grounds. What was it made of? Wood would surely break; it was not iron. It was strong, the dark creature was meeting my stokes. The dark hoods were covering them completely over their faces; I could only see yellow slitted eyes peering out.

I felt the cold metal of my *sgian dubh* hidden beneath my corset, its presence a steady reminder of the power I could wield. As my sword clashed against the creature's staff, I saw an opening—a brief, fleeting moment of vulnerability. Without thinking, I turned, my fingers brushing the hilt of the dagger. I pulled it free, the motion fluid but desperate. My heart pounded as I threw the blade with every ounce of force I had, watching it sail through the air in a blur of silver. Time seemed to stretch as it twisted and spun toward its target. A sharp crack split the air, followed by a flash of bright white light—lightning crackling, a searing warmth radiating from the point of impact.

It hit the creature in the centre of where, if it were human, would be a heart. There was an ear-piercing screech. Both Marcus and I held our ears and dropped to the ground. The creature I'd hit was reeling backward, bending its back as far as possible, letting out the scream. A white fire reached from the *sgian dubh* out into the limbs. From the noise and what I could see, it was burning the creature from the inside out.

The white light followed up its chest up into the neck and face; teeth showed in the darkness, long and jagged, while the yellow-slitted eyes were wide open and bright.

I glanced at Marcus, his own eyes wide in shock, his sword still raised, but his gaze locked on the creature. The white light blazed from the thing's chest, illuminating the courtyard in an eerie glow. His breath was shallow, as if even he couldn't fully comprehend the horror unfolding before us. Slowly, his eyes drifted to mine, searching my face for answers I didn't have. At that moment, it wasn't just the creature we were facing. It was the realisation that we were no longer fighting just for survival—we were fighting something ancient, something unknown. I swallowed hard, trying to steady my breath, but the world still felt like it was spinning.

Suddenly, his gaze shifted. He let go of his ears, rolling with his sword out, stabbing the other dark creature as he dove at my back, staff ready to strike. I had instantly rolled as I saw Marcus's sword in his hand, ready to strike. Both our swords impaled the creature, Marcus's blade lit with a blazing red fire mine, matching with white. The light was blinding. I held on, both my hands gripping my sword. The creature was squirming, light burning like the one before, fire engulfing it. "Hold on, Alix!" Marcus pulled his sword loose, stood and swung, slicing the creature's head. Black ooze spurted to the ground, and he lifted his leg and kicked, unimpaling the creature from my sword and landing it in the courtyard. The screeching ended, I rolled, looking over the edge to see the black ooze pooling on the white stones, the body disintegrating into nothing; only the black cloth cloak remained and its staff. I vomited over the ledge. A warm hand clasped my shoulder. "Ye all right, *mo phiuthar*?"

"Nay, what was that?" I asked.

"I donna ken, I wouldn't much like to see it again."

He reached out a hand and lifted me to my feet. We cleaned our swords and ran up what was left of the staircase towards the library. We reached it and it was glowing. Its great oak door opened as we reached it, slamming shut behind us. We looked at each other, shrugging our shoulders, odd.

"Claire! Liam!"

"Alix! We're here! Hurry, Liam's hurt!"

We ran over to her voice; stone and books had landed on them. Liam's head was bleeding, but not much. I glanced over at Claire, who smiled.

"I'm ok, please see to him." She was holding his head in her lap, brushing his head. I nodded. I turned to have a better look: he'd been hit hard. I couldn't feel anything more than the lump forming. Closing my eyes, I imagined I could see the bruising below and the swelling. I focused my power there.

Focus, what should it feel like, Alix.

Gotcha. I moved the fluid throughout, absorbing it into the flesh. The lump was shrinking, and the bleeding from the site stopped.

"Marcus, can you clear the mess? We need to get him up." I continued to examine Liam, pausing to check I hadn't missed anything. Marcus and I got him up onto one of the lounges and laid him down. He was too tall and his legs hung over, but his head was cushioned. With Claire close behind, he opened his eyes.

I scanned Liam's face once more, feeling his pulse beneath my fingers. The wound on his head was already beginning to close, but he was still pale, his breath shallow. His eyes fluttered open, a flicker of recognition passing through them before his gaze became unfocused. "Where am I?" he mumbled, his voice weak, almost lost in the noise of the battle still echoing in my ears. I let out a sigh of relief when he managed to lift his head slightly, his mind still intact. His body, however, needed rest. I gently pushed him back onto the cushions, smoothing the hair from his forehead.

"You'll be fine," I whispered, but even I wasn't sure if I was reassuring him or myself.

As I turned, something caught my eye—Claire was standing, but her face was ashen, her arm clutched tightly against her chest. My heart skipped a beat as she collapsed, crumpling to the ground like a rag doll. Time slowed as

Marcus rushed forward, his hands reaching for her just in time, pulling her close before she could hit the stone floor. His face was a mask of determination, but his grip on her seemed gentler than I'd expected, as if afraid that if he held her too tightly, she might break into pieces.

"Claire!" I shouted, rushing over to them, but my mind was already racing—what happened? Was she hurt worse than she let on?

We got her to another lounge, and I had a look. Her arm was broken, she was in pain and shocked. I mended her bone, making a sling out of a nearby curtain. Marcus walked over to the nearest window, and the glow of the library lit the outside of the window. A shield? He nodded and walked out the double doors.

He returned shortly.

"It's over. Whatever they were, Mal reckons there were only three. We got two, and he and Tommy got the other. Tommy and Sean are riding out with the dragons to make sure it is clear. The auld ones will make some shield over the castle, keeping whatever it is out," he said. "I tried to explain the library, but no one knows about it. Cian seems to think it's a spell the auld ones placed to keep the family safe, but it's old magic, not something they have seen here before."

"Aye, well, these two need rest. I think we should keep them here. It's warm, protected, and easy to defend. I need to get to my bag. Can you watch them while I go? If they wake up, give them some water."

He nodded. I grabbed my sword, making my way to the double doors. As I touched it, I thanked it, or whoever it was that protected it. Walking the long way around the library, I could see Mal pacing the wall. His dragon was in the courtyard, looking out. I walked towards him. "What were they?" I asked.

"I do not ken. Nothing I've seen before, I couldn't get a good look. They were covered in a dark cloak. Marcus said you burned one from the inside? Like lightning hitting a tree?" His eyebrows lifted, his dragon tilted his head listening.

"Aye, I threw my *sgian dubh*, there was a crack, then a blaze of white light, it hit the dark creature and… it screamed a god-awful scream. The light burned through its veins or bones, I dinna ken. It was horrible…"

"And the other?"

"It came at us. Marcus stabbed it first; flames were travelling up his sword, then I stabbed it with mine. It screamed, and the light travelled through it. I held it as Marcus beheaded it. Black gloop went everywhere; we tossed it into the courtyard. Before we could get there, it was gone, only a cloak and staff left."

He nodded. "Aye, the one we got was similar; nothing would touch it until I lit my sword, then it began to back away. Tommy held it long enough for me to behead it, too. It also disappeared."

I rubbed my eyes. I was tired. Exhausted from healing and the fight. "Marcus is watching Claire and Liam. I need to get my bag."

He nodded again and brought me close in an embrace, his arms wrapped around me. He took his cloak off and tucked me in, sitting me on the wall next to him. "In a moment, *mo phiuthar*, it can wait." He paused, looking down and brushed a stray hair from my face. "Did he ask ye?"

I looked up into his blue eyes, smiling. "Aye... how did ye ken?"

"I told him he had my permission to ask, Marcus reckoned you'd punch him and not answer. I ken you weren't keen on ever settling down, but I've seen the way you look at each other, and if that's not worth fighting for, then I do not ken what is. Plus, I rather like him, great warrior if we need one." He was laughing. "Battle strategies you ken... close ye eyes, *A ghràidh*, we have the watch."

Chapter Twelve

MALCOLM WOKE ME IN THE EARLY hours of the morning. I could see two figures walking towards the castle. I looked up at him.

"Aye, off ye go, lass."

I ran down the stairs, watching, observing their gait, looking for any injury. They looked tired. Sean had his pack in his hand and was walking with his usual long stride. Tommy had his pack over one shoulder, his sword strapped to his back. I made my way down, walking faster than normal. They looked up. Sean nodded and began walking to the back entrance.

Tommy's figure drew closer, his weary form moving with a quiet determination, the weight of exhaustion pressing down on him like a shadow. His face was grimy, streaked with sweat and dirt, his usually confident stride slower, but still steady. As he neared, the silent intensity in his eyes spoke volumes, though the exhaustion in his body made his every step seem heavy.

He dropped his bag with a soft thud and took a step forward, his hands reaching for my face, his touch both rough and gentle. The callouses from battle pressed against my skin, the warmth of his hands melting the chill I hadn't noticed had crept into my bones. I closed my eyes briefly, feeling the heat of his palms against my cold cheeks. Had it been so long?

With a soft brush of his thumb, he wiped away the grime from my face, a simple gesture that sent an unexpected shiver through me. A small, tender smile spread across his face, and before I could speak, his lips were on mine.

The kiss was sudden, fierce, and all-encompassing, as if everything that had been left unsaid between us was now spilling out. I wrapped my arms around his neck, pulling myself closer, the pressure of his lips grounding me. The urgency of the moment, the raw emotion, left me breathless as he pulled back.

I could taste the remnants of battle—sweat, blood, dust—on his lips. But underneath it all, there was a warmth.

A cool breeze chilled the air. He picked up his bag, and we walked back up the stairs into the castle, looking around at the rubble left behind from the battle. Three creatures did all this damage. As we reached the well, Tommy walked up, splashing freezing water all over his face and hair. He looked like a wet dog shaking his coat. We made our way to the library to the others. The doors were still closed firmly, a golden light covering them. As we got closer, they opened.

In the main lounge, I could see Sean sitting upright on the lounge, while small fairies surrounded Claire, all doting on her, bringing small drinks and cakes—one was even brushing her hair. Marcus had been sitting on a chair near the fire, legs up over the armrest, mouth open and snoring, covered in dirt.

"Alix, Tommy, you're alright." Claire smiled and came over, grasping my hands. "Thank you, Alix…. Miss Alice made us up some rooms in the library quarters just up the stairs and to the left, yours is in the far one at the end. Tommy, there is a room for you second one from the end." She turned her head, listening to one of the fairies near her ear. "Thank you, Bree. There's hot water too in the rooms, and food. You both look terrible. Alix, we are fine, and Marcus looks like he will sleep for days or until the fairies kick him out for the smell." She smiled and walked towards Liam, handing him a warm cup of something. Apart from the bruising bump on the head, he looked good. He, too, had been cleaned and was in fresh clothes. We made our way to our rooms. Tommy kissed my hand, leaving me at the door to my new room.

The room was unlike anything I had seen before, a peaceful haven amid the chaos. Delicate flowers and tendrils of ivy cascaded from the ceiling, their scent filling the air. By the window, a wooden bath steamed gently, the water alive with the vibrant hues of petals and fragrant herbs. I could see fresh clothing from my room, folded on the bed, along with a towel. I looked around, looking for the mysterious Miss Alice, but found no one tall or small.

I stepped over to the bath, shedding my clothing. It was incredibly warm. The water stung my cuts and eased my bruising, and as I washed the grime from my hair, I was immediately feeling more relaxed and fresher. As I climbed out, the water emptied and the bath disappeared; my filthy clothes and boots were gone too. I dried and dressed, and a brush appeared on the table near the window. I loosely braided my hair.

Looking around, I still couldn't see anyone.

"Thank you for everything, especially the bath."

I turned and smiled. Two mugs of hot chocolate sat by the bed. As I was walking over, there was a knock on the door. I answered, expecting to find a rather large fairy housekeeper, but instead, it was an emerald-eyed man, face red from shaving, and hair damp.

"Do you also have a magical room?"

I gestured to the two mugs.

He laughed, grabbing one. "I thank ye, Miss Alice, that will be all." He walked over to the window seat with the two drinks.

"Do ye know Miss Alice?"

"Aye, who else do you think ran the castle all these years… your grannie?"

"I… um, never thought about it. I was a little distracted with all the family secrets, ye ken."

He was smiling, drinking his chocolate.

***

The time had come to leave the quiet of the glen behind, and with it the weight of everything that had passed. I climbed onto Cian, the dragon's scales cool under my fingers. The pack settled across my back, and I felt the familiar rhythm of the dragon's movements beneath me. Each flight felt more natural now, as if the bond between us had solidified with each passing day. My body had grown stronger, more attuned to his every rise and dip in the sky.

As we soared above the Cuillin Ranges, the jagged peaks below us bathed in the pale light of morning, a sudden peace washed over me. The dark glens and lochs of Skye spread out beneath us, a landscape so familiar it felt like home. We crossed the sea, the cold wind biting at my cheeks as we neared the Bruce's croft, where the land seemed to breathe with a welcoming exhale.

Our horses were waiting for us. Tommy, Sean, and Liam would continue to Eire before making their way to Moar as guests of Brian in a week. The MacLeods would continue by horseback in time for the gathering. We parted ways with the others in the evening. I watched as they flew into the sunset and to the west. A cool breeze and the scent of wildflowers brushed my face as Tommy glided into the mist.

One week.

We made our way through our lands towards Moar, meeting a few clansmen making their way to the gathering. The pines smelled strong along the path, and the woods were alive. We climbed the moors and the valleys, stopping only to rest at night, where we discussed our attackers in the glen. We duelled, sparred, and compared techniques through the days. We passed no fairy folk. It was as though they had retreated further into the woods, where only the animals and the birds remained. A lone horseman was waiting for us on top of the last Munro as we rode alone.

He was atop a large dark horse, its mane braided. The man himself was large and strong, dressed in his finest warrior clothing, kilt, and plaid waving in the wind, glimmers of silver and gold hair lit in the sun. He raised a long sword into the sun in welcome. I turned to my brothers, and together, we lifted our swords high, a signal that was both a greeting and a declaration. The boys ignited their blades with fire, while mine shimmered in the sunlight, its reflection a silent bond between us. The MacLeod had been waiting for us, standing proud at the peak.

With a swift kick to my horse's sides, I urged her forward, the path narrowing as I approached the top. There, waiting like an anchor in the storm, was Da. His large frame loomed against the horizon, and as I slid off my mount, I felt a rush of emotions I hadn't anticipated.

Without a word, he reached for me, his hands strong but gentle as they cradled my face. The world fell away for a moment, and I was simply his daughter again, safe in his embrace. "Da," I whispered, feeling the weight of his calloused hands and the deep bond between us, a touch that said more than words ever could.

"Mo nighean, mo chridhe Alexandria." My daughter, my heart, Alexandria. "It lightens my heart to see you home, lass."

"Aye, and what of us, ey?" Malcolm and Marcus stood tall, wearing similar serious faces, and they stared down the MacLeod. He turned to meet their eyes.

"Aye, well, that depends if I heard right, you two bollocks have let your sister go wild, riding dragons, killing assassins, lighting fires, damaging property…" He walked right up to them, and the brothers looked at each other, unsure what to say. "And then there's the matter of the Patrick boy from Eire." He tapped them both on the back of their heads and walked away, bellowing with laughter. "Claire, lass, it's good to see you. I have a book set aside I reckon you'd like. And what are you two still standing there with your cobs open? I'd like to make it back before Mrs Mac's apple tart is gone."

At that, we all laughed. It was good to be home.

The ride took half a day, and as we shared stories with Da, I couldn't help but notice the changes in him. His face was etched with lines, deeper than I remembered, as though the time apart had added years to his shoulders. We fell into easy conversation, but my thoughts kept wandering ahead, toward the home we had left behind.

As we neared Caisteal Moar, I saw the first flicker of light in the distance—the soft glow of campfires scattered across the land. The air was thick with the scent of smoke and fresh pine. Clansmen and their families had gathered, their tents and makeshift homes dotted across the grounds, a sea of faces all in motion. Children ran with laughter ringing through the air, their small voices bright against the hum of activity. Mothers tended fires or washed clothes, while fathers prepared for the evening meal.

The sight of so many people gathered in the heart of our lands stirred something deep within me, a sense of homecoming so intense it nearly took my breath away. The keep rose in the distance, glowing with the warmth of family and tradition, its walls standing proud against the fading light of day.

We had returned just in time for the celebration to begin, though it felt almost surreal. The buzz of the clan outside, the laughter and singing, seemed so distant compared to what we had just endured. Dinner would be held in the main chambers upstairs, but I wasn't sure I was ready to join in just yet. My mind still lingered on the battle in the glen, on the moments of uncertainty.

But then, as we reached the stables, something changed. A hush fell over the camp as if the land itself was holding its breath. From the distant hills and the treetops, I saw them. Dark shapes cut against the sky—dragons, their massive wings beating slow and steady through the clouds. The sight was so sudden and breathtaking that I almost forgot to breathe.

They circled above the keep, their eyes gleaming like embers in the fading light. Even from a distance, I could feel the weight of their presence, the air around me crackling with their power. It wasn't just a reminder that they had returned—it was a declaration. The dragons from Skye had come home, their watchful eyes scanning the land for any sign of danger.

I looked up at the sky again, the dragons now fading into the mist, their silhouettes disappearing as silently as they had arrived. Their presence, though, lingered—strong, silent, and watchful—ensuring that we were safe, and that no harm would reach us.

Dinner that night was quieter than usual. Though the fire crackled in the hearth and the laughter of the family filled the air, there was an unspoken understanding between us all that the dragons, those mighty guardians, were keeping a silent vigil over the keep. The attack in the glen had brought much to light, and we all knew the danger wasn't over yet. But tonight, we were safe thanks to the dragons, who would always be there, watching from the shadows.

Chapter Thirteen

I WOKE TO THE SOUND OF PIPES reverberating off the stone walls of the castle, their haunting melody reaching deep into my soul, a song of strength, longing, and home. The sun was still low, casting a soft golden glow over the landscape, but a thick, almost mystical mist crept slowly from the moors that surrounded us, rising like a living thing—swirling from the earth, wrapping itself in tendrils that climbed to meet the sky. I stood for a moment at the window, drawn in by the beauty and the promise of the day ahead, feeling the pulse of the land beneath me.

I dressed quickly in the MacLeod colours—a deep blue tartan that echoed the sea to Skye—and secured my sword and dirk at my side. My mother's ring glinted on my right hand, the copper setting catching the light as I slipped it on. I braided my hair before making my way down the stone staircase, my footsteps echoing in the cold air.

As I made my way to the kitchens, the warm, welcoming scent of fresh bannock filled the air, mingling with the sounds of clattering pots and the cheerful hum of the maids as they worked. Laughter bubbled from the hearth where a fire crackled, sending occasional flickers of light across the stone walls.

Marcus appeared suddenly, running out the side door, a wide grin plastered across his face. Without warning, he tossed a bannock in my direction and I barely caught it.

"I think we'd better leave before Mrs. Mac's fiery temper takes another bite out of me," he said, winking as he bit into his own bannock, oblivious to the crumbs falling from his mouth.

I laughed, shaking my head. "You've a death wish, you know that?" I said, slipping past the kitchen door and out into the yard with him.

Today, the grounds were alive with energy, the early morning air filled with the roars and cheers of spectators gathering in the clearing. The men were showing off their strength in the age-old contest of stone throwing. The clan men lined up, each walking forward with a stone in hand, their muscles rippling beneath their shirts as they hurled the rocks with impressive force, sending them sailing through the air like darts. The crowd roared with each throw, some cheering their family members on, others teasing those who fell short. Stone throwing was as much a tradition on our lands as the sound of the pipes.

I watched with pride as my brothers stepped up one by one, their faces set with determination. Callum's stone soared far, a victory that would be difficult to match. The crowd cheered, and I joined in, clapping as he threw the final stone. Even the Clan MacLeod's fiercest rivals could do nothing but watch in admiration.

Next was the caber toss. I watched as the men walked over to the large logs. Angus Grant and Dougal Fraser were competing, talking as they adjusted their kilts. All three of my brothers would compete, all a head taller than Grant and Fraser. I watched as Marcus heaved a large log, his face masked with concentration as he launched it into the air. I held my breath as though time was pausing as it fell perfectly straight, landing upright and pointing towards the heavens above. That would be hard to beat. The crowd was cheering, and I clapped along.

Today I was to keep watch, to guard the MacLeod, but also to show my presence as his daughter—dignified, proper, and Lady of *Caisteal Moar*. Fathers from other clans introduced their sons to the MacLeod, prospects of marriage and lands, displays of strength and brawn. Unfortunately for them, the MacLeod brothers were a force to be beaten, their strength winning each of the three games today. The night was filled with music and dancing, decent food, and whisky.

Young girls followed Marcus and Malcolm around the hall, listening to their stories of battles, real and otherwise. Claire and I entertained ourselves at the back of the hall, the occasional dance with whomever Auntie Genevieve had pushed on us. Auntie Niamh laughed as she watched us from the dais, Brian at her side as they talked to Grannie. The music went late into the night. I sat on the parapet with my dog Cody, listening to it fade in the night and watching the people leave to camp under the stars or their cottages below.

***

The archery competition was next, and I stood on the sidelines, watching with mild amusement as Fraser and Grant took their turns. Neither of them was particularly skilled with a bow, though they put on a good show. They hit the stationary targets but missed every single moving one, their faces flushing with frustration each time their arrows veered wide of the mark. It was clear the competition was a foregone conclusion, and I could already feel the eyes of the crowd turning to me, waiting.

I glanced at the MacLeod, and I saw a spark of challenge in his eyes. I nodded back, a silent invitation for him to watch. A playful thrill stirred within me, and I found myself ready to prove more than just my aim.

Before Auntie Gen could offer any protest, I vaulted over the side of the platform and onto the field below. The crowd parted with a murmur of surprise as I strode confidently to where the archers stood, my heart beating faster with each step.

"Lady Alix, have you come to bestow a kiss for luck?" Fraser called out, his voice full of teasing.

I gave him a playful wave, my lips curling into a half-smile. "I think I'll do just fine without a kiss, Fraser."

Grant raised an eyebrow, the bow in his hand still cocked. "Aye, but I didn't think womenfolk could manage with such things."

I grinned and took the bow from Marcus, giving him a knowing look. "Oh, I'm sure I'll manage."

Marcus glanced at me warily, a flicker of concern in his eyes.

"Do ye know how to use it?" Fraser asked.

"It can't be too difficult," I said casually, already positioning the arrow. "But if I need help, I'm sure someone will show me the ropes."

I drew the bow back slowly, feeling the familiar tension in my fingers, the weight of the wood in my hands. The scent of pine trees and ripe apples from the nearby orchard filled my lungs, grounding me in the moment. A steadying breath, a moment of calm—and then I released.

The arrow flew true, striking dead centre of the target with a satisfying thud.

The crowd gasped, and I could hear Claire's cheer rise above the rest, her voice ringing out with pride. The men around me were equally stunned, some offering reluctant congratulations, others wearing expressions of quiet astonishment. It was clear my challenge had rattled their egos.

"What are you doing, lass? Aunt Gen's face is fuming," Marcus hissed under his breath, clearly trying to keep his voice low.

I didn't glance his way. "I'm bored, Marcus. Tired of playing the perfect lady for them. I need to hit something. Besides, I'm sure it's frowned upon if I start beating up suitors, eh?" I gave him a wink, but my eyes were fixed on the next target.

I walked toward the line of standing targets, five spaced apart at even intervals. Easy enough for me. The crowd murmured, and the men closed in around me, offering bits of advice—though nothing I needed. I smiled politely and, without hesitation, cocked the arrow. I breathed in, savouring the scent of pine and straw that mixed with the sweet, heady smell of apples from the orchard.

On my exhale, I let the arrow fly. It struck true, right in the centre of the target.

Claire was the first to cheer, clapping and yelling my name as the crowd erupted into applause. The men around me were equally vocal in their congratulations, though there was an underlying sting to their words. Their pride had been wounded, and they had no idea how to cope with the fact that a woman had just outshot them.

I tuned out the noise, my focus narrowing as I walked steadily to the next target. Without waiting, I cocked the bow again. I took another breath, steadying myself. *Pluck.* Silence. The arrow flew, and it struck true again: dead centre.

The cheers grew louder this time, some surprised, others more genuine, as the men around me exchanged glances. I could hear my father's voice over the rest, loud and proud, and my brothers' shouts of encouragement followed closely behind.

Fraser and Grant approached, looking somewhat deflated but determined to save face. "Well, lass," Grant said with a forced smile, "standing targets are a tad simple, are they not? Let's see how you go with the moving ones."

I nodded, already walking toward the next challenge. The moving targets. This was what I'd been waiting for.

The air seemed to still around me as I turned to MacLeod, offering him a silent nod. His eyes flickered with an approving glint, and for a brief moment, I saw something like a smile tug at the corners of his mouth.

I focused, blocking out the sounds of the crowd as I knocked my first arrow. The clay targets flew into the air—high, fast, and scattered—an extension of my arm and breath. I let four arrows go in quick succession, each one finding its mark, striking the targets in perfect sequence.

The crowd fell silent, the anticipation heavy in the air. I stood there for a moment, letting the stillness settle over me. Then I turned toward Marcus, handing him back his bow. I didn't need to say anything; the look on his face said it all.

The crowd exploded into cheers, my brothers' voices ringing out above the rest. I caught sight of MacLeod standing tall, his head nodding in approval, a broad smile spreading across his face. The other Lairds beside him had their mouths agape, no doubt trying to decide whether they should start considering me as a potential daughter-in-law—or an opponent to be reckoned with.

As I made my way down towards the main keep, the air became thick with the smell of roasting meat from the kitchen below, promising a feast worthy of their occasion. Tonight, the men and warriors would pledge their allegiance to the MacLeod.

Aunt Gen met me in my chambers, her smile wide as I entered the room. "Alix, did ye really have to show all the men up today?" She raised an eyebrow, her voice playful but with a hint of reprimand. "Ye couldn't have missed just one target, perhaps?"

I shot her a teasing look. "Aye, and be dishonest? Was it not you who taught me how to use a bow in the first place?"

"It was," she replied, her laugh ringing out, her face lighting up with youthful mischief. "And too good a job I did, if I do say so myself."

Her laughter was infectious, and I couldn't help but join in. It was always a comfort to hear her laugh, as if time stood still and we were back in those quieter days before the weight of my future settled on me.

"Come, let's get you dressed," she said, motioning for me to sit. "I've made a few adjustments."

I watched as she moved to the wardrobe, a flutter of fabric following her as she picked out my attire. The woollen skirt I wore was shorter in the front, stopping just below my knees, offering more freedom of movement than I was used to. It was practical, but the deep blues of the MacLeod colours still shimmered with the faint elegance of my heritage. My leather boots, high and sturdy, peeked out from beneath the skirt, their polished surface gleaming with quiet strength.

A leather corset was next—strong but flexible, fitting snugly over my cream blouse. The blouse itself was simple, but the sleeves cuffed midway with copper bands, intricately etched with patterns of leaves and flowers. The design felt personal, as though the very earth was wrapped around my arms.

A leather belt crossed over my waist, the integrity of its braided form holding fast. At my side, my steel dirk was polished and sharp, the only weapon permitted in the Hall. It felt like an old friend, secure and steadfast.

Genevieve fastened the MacLeod arisaid around my shoulders like a cloak. It draped down my back, its weight both comforting and noble. The copper brooch that held it in place was a work of art, deep knots entwined with standing stones and thistles—symbols of strength, of the land, and heritage. I traced my fingers over the brooch, remembering how my mother had brought it from Orkadia. It had always been hers, but now, it was mine to wear.

Genevieve's eyes softened as she adjusted my hair, the strands cascading down my back in loose waves. She braided the front to keep it out of my face, but left the rest to flow freely: practical, yet graceful.

A crown, delicate yet powerful, rested on my forehead, made of winding copper knots, thistles, and stars. The crown had been a gift from Aunt Gen when I turned sixteen, a symbol of my coming of age, and it had always held a special place in my heart. As I caught my reflection in the mirror, I noticed the same intricate patterns—thistles and stars—were carved into the leather of my corset, a subtle detail I had never noticed before.

"Well then," Aunt Gen said with a satisfied nod, stepping back to admire her work. "You look every bit the lady of

MacLeod, though perhaps with a bit more fire in your eyes than they might expect."

I met her gaze in the mirror, my reflection now fully complete. For a moment, I saw not just the daughter of MacLeod, but a woman who had taken her fate into her own hands.

"I think they might have underestimated me," I said softly, a flicker of defiance in my voice.

Aunt Gen smiled, her expression proud. "Come, Alix."

With a final glance at my reflection, I turned and walked towards the door. Genevieve followed close behind, and together, we headed toward the Hall.

***

The MacLeod stood tall on the dais, his presence commanding the hall. The chairs and tables had been cleared, and the room was alive with the scent of evergreen branches, wildflowers, and thistles, all draped across the walls and ceiling. It felt as though nature itself had joined the gathering. The hall was packed with clansmen, warriors, and visitors, all dressed in their finest attire. The women, dressed in fine ribbons and furs, filled the upstairs alcoves, gazing down on the proceedings, their whispers barely audible against the murmurs below.

The formalities were about to begin.

Uncle Brian entered the room, wearing his full war chieftain regalia. The crowd parted in respectful silence as he made his way toward the dais. With each step, the room seemed to grow quieter, the weight of the moment settling in. When he reached the MacLeod, Brian drew his dirk and dropped to one knee. The hall fell into absolute stillness as his voice rang out in Gaelic—a solemn vow of loyalty and fealty.

"I swear by the holy iron that I hold, by our gods the new and the old, to give ye fealty and pledge ye my loyalty to the Clan MacLeod. If ever my hand shall be raised against ye in rebellion, I ask that this holy iron shall pierce my heart"

The Chieftain's gaze softened as he accepted the oath, and he raised Brian to his feet. They drank from a copper goblet, and Brian stepped back, taking his place behind his brother. The same ritual was repeated as each of my brothers knelt, the air heavy with their solemn vows.

And then, it was my turn.

Though Aunt Gen had taken the oath before—her loyalty pledged long ago as a woman of the clan—this was my first time. Her hand, warm and steady, squeezed mine as I moved toward the dais, a silent encouragement. There was something in her eyes; a knowing, a recognition that I was stepping into something I could never fully escape but would always be a part of. She had walked this path already.

I could feel my heart racing in my chest as I walked down the empty aisle. Each step felt like it echoed through the hall. My brothers, who had already taken their oaths, stood at the sides, their faces unreadable. This was my moment.

I knelt in front of the MacLeod, my dirk drawn, the steel cold and familiar in my grasp. The weight of the moment pressed down on me, the eyes of the hall heavy on my back. I could feel the silent expectations, the shared history, the pride and responsibility of being one of the MacLeods. I looked up to meet my father's gaze, feeling the intensity of his silver eyes focused on me. His face was calm, but I could see something else there—perhaps pride, hope.

My voice rang out, strong but steady, as I spoke my vow.

"I swear by the earth beneath my feet and the sky above me, by the auld ones, the fae, gods new and old. By this iron that I hold, I swear to stand with you, my father, and my chieftain, in all matters of both clan and kin. I pledge my loyalty, my strength, and my heart. I pledge to defend and protect our people, whether by my bow, hands, or sword. For as long as my feet are on these lands, you have my protection and my sword. Should the day come I do leave, know I uphold this oath in all decisions I make to protect all those who cannot protect themselves. And should my hand ever be raised against ye in rebellion, I ask that this iron shall pierce my heart."

The silence that followed was profound. I could feel the weight of my father's gaze, the unspoken understanding in his eyes. Slowly, he reached down, taking my hand in his and helping me rise. He kissed my mother's ring, the same ring she had worn, and then stood tall beside me.

"And may you always remember that family is our greatest strength, *mo chridhe*," he said softly. The warmth in his voice made my chest swell with pride.

I moved to stand with my brothers, my place now irrevocably marked in the history of the clan. The hall erupted in murmurs of approval, but for me, it was the quiet that felt the most powerful. This wasn't just a vow. It was a bond; one that would carry me through both trials and triumphs, a promise that would echo through generations.

Looking around, I saw Aunt Gen nearby, standing tall beside her family, her expression a mixture of pride and something deeper—perhaps an understanding of what I had just pledged. She had already taken this oath. She had lived the life I was now stepping into, and I knew she saw me in a new light, just as I saw her.

The warriors of the MacLeod clan stood tall, their faces proud and solemn as they observed the oath-taking. I could see Claire and Niamh dressed in the MacLeod colours, their eyes filled with respect. Nearby, I spotted Sean and Liam, dressed in the warrior clothing of their clan. They were from Aunt Niamh's clan in Eire, and their presence was another symbol of the bond between clans solidified by Niamh's marriage to Uncle Brian.

The Grants and Frasers were, much to my annoyance, still here, as were some of the smaller clans we offered protection to, sons a-plenty. Most of the young ladies of the hall were swooning over my brothers, some almost drooling. I gave a look to Claire that she would recognise, and I could see her containing her laughter.

A gentle breeze stirred through the hall, rustling the evergreens and wildflowers that adorned the walls and ceiling. The subtle movement of the plants seemed to echo the sudden shift in the atmosphere.

Some of the women in the gallery turned their heads, eyes wide with curiosity, while others, still caught in their swooning, abruptly snapped out of it. A few gasped, eyes bulging in surprise as they glanced toward the entrance. I felt the air grow heavier, and instinctively, my gaze dropped to see who had arrived.

The air grew thick with tension as Tommy entered. My heartbeat quickened, a mixture of confusion and anticipation stirring inside me. I glanced at Marcus, his brow furrowed, and saw the concern mirrored in my own expression.

Tommy's presence filled the room as he strode toward the dais, every step deliberate, each movement betraying the strength beneath his grace. His golden hair caught the light, and his emerald eyes, usually full of mischief, now held a quiet intensity. His kilt, dark as the forest, swayed with his movements, and the dirk at his side gleamed like a silent promise. There was an elegance to him that belied the warrior's fire in his chest—his smile, warm and genuine, drew the room's attention, but it was the weight of his presence that left no room for doubt: this was a man who could command both respect and affection.

He stopped at the Chieftain and knelt. Marcus took a step closer to my side and whispered, "He shouldn't be here; they have grounds to attack if he doesn't swear the oath." I turned my head sharply to meet my brother's eyes, concerned and worried. What was going on here?

Tommy pulled out his dirk, raised his hand holding the glittering blade in the light. He waited a moment, then stood, sheathing his blade. The hall was silent as he met my father's eyes.

"My Lord, I come as both kinsman and ally. My oath is to the name I bear, not to any other, but I offer you my protection, my strength, and my loyalty. As Laird of my own lands, I give you my word that I will stand by you and your clan whenever you call on me. Today, I give ye freely my obedience, I hold myself bound to your words for as long as my feet walk on MacLeod land."

The MacLeod looked firmly at Tommy, nodded, and put his hand on his shoulder. "We are honoured by this offer of friendship and goodwill, and I accept this, holding you, as always, in good faith as an ally of the Clan MacLeod."

"I also come to you with the utmost respect and sincerity." Tommy paused, moving his eyes to meet mine with a look of one going to war before returning them to the silver eyes of my father. He was speaking in Auld Eris and loud enough for only those close to hear. "Your daughter, Lady Alexandria MacLeod, is the strongest woman I know. From the moment we met in battle, her spirit has captured mine. Her courage, her laughter both fill me with awe. I wish to stand beside her, to protect and honour her, though I know she is more than capable of doing so herself. I offer her my heart, my name, my lands, and my sword, and ask for your blessing to call her my wife."

Both their eyes were locked. People were resuming conversations as the Chieftain had listened. I could hear Fraser and Grant arguing in the distance. My heart was beating so loud it felt like it would explode. I looked around, and Claire and Niamh were smiling. Sean and Liam were looking around, likely for the best chance of escape should it come to it. Malcolm was slowly nodding his head with a grin. I could feel Marcus let out his breath, but felt his presence closer than before.

The silence in the hall stretched, the weight of his words lingering in the air. Finally, the Chieftain nodded to Tommy and placed a hand on his shoulder. "Friendship, help and honour, I can freely give ye, and assistance of my clan in time of need... But the hand of my daughter is not mine to give. Ye have my permission and blessing, but the choice is hers, and hers alone."

I stood there, feeling the weight of the moment press against me. Tommy's words echoed in my mind, and the Chieftain's blessing felt like a turning point. My heart raced, unsure of what I should feel, but certain of one thing: my life had changed forever. What came next was mine to decide.

The Chieftain's voice cut through the heavy silence, his words carrying the weight of the ceremony but also an invitation to move forward. "Now, let us celebrate," he declared. "Our strength lies in our unity and our honour. The MacLeods are here!" With that, he raised his sword high, and the hall erupted into cheers. "*A dhion agus a dhion*!" The MacLeod motto rang out, filling the space with its powerful echo. The tension broke, and the festivities began.

The room erupted into a whirlwind of noise and movement. The bard's voice rang out, strong and rich, while the sound of the pipes filled the air with their sharp, joyous notes. People spun and twirled across the floor in lively dances, their feet stamping in rhythm with the music.

The scent of roasting meat now mingled with the earthy aroma of ale and whisky, wafting from the platters that the maids carried around. The sounds of laughter and clinking mugs blended with the hum of conversation, and the warmth of the fire crackled in the hearth.

Amidst it all, Claire suddenly grabbed my arm and spun me around, her laughter ringing out like a bell. "I ken it, Alix, I did." She grinned, her eyes sparkling with mischief. "And I ken ye feel the same way."

I shook my head, laughing. Before I could answer, we were stopped by Fraser and Grant.

"Ladies, we brought ye some wine!" Fraser yelled. "Aye and a dance, lassies"

"What he means to ask," Grant said, grinning, "is if you two fine lassies would care to join us for a dance?" He raised an eyebrow in a teasing challenge, his voice carrying over the music.

"Sister, cousin, I've been lookin' for ye," Callum said, his voice booming over the chatter. He looked over, then winced as he bumped into Grant. "Och! Didn't see ye were already speaking to someone."

He paused, his face turning slightly sheepish as he addressed Grant and Fraser. "I apologise, lads," he said with a quick wink. "Decent work today, I hope ye aren't too sore after bein' bested by my sister here." He gave a teasing grin, his words laced with pride.

Grant and Fraser exchanged glances, clearly uncomfortable under the attention. "Not at all, sir... I mean, my lord," Grant stammered. "I think Da is calling us." Both men walked away.

"Did you really need to scare them off so quickly? We hadn't even begun to torment them!" I winked at Callum, who laughed.

"Aye, and that, ladies, is exactly why I interrupted. Now I believe, Claire, you owe me a dance." He bowed low, offering his hand. Claire twirled and grabbed it, and they made their way closer to the music. I watched for a moment the two of them dancing in the distance, Callum's two boys were running between the kitchen maids, cookies in their hands, escaping Ms Mac. His wife, Isobel, was dancing with Marcus, which was becoming quite entertaining when the boys tried to hide under her skirts.

I was laughing to myself when a gentle breeze, carrying the scent of wildflowers and mountain air, brushed against my face. A hand pressed lightly against my back, and I turned, surprised to find Tommy standing there.

"There you are." Holding my hands in his, he kissed them. "I declare my intentions in a hall filled with armed men, risk my life and all to find you talking with those puppies who canna even talk to ye brother."

"And when were you going to tell me about being a Laird?"

"Och, well, you never asked, and I got a wee bit distracted, ey, but if it will entice you to marry me, then I best tell you… I'm a Laird." He winked as he said it.

"You're an eejit. Now, are you going to ask me to dance, or should I go find Fraser? He seemed quite interested before Callum scared him off."

Tommy laughed and grabbed my hand, whisking me towards him. "I don't think so, *a chuisle mo chroí*. I seem to recall you settling for an ordinary warrior from Eire not too long ago."

"Aye, I can still change my mind, ye ken. And I'm verra good with knives."

He spun me around and caught me, his hand brushing my face. "You still sure, Alix?"

"I've never been surer of anything in my life, Tommy."

***

The dancing continued late into the night. I danced with Tommy and the others until Marcus suggested we go to the roof. We left in pairs so as not to cause too much notice. As Claire and I were leaving, Da called me over. Claire saw her mother and went over to wait for me. "You look very bonnie tonight, *mo nighean*."

"Thanks, Da."

"The Patrick lad is a fine man, honourable and brave like his Da. Ye brothers and Brian speak highly of him. I can see you've made up your mind, Alix. Ye mother had the same look when I asked her."

"Aye, Da, I have. It feels right, terrifying but right."

"No man will ever be good enough for ye in my eyes, but… if he brings ye joy, then he's the one for ye, Alix." His voice softened, and I saw something else in his eyes, a depth of love for me that made my chest tighten. "If he can make ye smile like that, then he has my blessing."

I wrapped my arms around him, suddenly feeling like the young girl I was when he gave me my first sword.

"Once the extra people leave, we can work a bit more on yeh magic. Now get your cousin and sneak off to the roof, aye?"

"Wait, how, did you…?"

"It's like the rope again, do you really think you and your daft brothers were the first MacLeods to discover all the secret escape routes from the keep? You ken who my sister is, don't ye?" He started to laugh.

My heart still swelled with warmth from Da's words. I shook my head, trying to shake off the emotions, but it felt like something had changed in me. As I curtsied to him, a tear threatened to escape, but I swallowed it back. Claire was already tugging at my hand, eager to head to the roof, and I followed her, trying to focus on the moment ahead.

We headed off hand-in-hand through the secret passage in the library tower, hidden behind an old tapestry of a wolf and a stag. We pushed the door open and closed it behind us, sealing the light. A small glowing flame bobbed on the staircase, lighting the way. We followed it up the torrent to the next door. With a gentle push, we had it open and stepped out into the flat roof high above the hall. Up here, we could hear the music below us. Malcolm and Marcus had lit small flames around us. We pulled out the flasks of whisky we had grabbed, and the boys had trays of apple tart. Likely, Marcus had seen Ms Mac's softer side on the way out.

The night was slipping away slowly, the warm glow of the fire flickering against the chill night air. We spent hours laughing, eating, and drinking, the music from below a distant hum. Even Marcus and Sean had finally given in to the comfort of sleep, their bodies sprawled near the fire. Claire and Liam were deep in conversation about books, while Malcolm finished off the last of the pie.

I was twirling slowly, my feet tracing patterns in the stone, lost in the melody of distant bagpipes, when suddenly—a loud crash. The sound split the air like thunder. My heart skipped a beat, and I froze, searching the darkness for the source. Tommy's hand tightened around mine, and the night that had been so light just moments ago seemed to shift, like a shadow had fallen across it.

Malcolm shot up and walked to the edge; the walls were high, hiding the flat roof. We looked out to the edge of the clearing. The crofts were quiet and still; everyone had gone to their beds. There was another loud crash, far away but loud. Marcus and Sean shot up, swords ready. We still couldn't see anything.

Malcolm's tone shifted from playful to grim, and I felt the sudden weight of his words. "Sleep while we can, Alix. But be ready," said his voice, low and steady, though there was an edge to it now. His eyes scanned the dark, never staying still. "I've a bad feeling about what's coming. It's been too quiet for too long." He shook his head as if he could shake off the unease creeping up his spine. His gaze flicked to Tommy. "We can't afford to be caught unprepared."

Malcolm pulled me close, his grip firm and reassuring. "Sleep, Alix," he said softly. "You'll need to charge. The dragon's wards will keep them away until we are ready. I'll wake Da. The *Scathach* will keep watch for now"

"Tommy, take the girls back to their rooms. I'll meet you back at mine. Marcus, wake Auld Mac; we'll need the horses ready in the morning. Then wake Callum, he'll need to know."

"Alix, now please, we have everything sorted, we'll get you when it's time."

I nodded and we headed back through the castle to our rooms.

Tommy's eyes softened as he took my hand, his thumb brushing across my skin. "Rest, *my lady*," he murmured, his voice low and reassuring, though I could hear the strain in it. "I'll be back once I speak to Cian. I'll let you know once I do, ken." He leaned down and brushed a kiss across my forehead before he turned and left, the door closing softly behind him. I lay back on the bed, the soft sheets feeling too heavy around me. My eyes fluttered shut, but sleep didn't come. The quiet of the room felt suffocating, and my mind raced with unanswered questions. What was coming? Why now? Something was looming, something I couldn't shake, and I didn't know if I was ready for it.

Chapter Fourteen

ALIX! IT'S TIME!"

A voice rang through the fog of my dreams. My eyes fluttered open, and for a moment, I wasn't sure if I had heard it or if it was just the shadows of sleep still lingering. A blur of red hair flickered in front of me—then nothing. I blinked again, but the room was empty. Just silence. I lay back, my pulse quickening. Was I dreaming?

Suddenly, the door swung open with a creak, shattering the stillness. "Good, you're up. Get ready. The council is meeting." Marcus left as quickly as he came in.

Looking out the window, I could see dark smoke in the distance behind the woods, rising above the horizon. I changed into my full leathers, cloak, boots, braided my hair tight and strapped in all my *Scathach* weapons and sword.

We climbed the stairs to the war chamber. The heavy oak doors creaked as we entered, their groaning echoing through the stone walls. The room smelled faintly of wax and parchment, a reminder of the many decisions made in this very space. The fire in the hearth crackled softly, but the murmurs of tense voices drowned out its warmth. The air was thick with the weight of unspoken concerns, and I felt a shiver race down my spine. I hadn't been here in years—since I was a child, when these walls had seemed so much larger. Now, they felt like a cage, pressing down with the history of so many battles fought, so many decisions made by men with no other choice but to act.

The room was filled with voices—too many opinions, too many ideas about what was to come. My fingers brushed the edges of the carved table, tracing the familiar contours of the land I had grown up on. The valleys and rivers, the mountains and meadows, they were all etched into the wood as though they were part of us. But beneath the beauty of the table, I could feel the tension in the air. My mind raced, but my fingers remained still as I tried to ground myself in the present moment.

I rested my hands on the old ash oak. Looking down at the delicate landscape of the MacLeod lands, each valley, Munro, river, meadow, and falls, Skye, the Cuillins, the glen and the old man Storr. My fingers traced the ruins along the edges, carved deep long ago. There were single standing stones throughout the table, situated in the map… odd. I looked at Marcus, who shrugged his shoulders.

Brian's voice broke through the silence. "We do not ken who we're up against."

"Aye, brother, I have a good mind who it is and why they've come."

Who were these people? Were they people? Could they be the same who attacked us in the Ewan?

"Britannia, Brian, I ken it's them who have come back."

There was a long pause as everyone in the room absorbed the weight of his words. The fire crackled in the hearth, its flames flickering against the cold stone, but the silence felt even heavier. I could feel my heart beating faster in my chest, the words hanging in the air like smoke.

"Aye." Brian broke the silence. "And who is it they've allied with? The Black Coats?"

The room stilled again. The mention of the Black Coats sent a chill down my spine. I looked around, seeing the same unease reflected on the faces of the men at the table. This wasn't just a battle; this was something else entirely.

"We've sent scouts to find out what and how many we are dealing with," Malcolm said.

"The Scathach are here and ready," Brian said, his voice firm. "We'll leave enough to hold the keep, but the rest will follow me. We'll march here, to this point—" he tapped the map, "—and wait."

His finger lingered on the map for a moment. I could see the tension in his face, the subtle tic in his jaw that betrayed his nerves. Brian was a warrior, but he had seen too many battles where men like him had died before their time. He had a plan, but even he couldn't hide the uncertainty in his eyes.

"It will give us the advantage of the hills," he continued, "but we'll need to split and shield in the woods. The trees will slow them down. If we're lucky, we'll get the high ground before they can strike."

Malcolm, leaning over the table, furrowed his brow. "And what if we're not lucky?"

"The riders will wait here for orders and charge," Brian said, pointing to another standing stone on the map. "But if they have more foot soldiers than we expect, it might be better to flank them from the sides. We can't risk having the hills compromised."

"Aye, but if we're flanking from the sides, we risk losing the element of surprise," Malcolm countered. "We need that advantage. We can't afford to be outnumbered. And if they have the Black Coats, they'll have magic on their side."

"Magic?" I couldn't keep the edge out of my voice. "We've dealt with that before."

"Aye, but this is different," Brian said, his eyes dark. "We haven't faced them in years. We don't know what they've learned since."

"Aye. Grant, Fraser, your men will join ours. Foot or horse?" the MacLeod asked.

"Both—those who have horses will ride, the others on foot. I have a few good healers. Where do you want them?" Fraser answered, now looking at the MacLeod.

Grant's eyes were narrowed, his mouth set in a tight line as he listened to the plan unfolding. He wasn't saying much, but I could tell he was thinking—his hands were folded in front of him, and his knuckles were white. Beside him, Fraser was adjusting his sword belt, his gaze flicking between the table and the map, but his expression was unreadable.

The tension in the room felt like it had a physical weight, pressing down on all of us. Even Grannie, usually so calm and composed, was silently chewing the edge of her lip as she watched the men argue.

"They'll be with me. Here." He pointed to another standing stone, higher up on one of the Munros, surrounded by the auld oaks. "I'll be able to see, redirect if needed. Ma, you'll run the tent with me, eh?" Grannie nodded, clearly these were her orders to leave as she grabbed her bag and exited through the side door. She would begin to set up the healers' quarters. I could hear her ordering servants around, hot water, clean bandages, and herbs.

"*Mo phiuthar*, the keep is yours. Take the children and those who cannot fight through the old tunnels to the mountains. Get them to safety."

"It's already done, brother, Niamh and Claire left in the last hour, Ms Mac along with them. I will stay."

"Aye, I thought as much." The MacLeod and Brian exchanged looks and nodded.

As the discussion continued, I couldn't shake the feeling that something was missing. Everyone here had their roles to play—warriors, healers, scouts, commanders—but what was I? Where did I fit into all of this? My eyes flicked to the standing stones scattered across the table. Each one marked a place of power, a part of our history, but they were also reminders of everything we stood to lose.

My heartbeat was growing faster. I wasn't a child anymore. I was a warrior. What was my role?

The double doors swung open, and a cold breeze blew through. Tommy's hair was tousled from flight. He had full fighting leathers and armour on, with both swords strapped to his back, knives to his legs, and one to each boot. Stern and focused, a warrior of auld. Emeralds were blazing, and he approached the table. "Ten thousand at least, marching from the south. A third have horses, many look like farmers with no formal training, their commanders a few hundred black coats."

The room went silent.

Black Coats. Again.

Britannia's?

"I couldn't get close enough to see the leader; the men came from far south beyond the lowlands and the wall"

The MacLeod clapped him on the shoulder. "Aye, thank yer and yer men."

"I have fifty men and dragons from Eire, not long arrived. We are at your command, sir."

MacLeod nodded. "Right… Brian, you'll lead the riders and the warriors on foot; Malcolm will go with you. Tommy, you have the sky. Marcus, you have twenty men and dragons, those who are ready to join you both in the sky. Grant, Fraser, we'd be honoured to have ye men where you best see fit. Callum and I will be with the healers and the archers."

"Sir."

"MacLeod."

"Brother."

Da's fingers hovered over the map, tracing the paths of rivers and mountain passes. He paused over the ridge, his brow furrowing, as though contemplating the lives that would be lost depending on his decision. He nodded, scratched Cody's head, and left the room towards the parapet. Marcus looked at me, shaking his head. Too late.

"Da!" I flew out through the double doors behind him.

"Father!" He slowly turned around. Eyebrows raised, eyes sold silver staring into mine.

"Aye, Alix."

"I wanted to ask, where should I be in the battle?"

"You, lass, will be following your people to the mountain."

"I will not! I am better used elsewhere."

"No, ye willna be fighting."

"Aye, I will."

"If you do not go with your people, you can stay in the castle where your aunt can keep an eye on ye, but you willna be going anywhere near the fighting"

"And why not?"

"Because I said so."

"Aye, and all my brothers can; there are men, warriors, smaller and younger than me. Far less experienced."

"They are men, you are my daughter!"

"And if I wasn't, then what, no worries, I'd be allowed or not your problem, ey?"

"Well, you're my daughter, so you will never know. I say no, you're not flying, riding, or fighting against the dark coats or the Britannia's men." He was angry, speaking through his teeth. So was I, and I could be just as stubborn. I walked up as close as I could, bringing myself to full height.

"I have faced them before and killed them, while you and your men were here drinking whisky."

"You got lucky and that is exactly why I willna risk ye again."

"Lucky! I am a *Scathach* warrior! I have done the same training as your men, if not more. I have more than proved my skills time and again."

"You are my daughter, Alix. You will stay here." His voice was low but sharp, a command wrapped in love.

I stood my ground, fists clenched. "And I am a warrior. I will fight. What will you do? Hide me away like a child?"

His eyes narrowed, his jaw clenched. "You *are* my child."

"Then let me fight! Let me be who I am, Da. I've trained for this. I *deserve* to be there."

He took a deep breath, then let it out slowly. "I will not risk you again. Not after what happened before."

The words cut through me, and for a moment, I faltered. But the stubbornness inside me wouldn't let me back down. "What happened before wasn't luck. I can handle this."

My feet were firm on the ground, my head up. Hands clenching together. "I am a MacLeod, I am a *Scathach* warrior. I will fight."

He took a deep breath, "You are a MacLeod. I am your Chief whom you swore loyalty to. I order you to stay at Moar." His teeth were clenched; he was angry.

We were staring at each other, steel and storm.

Callum's voice cut through the storm of anger, low but firm. "Alix, come." He didn't need to raise his voice—he knew how to reach me when the world felt like it was closing in.

I hesitated, my chest still tight with rage, but something in his gaze made me pause. He wasn't just pulling me out of the argument—he was grounding me.

"As you say, MacLeod." I stormed past Callum, not even looking back. My heart thudded in my chest as the doors slammed behind me, but I knew one thing for sure: no matter what Da said, I wasn't going to sit this fight out. I wasn't going to be kept in the shadows.

***

I threw my doors open, grabbed the jug, and smashed it against the wall. The sound of it shattering seemed to echo in my chest. As I lifted the basin, it was grabbed from me.

"Let. Go."

"No." Callum's voice was firm as he pulled it away.

I spun around, fist raised to strike him, but he caught my hand, his grip tight, unyielding. "Calm down, Alix."

My breath came in ragged gasps, my chest tightening with anger and helplessness. I ripped my hand free, storming to the window, my gaze fixed on the horizon. "Why? Why can't he just see me? I can do this…"

"He does, *mo phiuthar*." Callum's voice softened. "But you are his daughter. He doesn't want to lose ye."

"Aye, well, he doesn't have a problem with any of you going to battle," I snapped, turning back to face him.

"We are sons, Alix. It's different. It's expected. You…" He hesitated, his gaze steady. "You are who we are to protect. That's all he wants. To keep ye safe."

"Safe?" The word stung, a bitter taste in my mouth. "Safe or locked up?"

"If he wanted you locked up, you'd be in the tower, lass," Callum said, stepping closer. "It's one thing teaching ye how to fight, it's another to see you fighting for your life on the field."

"Then what was the point, Callum? What was the point of all those years of training?" My voice trembled, frustration choking me.

Callum's eyes softened, and he reached out, resting a hand on my shoulder. "What's our motto?"

"*A dhion agus a dhion,*" I muttered, feeling the familiar weight of the words settle in my chest.

"To protect and defend."

"Aye, to protect and defend. He taught you to protect, for when you need it. To defend yourself and others. And for you to protect those who can't. You are a Lady of Caisteal Moar, Alix. You will always protect those around you." He paused, giving me a long look. "But if he can, he'll always do everything he can to protect you. We all will."

I turned to face him, my chest tight with a mixture of gratitude and sorrow. His deep blue eyes, so like our mother's, were full of understanding. I threw my arms around him. "I will protect you, too, *bhràthair*. Stay safe."

***

There was a knock at my door, and before I could even answer, Aunt Genevieve entered, already dressed in full battle gear, her face painted with bold strokes of black, blue, and white. Her eyes burned with the intensity of a warrior ready for the coming storm, and her presence filled the room like a sudden wind, sharp and fierce.

"Right, time to get ready," she said, her voice steady and commanding.

Ready for what? We were both confined to the keep, the battle far away. The question was unspoken, but I could feel the tension rising between us. She saw my confusion but didn't pause, already moving to guide me.

"Sit," she ordered. I obeyed, still processing the sight of her—my aunt, in full war regalia—standing before me like some kind of living, breathing storm.

Without a word, she moved behind me, taking my hair in her hands. She worked quickly, braiding it tightly, weaving an indigo ribbon through the strands until it formed a crown. "Tight," she muttered, "so it can't be pulled."

I felt the weight of her hands, both soft and firm, as she finished, then turned to face me. There, on her tray, sat an array of powders—shades of blue, black, white, and gold. She dipped a brush into the darkest powder and, with swift, practised strokes, began to paint three faint lines down my cheeks, from my eyes to my chin.

"War paint," she explained, almost as if reading my thoughts. "A mark of strength. Resilience. Honor. Valour."

I swallowed hard, still unsure of what to say. I'd seen warriors before—men and women, covered in paint and armour—but somehow, seeing it on myself, hearing the words attached to it, made everything feel more real, more immediate. But the war paint was nothing compared to what she did next.

Genevieve took a smaller brush, dipped it into white powder, and began to paint delicate knots and lines across my forehead. She spoke as she worked, her voice low and steady. "These symbols represent the elements—water, earth, fire, air—and healing. They are the foundation of who we are. And the power we carry."

I watched her hands, entranced by the ritual, but the words she spoke were even more powerful than the symbols she painted.

"Water, earth, fire, air…" I whispered, echoing her softly. The words had an ancient quality, like a prayer or a chant.

But it wasn't just magic she was painting on my skin—it was history. Legacy.

She then dipped a third brush into gold powder and flicked tiny splatters across my cheeks, across the lines she'd painted, creating a shimmering effect. "For the auld gods. And for those who watch over us," she said, her voice quieter now, as if speaking to those who might be listening from afar. "To give us courage and bravery for what must be done."

I felt the weight of those words, like they were imbuing me with something.

Finally, she picked up a copper necklace, delicately interwoven, with runes carved deep into the metal. As she clasped it around my neck, I felt a surge of energy— something ancient and alive.

When she stepped back, I stood, her gaze now fixed on me. It wasn't just the war paint or the necklace, though— they were only a part of it. It was the way she was looking at me, like I had just become something more.

Before I could ask any more questions, the door opened again, and Auntie Niamh and Claire entered, both already dressed in full fighting gear. Their faces were painted, their expressions hard and ready for whatever was coming. They moved to join us, standing together in a line.

Aunt Genevieve looked around at each of us, and her voice rang out, strong and unwavering. "Our bloodlines run deep with magic. We are both *Scathach* and *Valkyrie*. From the North and the West. From the Glens to the Stones. Today, we rise."

The words echoed in the room, and my heart began to race. Scathach and Valkyrie.

"A dhion agus a dhion," Genevieve said, her voice resolute.

I blinked, the weight of the phrase sinking in. "*A dhion agus a dhion,"* we repeated, the words on my tongue firm as iron.

There was a long silence, and the ritual settled around us like a cloak.

***

I walked to the end of the courtyard, and the men were ready to go. My brothers were waiting; they took a step back as we got closer. Grannie had not long finished blessing the warriors' safe return, the hair of all three of them ruffled and sticking out in the same direction. I hugged them all. I turned to my father. The MacLead, in all his warrior's glory, stood by his horse.

"I'm sorry, Da."

"It is nothing, *mo nighean*. I see you let your auntie paint you like a she-devil, then." He was smiling, trying to make light of our fight.

"A *dhion agus dhion*, you have my sword and my shield. I will defend our people."

He lightly brushed my face with his hand. "The heart and spirit of a true warrior, much like ye ma." He paused. "Will ye give me your blessing?"

I nodded. He knelt to the ground, my heart heavy as I placed my hand upon his head. My voice trembled slightly as the words spilled out, a blessing older than our family. This was a prayer I had heard all my life, but today it felt different, heavier—my father was leaving and this could be our final goodbye. For him, for us, for everything we stood for…

"May the road rise up to meet you.

May the wind be always at your back.

May the sun shine warm upon your face;

The rains fall soft upon your fields, and until we meet again,

May God hold you in the palm of His hand.

Beannachd Dia dhuit."

He stood and climbed upon his horse. There was a dark shadow that flew above, landing a few feet away, Cian. Tommy jumped down. I walked towards him. He nodded at the MacLeod as I got nearer. The battle would be soon.

"A chuisle mo chroi, I see the Valkyrie have arrived." He had a wide grin on his face.

"You fight, and you come home." My voice shook as I spoke, my hand resting on his chest.

His eyes softened. "Aye, where else would I rather be?" He bent down and kissed me, slow, strong, and deep. Breaking away, he reached into his vest pocket. "Now, I have something for ye. It's not much, but I had to go home to grab it." Tommy slid a ring onto my finger. I felt its cool weight settle on me, as though it were a promise—a reminder that no matter what happened, part of him would always be with me. The stone was round, misty and had a deep green that rippled through the middle. It was like looking into water in the early morning, a grey mist covering the water below, and its dark kelp breaking through. It was beautiful. Simple gold encased it, and small ruins were carved into it. It fit perfectly on my finger. The green stone seemed to pulse softly, like a heartbeat. I held my breath for a moment, unsure whether I should smile or cry. I looked up into his emerald eyes. "Don't hold back, *mo nighean,* remember they will not show mercy... the Black Coats do not ken its meaning."

His hands brushed my face gently. *"Tha Gaol agam ort le cridhe."* I love you with all my heart. He smiled. "I'll see you soon *a chuisle mo chroi."*

"Wait, you never told me what that one meant?" I asked.

He smiled. "Beat of my heart, *my lady,* my everything." As Tommy kissed me, I felt the weight of everything: our love, the battle ahead, the unspoken worry that he might not come back. His lips were warm, but there was a sadness in the way he pulled away, like he was trying to memorise the feel of me before he left. I held his gaze for a moment, my heart thudding in my chest. This could be the last time I saw him. His thumb brushed over my knuckles where he had placed the ring on my finger, his touch warm, but his eyes full of that same sadness I felt in my chest. I couldn't allow myself to think that way. But the thought gnawed at me anyway.

The courtyard was suddenly too quiet, the sound of hooves filling the space where our voices had just been. Tommy turned, his face set in a grim line, and climbed onto Cian's back. Cian let out a huff of mist. "Storm rider, stay true, do not be fooled." And he leapt into the sky.

Then, with a final nod, the other warriors turned toward the gates. The air hummed with their departure, and I knew that once they crossed that threshold, there was no turning back.

***

My aunties and Claire were at my side. "It is time." We signalled the Scathach warriors to lower the gates. The men left would help us defend the keep and the secret path to the mountains our people had left on.

Niamh and Claire's dragons circled overhead.

We made our way to the watchtower, from here we could see over the grounds. On the highest hill in the valley, I could see the healers' tent. My heart thundered as I scanned the valley below. The healers' tent stood against the backdrop of rising smoke, a grim reminder of the price of this fight. My Da's figure loomed on his massive black warhorse, a beacon of strength—but even he could not protect everyone from the chaos descending upon us.

The dragons would be flying high above, waiting in the distance. Brian and his men were standing tall, waiting for the enemy to come through the woods to attack. I couldn't see the archers but knew they would be hidden. Smoke billowed in the distance, the acrid smell of burning crofts drifting on the wind. I could see the flickering orange glow in the woods where they had set the homes ablaze. Crofts could be rebuilt. But the people—no, they couldn't be replaced. Not the way they had lived, fought, loved. Not the families. It was a relief that we had got ours to safety.

The first boom echoed through the valley, shaking the ground beneath us. A massive tremor rippled through the woods as trees crashed down. A sea of birds erupted into the sky, filling the air with the sound of flapping wings. The war drums started; slow, deep, a relentless rhythm that made my chest tighten with dread. More trees were falling. Through the opening, now significantly larger, a sea of black pooled through. Men and those in black coats. As they filled the valley below, more trees were shaking and falling.

A massive grey beast slithered over the men, its body twisting like a giant, sinuous snake. No legs, just writhing coils of muscle and scale. Its head, smaller than a dragon's but larger than any bear I'd seen, reared up, snapping its mouth open. Rows of razor-sharp teeth gleamed in the sunlight as it snatched a deer, tossing it to the ground with a sickening crack.

Claire gasped as another beast appeared, ripping the deer towards itself and proceeding to eat it. The deer's leg remained hanging from a tree, dripping blood on those who walked past. Men on horses were beginning to file through, avoiding the worm-like creatures. A Black Coat on a large black horse followed behind, holding its staff high for all to see. One of their commanders.

The valley was filling up, our men at the bottom of the healers' munro stood firm, riders on the crest and dragons hidden in the skies above. My heart pounded in my chest, a steady drumbeat that echoed in my ears. Every man I loved was out there, risking everything. How many would return? How many would fall? My breath caught in my throat, but I couldn't look away.

Another worm-like creature came through, knocking down the trees in its way. It kept sliding, working its way through its army. It was building up speed coming towards our lines, then lifted itself up and smashed down into a flank of our men. "*Ifrin,*" both Claire and I voiced. Easily twenty of our men were underneath the creature, another I could see in its mouth. Their commander lifted its staff, and they attacked.

Those on foot held the moore the archers were attacking the giant worms, men had climbed on the one who had attacked, and they were stabbing it continuously with their swords. I could see a flaming arrow rise in the distance from the woods; it landed between the giant worm and the Black Coats' army. Two more landed close by in a line; they set alight. A river of flames was dividing the two armies. About a third of the Black Coats' army had already begun to attack our men; the river of fire had cut them off from the rest of their kin.

I could see the MacLeod high on the healers' moor, his sword lifted and pointing down. Brian signalled back with his sword. From either side of the crest, the riders came down and loud war cries filled the air. They were fast, a blur down the crest. I could make only one rider; his sword was high, leading the men, and it was on fire. A blaze of flame lined the air behind him. Malcolm.

The Black Coats' army panicked and closed ranks. The riders were pushing them together, backing them into the river of fire. Malcolm controlled the flames around him, bringing them forward. As he rode around the army, he burnt those who attacked, their bodies lighting the ground they landed on. Panic was good; the commanders were shocked, their army moving closer together, and they were struggling to bring their men to order. The worms were uncontrolled, trying to escape the flames, and the riders were pushing the army back further, closer together.

Another flaming arrow, this time from above, landed near our riders, and they moved back. Another five arrows landed, circling the army. A river of flame lit up. The riders pulled back, Malcolm commanding them back to the crest. The flames engulfed a circle around the army. The men on the moor were making progress. Many of the army's men were falling. I could see some of our men bringing the injured to the healers' tent. The first worm was down, hundreds of arrows in its head and back, its tail black and charred from fire. I could only hope it was dead.

Malcolm had put out his flame, his men high on the crest, watching as the enemy was surrounded in flames. It had been too easy to divide the army below. They hadn't come all this way to be defeated. Another worm fell, its massive body crashing across the river of fire. The flames sputtered out in its wake. The enemy surged forward, using the creature's carcass as a bridge.

The commanders were pushing them out. Then one of the commanders lifted his staff high, pointing into the sky above, and a green light shot with a crack. I followed its train into the sky. Another green light came behind, colliding with one another, and a deafening scream of pain echoed. No, it couldn't be. A flash of green light ran out of the clouds, and a dark mass fell to the ground. A smaller shape falling behind.

Dragon.

Rider.

As I watched the dragon plummet to the ground, my heart dropped with it. I looked for the smaller shape. Something had been trying to slow it down, to stop it from meeting the ground. The body was lifeless, slowly falling to the earth. Another dark shape was diving towards it, it was though time was slowing, trying to stop the body from meeting the ground. The dragon was close, but the ground was coming up to reach it.

Pull up.

Pull up.

Cian.

I could see his dark green scales, glinting in the sunlight. No, not Cian. I couldn't lose him. Not like this. The ground was coming up fast—too fast. If he didn't pull up, he would—no, I couldn't think it. Not like this.

Cian wove through the air, his wings snapping with grace as the green beam whipped past him, missing by inches. Another shot came, and this time he dove, pulling up just in time to dodge it. My heart stopped in my chest, watching him dance with death in the air. Arrows came from every direction, raining down on the commanders, but Cian's movements were a blur—every turn, every roll a desperate escape from the inevitable. Cian's movements had saved them. I watched as they levelled out and dove.

The body of the rider had slowed, and the air around me froze as I watched it land on the dragon below. I could hear the painful roars of the dragons above, and one very pissed, angry, and distraught Cian.

He dove towards the commander. He was sitting on his horse, head and black cloak leaning back, he looked to be laughing. Cian was flying directly at it; the men around dispersed in all directions. The commander stood still, staff pointed at Cian, green light pooling at the end. The beam was let loose, green light shooting towards them. My hands gripped the sharp stones of the walls beneath me, cutting into my hands, blood trickling down them. I couldn't breathe. Cian twisted, missing the light. It came again, he twisted. He was close, meters away. I could see his jaw open, his head lowered, and his tail bending up. His rider was running, both swords drawn. He reached Cian's head and jumped, swords ready. The commander had not been expecting it, and its staff fell to the ground. The rider's swords met the commander, crossing, and they severed the head of the Black Cloak.

As though time had paused, the head fell silently to the ground. The rider landed on one knee, swords outstretched behind him. The sun hit his golden crown as he knelt, his head bowed in respect to the fallen commander. Cian hovered above them, his wings beating slowly as he waited for the signal. The air felt thick with the tension of the moment.

Tommy stood up, sheathed his blades, and walked towards the staff, one hand outstretched. The staff rose into the air and began to shake and glow, exploding. Pieces of the staff flew out, hitting the army running away. Men dropped as they ran, face down into the ground, shards in the back of their necks. Cian had turned and was coming back, as he slowed towards the ground, Tommy leapt up onto his tail, running towards his wings. They took off, slowing down towards the cavity where the dragon and rider lay. Cian let out another painful roar and flew high into the sky.

A hand, warm and steady, rested on my shoulder. I looked up into Genevieve's calm blue eyes, and she nodded, her expression tight with understanding. I saw Niamh holding Claire, her face pale, eyes wide with grief. The loss of a dragon was a wound deeper than any sword strike— these creatures were their family, their kin. But there was little time for grief now. The battle raged on.

***

I looked back out to the glen. All the riders were coming down the crest, arrows flying from the trees behind into the army. It was sword against sword, and the archers were focused on the last worm. Riders on the commanders. A dragon came towards the worm and, with a breath of fire, roasted it. I could hear it squealing as it was engulfed. We could smell the burning flesh from where we stood. Marcus on Igor.

Claire grabbed my hand. "Alix, they're coming."

The castle walls shuddered beneath my hands. No crash. No green light. My heart skipped a beat. *What was that?*

I turned away from the battle below and sprinted to the other side of the tower, desperate to see what was happening. The ground beneath my feet trembled again, and I froze. A horrible, grinding sound echoed up through the stone. One of the worms was burrowing its way up.

Ifrin tunnels, I thought, my stomach tightening. It was digging through the earth.

Another violent rumble shook the keep as the massive beast shot upward from the ground like a giant serpent. The dirt and dust swirled around it, and for a moment, I could see its black scales glinting in the fading sunlight.

Please, let there be enough stone. We can't afford another breach.

Genevieve's sharp gaze met mine, and she nodded, already moving ahead.

"Archers to the ready! Fire on my mark!" Her voice rang out, steady and commanding. She had defended the keep before. She knew what needed to be done.

"Claire! Highest tower now! You're our best archer, but I need ye safe!"

Claire didn't hesitate. She darted up the stairs.

"Niamh—*from the sky*!"

Niamh didn't wait for more orders. She sprinted to the roof, her movements swift and fluid. She leapt into the air, her Silver Dragon catching her mid-flight, and together they soared toward the worm.

"Alix, you ready?"

Genevieve's voice cut through the chaos, firm and unwavering.

"Aye, *a dhion agus, a dhion*," I replied, my voice steadier than I felt. I nodded, making the sign of protection over myself.

I moved to the parapet, my boots scraping on the stone. The bow felt heavy in my hands, but the fire buckets nearby reminded me why we were here.

"On my mark," Genevieve's voice commanded, and I could hear the weight of her experience in it. She *was* the Valkyrie commander.

The ground rumbled again—more tremors, more shaking. Another worm was coming. But the first was still halfway through its tunnel. It was our chance to trap it.

I pulled my arrow, lining it up with the beast. It had not fully emerged, but we had to act fast.

"Steady…" Genevieve's voice was low, a thread of tension running through it.

The worm's head twisted upward, and a gut-wrenching screech reverberated through the earth as it tried to wriggle free. I could see its belly bulging.

"*Fire!*" Genevieve commanded, and I released the arrow.

It was squealing. Flaming arrows hit true; its belly was covered, a final arrow gilded steady, the moving worm arched in pain. The arrow hit it directly in the eye, flame following its path, and it continued to the back of the head.

Claire.

The beast dropped dead to the ground. It hadn't made it far enough out of the tunnel; if anyone had been in the tunnel, they'd be trapped. The second worm's head popped through; it was smaller and quicker.

"Reload!" Genevieve's command rang out sharp and precise, slicing through the air like a blade.

My fingers worked quickly, knocking another flaming arrow to my bow.

"Steady…" My voice was a whisper, but my heart was a drum in my chest. The worm writhed in the tunnel, its body undulating as it tried to push through.

"Hold it…" I barely breathed, eyes fixed on the wriggling mass. Every muscle in my body tensed, as if waiting for the perfect moment.

"Now!" Genevieve shouted.

The arrow flew from my hand in a blur of flame. The worm shrieked, a sound that made my skin crawl as it flung itself out of the earth. *Ifrin!*

"Reload! Fire again!"

More arrows shot into the beast, sending it into a frenzy.

"Catapult ready! We're caving that tunnel in! Aim…"

The men pulling the catapult worked in sync, their movements swift but sure. They had done this before.

"Fire!"

The catapult released with a deafening crack, a massive boulder hurtling toward the mouth of the tunnel.

I exhaled, watching the stone smash into the earth. It was a momentary reprieve, but we had bought ourselves time.

"Reinforce the gates! The water, all of it—*complete lockdown*!" Genevieve's voice snapped through the air like a whip, and the castle sprang to life.

Beams of timber were hastily bolted into place, reinforcing the iron grates. There was no room for hesitation. We weren't giving them an inch.

The ground trembled again. My stomach dropped. *Where is it?* I scanned the horizon, but I didn't see the threat until it was too late.

At each side of the keep, the earth began to break open. *Clever, damn clever.*

"MacLeod!" My voice was urgent. "They're coming at both ends!"

She looked to me, then to the battlements, her eyes flashing with a quick, calculating plan.

"Archers! Focus on the one to the west! Grant, bring the tar!"

"Aye!" Grant's voice rang back, carrying across the chaos.

"We're going to light it up," Genevieve muttered, her words a grim promise.

She turned to me, her face hardening with resolve. "Alix, if it were me, I'd send as many through the tunnel as possible. Watch and take them. Keep the tunnel open. I want it to slide back into the earth, dead."

I nodded, a cold chill running down my spine.

Grant returned with men and tar, hot.

The worm emerged, heading for the eastern wall. As the men poured through the tunnel, I took my position along the parapet. My bow felt like an extension of my arm as I fired, each arrow finding its mark with precision. One down. Then another. And another. I kept moving, each shot a breath, a prayer.

"Now!"

Grant and his men poured the hot tar over the back of the worm.

"Light it up!"

A flaming arrow followed it, striking the middle of the beast. The fire burned it from the tail upwards, catching the tar. The beast dropped to the ground screeching, making its way across the grounds, diving into the tunnel. Light lit below, and fire bellowed out. The three men left turned to run back to the battle. One, two, and three arrows met their mark.

Another worm was making its way out of the ground. *Ifrin,* how many were there? As it came through, it dove toward the northern wall. The archers were struggling to take it. I dropped the bow and ran across the parapet. As I reached the end, I pulled my dirk loose.

"Alix!" Genevieve threw her dagger from the wall above, hitting the best in the chest. I leapt off the parapet, aiming for her dagger. My left hand stretched out, my own dagger striking the beast. I held both daggers and used my body weight to drag them to the ground, slicing the beast's belly open as I went. It screeched in pain. As I reached the ground, I pulled the daggers loose, turning out of the way of the falling innards above. The worm crashed to the ground behind me. I knelt and wiped the guts from the daggers, sheathed them, and looked up.

A brilliant green light cracked through the dust and stone, blinding in its intensity. From the chaos emerged a figure cloaked in black, his eyes glowing with malice. The Black Coat Commander moved through the smoke, his presence like a shadow on the battlefield.

"Now!" Arrows from all directions of the castle shot out. He swung his staff around and a green shield deflected the arrows, disintegrating them. *Mac na galla!* Son of a bitch! I drew my sword from across my back, it turned its head to look at the castle, then to me. I held my stance, let it come to me. I could see its rotten teeth under its dark hood. It walked over so slowly it was almost gliding across the ground. More men were coming through the tunnel. Genevieve would take care of them; this Black Coat was mine.

I smiled at it. "I'd kindly ask ye to leave my land, sir."

It cackled. "Nay, girl. It won't be yours for long."

"Verra well."

The ground trembled beneath my feet as the Black Coat Commander strode toward me, the darkness of his cloak trailing behind him like a shadow in the dust. I could hear the distant cries of battle, but they seemed muffled, as if the world had narrowed down to just the two of us.

His eyes, glowing faintly beneath the hood, met mine. There was no mistaking the malice in them. He wasn't here to talk—he was here to end this.

I gripped my sword tighter, the weight of the blade a cold comfort in my hand. My pulse raced, but I steadied my breath, focusing on the way his every movement seemed calculated, deliberate. He was sizing me up, just as I was studying him. We were both waiting for the first move, and I could feel the air thick with anticipation.

The Black Coat lifted his staff, the green light flickering at the tip. His lips curled into a cruel smile, and I knew what was coming. The staff came down in a swift arc, aiming for my head. I twisted, dropping my shoulder to dodge, the air rushing past me as the staff barely missed.

The heat of the battle surged back into my limbs as I spun on my heel, ready to counterattack. But he was already there. His staff whipped back up, blocking my strike with a flick of his wrist. The force sent a jolt through my arm, and I staggered back, barely keeping my footing.

"Not bad," the Black Coat rasped, his voice cold and mocking. "But you're not fast enough."

I swallowed the bitterness rising in my throat and lunged again, this time aiming for his ribs. My sword met the shield of green light before it even got close. The impact sent a sharp shock through my wrists, and I staggered back again, my teeth gritting with frustration. The shield was impenetrable.

He was toying with me.

The thought made my blood boil.

I could feel the sweat starting to drip down my neck, the tension in my limbs growing with each failed strike. My mind raced for a solution. *Find an opening. Stay calm.*

The Black Coat took a step forward, his staff sweeping low toward my legs. The blow was quick and precise. I jumped, narrowly avoiding the strike, but I felt his eyes on me, felt the way he was reading my every move.

He wasn't just fighting me. He was studying me, waiting for a mistake.

I forced myself to focus. *I won't give him that mistake.*

A moment of hesitation—a split second in which his gaze flickered away—was all I needed. With a roar, I closed the distance, bringing my sword down with every ounce of strength I could muster.

But his staff shot up again, knocking my sword aside with a force that nearly threw me off balance. He spun the staff in his hand, moving in a fluid, almost predatory motion. His eyes never left mine.

Before I could react, he swung the staff in a wide arc. I barely managed to duck under it, the tip of the staff grazing the top of my head. My heart hammered in my chest, and my lungs burned from the exertion. I was losing ground, I could feel it. Every move I made was anticipated.

His voice echoed again, low and mocking. "You should have stayed out of this, girl."

I gritted my teeth, forcing myself to stay steady. I couldn't let him get in my head. *Focus.*

The next time he attacked, I wouldn't just defend. I would strike.

He swung his staff again, aiming for my head. This time, I didn't twist away—I stepped in, close enough to feel the heat of his shield, and parried his blow with my sword. The impact sent a jolt up my arm, but I used the force to push myself forward, forcing him to stagger back.

For a heartbeat, we both paused, circling each other. I could see the faintest hint of surprise in his eyes. It was all I needed.

With a growl, I closed the distance again, bringing my sword down in a sharp arc aimed at his throat.

But at the last moment, he spun, his staff coming up in a violent sweep. I blocked it, but the force pushed me back, throwing me off balance.

The Black Coat laughed, a chilling sound that made my skin crawl.

I swung wildly, desperate, but he blocked each blow effortlessly. Every strike I made, he deflected with the same unhurried, precise movements.

He's not just powerful. He's patient.

My breath was coming in short, ragged gasps now. The adrenaline that had carried me through the first few moments of the fight was starting to fade, replaced by a creeping exhaustion.

I needed to end this, and soon.

His staff whipped around again, aiming for my chest. I ducked just in time, but this time, I wasn't thinking—reacting purely on instinct. My feet slipped on the stone beneath me, and I stumbled.

He saw it immediately.

With a swift motion, his staff jabbed forward. I tried to parry, but he was too quick. The blow knocked my sword from my hand, sending it clattering to the ground, just out of reach. My heart dropped into my stomach as I stood there, weaponless, facing this creature who was both a master of the fight and the magic that shielded him.

"Now," he murmured, his voice a death sentence. "You're finished."

For a moment, everything seemed to slow. The world narrowed down to just the two of us, and the Black Coat's staff hovered inches from my chest, glowing with deadly intent. The weight of the moment crushed down on me, but I didn't give in. I wouldn't.

With a sudden surge of willpower, I dove for my dagger, slamming my hand to the stone floor and retrieving it in one fluid motion. In a heartbeat, I was back on my feet, ready to fight.

He smirked.

"Better," he said, as if impressed. "But not enough."

As he lunged forward, I twisted around him. Landing behind, I released my dagger and stabbed it through the back of his neck. Light cracked and spread like lightning through his body, disintegrating as the light touched it. The coat pooled to the ground, and my dagger stabbed into the dirt. I pulled it free. There wasn't even blood, but the blade was hot.

"No, you will never win."

From across the yard, I could see another. I turned to face it. It looked around, then ran back into the tunnel. I could hear Genevieve from above commanding the men to fill the tunnel. The clicks of the catapult were in. There were bodies and remains of the worms were spread around the yard, but none were our men.

Looking up, Genevieve was walking the wall, a Valkyrie commanding the keep. Her eyes locked with mine, a flicker of command passing between us. Without a word, she turned, already in motion. Her presence cut through the chaos like a blade. Grant lowered a ladder for me to climb.

***

The silver dragon flew down into the courtyard, and Niamh jumped down, running up the stairs. "They're after something, or someone. They know we don't have it here." She was sure.

"Aye, what could it be?" Genevieve asked. I was cleaning my sword, looking out at the battle in the field. Dragons were flying lower, flames lighting up the enemy. Carcasses of the worms and a couple of dragons lay on the ground. Shadows of men covered the grass. It was beginning to drizzle. The MacLeod had moved and would be in his tent, healing as many of the men as he could. Brian was high above, commanding the men. I couldn't make out how it was going.

Footsteps hurried down the steps. "They're after The MacLeod!" Claire gasped, her voice tight with panic. "They're already headed for the river." She was pointing in the distance. Black Coats were making their way around the moor, heading towards the river where they would be able to climb up the back to the tents at the top. My heart skipped as Claire's words struck with icy clarity. They were after *The MacLeod*. My chest tightened. I wasn't sure we could stop them, but there was no choice. Not this time.

I snapped my head towards my aunt. "I am the fastest rider."

Genevieve nodded. "Ride to the river, command the auld ones to help."

"It will give us a chance, as long as there are no tunnels," Niamh said.

I sheathed my sword and ran across the walls, the courtyard and out to the stables. Auld Mac had left a few of our horses saddled in case we needed to escape. My silver mare, always faithful, tossed her head and pawed at the ground. "As fast as we can, *mo nighean*," I whispered, feeling her strong legs carry us as one. We flew out of the stables and across the fields, jumping the stone wall. The rain was spattering my face as we rode.

Faster.

Faster.

We were approaching the battlefield, turning along the edges as we rode towards the river. I was spotted, and some of the Black Coats began to follow me. They had horses now. More must have made their way into the glen.

Faster.

I could see the river ahead. The Black Coats were gaining on me. I could hear the pounding of their hooves, the hiss of their breath in the air. My heartbeat was louder, but I kept my focus on the river ahead. This had to work—there was no other choice.

As I approached the ravine, I could feel the dark shadows behind me slowing. My horse's feet were running on the river rocks, and we stopped in the water. I turned her around. Looking up, I saw a dragon flying towards us. I lifted my sword to the sky, the hilt cold in my grasp. The river behind me churned, rising higher, pulling away from the land. I could feel the Auld Ones answering, their power beginning to stir beneath the surface. My heart raced. And then, with a cry, I called to them.

"Auld Ones, heed my call! Protect our people from these shadows, rise from the river and the lands, show us your strength and resilience. I ask for your help!" I hoped my prayer would be heard.

My horse was restless, the river flowing stronger. The Black Coats and their shadows came closer. I moved to face them. Unsheathing my sword, I reared my mare up on two legs. The river was pulling back behind me. I could feel a wall of water building. "*A dhion agus a dhion!*" I yelled with my sword drawn to full height on my horse. As we fell back to the ground, I lowered my sword.

The water behind me swirled as if answering a call, the river shifting, bending with a power I could not see. A shimmer in the water... Then stags of liquid and light began to form—massive creatures, their antlers gleaming like silver in the fading light. They moved with grace, an unstoppable force of nature. The stags ran them down, continuing towards the battlefields. Their antlers shimmered as the light hit them. They were an unstoppable force of power and water. They crashed and swept through the Black Coats, staff snapping blue lights, disintegrating their bodies. "Thank you," I whispered. I turned to my mare. "We must keep moving, *a lennon*." I gave her a slight kick, and we were off. Around the ravine and up climbing the Healer's Munro.

I could see the tent, men some on cots and others on the ground. Screams of pain echoed down the hill. Clashing of iron followed. Was it too late? "Faster, *a lennon*, faster!"

When we reached the top, three Black Coats were there. Locked in battle with the MacLeod and Callum. Their staff hit the swords of both men. I leapt off my horse; she would find safety in the tent. I rolled to the ground, pulling a *sgian dubh* from my corset in each hand. Letting them go, I aimed true at one of the commanders. The blades pierced the commander's chest, and a burst of blinding silver and gold light erupted, sending heat through the air. It wasn't just light, it was raw power, crackling like fire and ice in a single moment. The commander bent backwards as flames began to flicker from its body, a scream wretched from its throat. Standing, I drew my sword. The two commanders heard the screams and turned to face me. I walked towards the burning commander, my sword lifted. I grabbed its hood, pushed it back, and a shrivelled face wrinkled but not old faced me, with yellow rotting teeth, and cat-slit yellow eyes.

It smiled. "You'll be the next one girl, they can't keep you hidden for long." Its voice was high, sending shivers down my neck. I lifted my sword, decapitating it. Its head dropped to the ground, face held in laughter. I kicked my boot into its chest, knocking it flat to the ground.

Another one appeared near Callum; he had two fighting him. The MacLeod was holding his own, but now three more had appeared. They were pushing him back further away from us. I began to make my way to Callum from the ground, and another appeared in front of me. We began to fight, sword and staff. Iron clashed as they met. Gold and silver sparks shot out on impact. I couldn't make contact. This one was quick. I was trying to look at Callum—Da, where was he? Then the staff hit me in the stomach, and I went to the ground.

"Alix! Behind you!" Callum yelled.

Another staff came down in front of my neck, then my chest, sideways, hoping to pull me back. I let go of my sword and grabbed it, pulling the would-be assailant over my head and into the ground. I stood with the staff still in my hand and plunged it down into its chest. Green and white light flared, spreading out in a spider web through its body. I pressed harder, all my weight behind it, jarring the glowing staff into the ground through its owner.

Lifting my head, I saw one of the Black Coats pick up a fallen sword and stab it through Callum's side. He fell to his knees.

"No!"

I could hear my blood-curdling scream in my ears. I was running, sword back in my hands. I swiped, attacking anything, anyone near me. Blurs of Black Coats merged with white light and blood. The air was thick with the scent of blood, and the clash of iron rang in my ears as I fought. Sweat stung my eyes, and my hands ached from the grip on my sword. Every time a staff collided with my blade, it felt like a shock of cold, sending vibrations up my arm.

At last, I made it to his arms.

"I've got you, *bhràthair* ." I held him before he could go forward. I lowered him to the ground. My hands were shaking. I pulled the sword free, ripping my coat off, and shoved it into the wound. His blood soaked my hands, slick and warm. Was this happening? Was I going to lose him? The world seemed to spin, a blur of motion around me, but all I could focus on was his face, the slight smile on his lips even as his life slipped away.

Focus, Alix, focus.

Blood wasn't spitting out of the site, which was good. My heart was pounding in my ears. Was it my heart? The beat was steady, strong, and pounding, strong. I looked at his face; he looked young, with deep blue eyes like the lochs of our land, and bright red hair waved against the green grass.

"Do not worry, I won't let you go anywhere."

He smiled and nodded. I could see the grass around us going dark with blood. "Grannie!"

I kept pressing harder, please, please stop. I was trying to feel what was happening. Stop the bleeding. I lifted my head, hoping to see Grannie; instead, I could see Da fighting his way through the Black Coats towards us. Four Coats' heads were missing, and on the ground around him. He was tiring, slowing, but still determined to reach us. I looked down into Callum's blue eyes.

"Isobel's with child." It was almost a whisper. "Tell Isobel… name the child Alix. And… tell her I loved her. Always." He had lifted his hand to my face, but it was slowly falling.

I grabbed it and held it against his chest. "You're not going anywhere, you'll tell her when we're home!"

A large dark shadow flew above us. Its rider jumped, landing between the Black Coats and Da. Marcus. Thank *Beila*. Both swords out and ready, he met Da, cutting down another commander. Only one was left. Marcus had him. Da ran over to us. There was a lot of blood slowly leaking through to the ground. He smiled, hands covering mine.

"You've done well, lass, you've slowed it… I'll take it from here, ey. Go help Marcus."

I was frozen, my hands covered in Callum's blood.

"Alexandria, I have him." Silver eyes were firm. I nodded and stood. Wiping the blood on my pants, I picked up my sword and ran towards Marcus.

This commander was different, taller, his staff was black, and his hood was higher.

"Ah… the twins. I wondered. Strange we should meet again."

"What do you want, you bastard?" Marcus spat, voice ragged, the fire in his eyes burning with hatred.

"Has your power come into full form, young'uns?"

"We have enough to kill you!" Marcus yelled.

"We shall see."

He leapt towards us, taking us off guard. His staff was swinging, turning the air around him green with light. It felt evil. He was much stronger than the others; he was taunting us with each movement.

Marcus lit his sword in flame, red and green pushing against one another. I attacked with my sword, sparking with gold, white and silver light of the staff with each collision, singeing the grass around us. We were moving back, forth, and around towards the very top of the hill. I could see those fighting below. How long had we been fighting this battle, and for what? Who were these creatures?

He stopped right in the centre and Marcus's sword of flames went through his chest. He was then kicked to the ground, and my brother pulled his sword free.

The creature's hood fell back.

Unlike the other one, it was not shrivelled up. It was older, with black hair and blue cat-like eyes, and his teeth were rotten.

He smiled and began to laugh, reaching for his staff to strike Marcus in his back. My sword was heavy, and my arms felt like lead. The commander stood up, Marcus's his magic was weakening, too—his fiery sword flickered like a dying star.

With one last breath, I summoned every ounce of strength, feeling the magic surge in me, just as I brought my sword down one final time. The creature shrieked, a terrible, gut-wrenching sound, before crumpling to the earth.

A binding light shot from my sword as it hit the earth below. The light rippled through the earth, connecting a line of my sword to the standing stone in front of me. I looked up, and a white light was beginning to break through the cracks in the stone. The body below had disappeared, leaving no trace.

As I looked towards the standing stone, another golden light shot out. A pulsing force pushed me back, slamming me into Marcus. We were both sent tumbling to the ground. As I pulled myself up, I saw a body walking out of the stones towards us. It glowed like a star; the brightness faded, but a faint white glow remained behind. It was a woman, wearing a green dress with long flowing sleeves. An arisaid crossed her chest in the MacLeod colours, tightened with a leather belt. A sword halted to it, its handles covered in runes and thistles. The blade glimmered like the glow behind her, also covered in runes.

"Where is he? Your brother. We don't have much time." Her voice was familiar, soft but firm. We stood and walked towards Da and Callum. She ran over, falling to the ground beside them.

Her hands lightly touched Callum's face. Da looked up at the glowing woman. His face relaxed when he saw her. She ran her hands over Callum's body, speaking in a language older than Eire's. Light glowed from her fingertips into him. I was kneeling beside them, holding his hand, and I could feel his heartbeat becoming stronger. The light around her faded as the light brightened within him. She stopped, her hand brushing his face.

"You're going to be fine, my sweet lad. Rest now. I'm here," she whispered. He looked asleep, the corner of his lips turned up like a secret smile. I looked up as she brushed her long, fiery red hair back over her shoulder. She reached over, grasping Da's hand. "Alastair, he's going to be fine." She smiled, her eyes glimmering lakes of deep blue.

"How long?" he whispered to her.

"Not long enough, *mo chridhe*."

He stood, reaching out a hand to help her. She was nearly his height. Their heads bent together, whispering. He kissed her head, cupping her face. *"Bidh gaol agam ort gu brath."* I will love you forever.

She smiled. "Always my love. It is time."

She turned to face us.

"Ma?"

"Yes, *mo nighean*. Come, Marcus, *mo chridhe.* I don't have long to explain. We must set the wards."

We followed her back to the standing stone.

"Our lands are old, our ancestors had great magic and many secrets." She was looking around. "I cannot explain them all just now; it will have to wait. These stones are more than rocks. They are our people's ancient wards—placed to protect us from the darkness. Without them, Caledonia would fall. The stones were placed through our lands to keep out evil. They align with the stars in an orbit for protection. The night the two of you were born, it was a moonless night, and evil broke the lines across Caledonia. We do not know how or why it happened. And there hasn't been a magic strong enough to restore it. We need to light the stones circle here; it will drive the rest of the Black Coats out.

"You both must drive your swords to the centre of the hill. Push your magic through it, Alix, like you did before, but stronger. I believe the two of you together can do it. One dark as night—" she touched Marcus's cheek "—and one of golden starlight." She tucked a loose hair behind my ear.

"My dears, you must strike the ground and pour your magic into it at the same time. It will be exhausting. I need you to keep going no matter what happens." She looked at the sun as it was beginning to set. "I will be with you. Your father, and I will protect you. Just hold on."

Da was now standing with her, their hands intertwined.

"I may not be able to come back for some time. Once the ward is restored, it will make it even more difficult. You must find me in Orkadia, I will find ye all again." She looked at the setting sun again. "You must do it now, my loves."

We nodded and stood forward. Marcus and I held our eyes, lifted our swords together, and brought them down. Bright red flames surrounded his sword, mine flames of gold, silver, and copper. We looked at each other, then back at the swords.

"Hold on, my loves, it's working."

I could feel shaking as heat pushed into the earth. Something was trying to push my sword out. It was taking all my strength to keep it in. The line appeared in the ground, shooting towards the standing stone in front, a web of lights illuminating with red, copper, silver, and gold light. Another line shot out of the stone in the ground. I followed it towards the stone on the crest. In the distance, the stone lit up, and time felt too slow. The line was making its way through to the next stone; as it reached each one, white light burst into the sky above.

My legs were about to collapse. I didn't think I could go on. A firm hand wrapped around me, holding me up. My magic was draining, my body aching. I looked across at Marcus. Da was holding him upright. Looking behind, I saw Ma. She was smiling.

"You're doing great, *mo lennon*, you're almost done, just a little longer."

They were holding us up and holding each other. Their energy and magic keep us through it. The line glowed and was almost back at the stone in front, a complete circle. As it reached completion, the first stone shot a bright light high into the sky, then a golden light filtered over the land, encasing it. Black shadows flew into the sky, hitting the light and disintegrating into nothing.

"Let go, my dears, together, you've done so well, so very well."

I pulled my sword free and collapsed into my mother's arms. Looking over, Marcus was the same. Da came close and held the four of us tightly together. The ground shook for a moment as a dragon landed.

"Ma!" Malcolm ran over, embracing us all. "I ken it had to be you, I saw the light." He had tears down his face.

"Oh, my dear lad." She wiped away his tears. She stepped back. "I must return now. I'm sorry, my dears. This war... It's far from over. It's just beginning. Orkadia—start there.

And Alix, hold on to those rings. They'll guide your magic and protect you. Promise me you'll keep them safe."

She turned and walked towards the standing stone. "*Ged is fada an turas, tha gaeol agam ort.*" Though the journey is long, I love you. She smiled, tears in her eyes, then turned and walked slowly into the standing stone. A golden light glowed, and she faded into the stone.

As we stood there, watching the stones glow with the final pulse of energy, a thought lingered in my mind. This wasn't the end of the war; it was only the beginning. The battle had been won, but what lay ahead… that was a question only the stars could answer.

"Come, let's take your brother home." Da turned us away towards where Callum was lying. Grannie was close by his side.

"She came then?" Grannie asked.

"She always does," the MacLeod answered.

***

The commanders of the enemy army had perished when the wards were activated, but the battle's aftermath still weighed heavily on us. Malcolm flew down on his dragon, meeting the others who would escort the men out of our lands. Above, dragons soared, their powerful wings beating as they filled in the tunnels where the worms had burrowed, burying their monstrous carcasses in the earth. It felt like the world was slowly returning to order, but it would take time.

The warriors on foot or riding brought the dead back to the keep, where their bodies would be washed and await burial in the cooler cellars below. Those who required healing were brought to the main courtyard, where a tent was erected. Grannie and Da would oversee this. The men who had been in the healers' tent were brought down in carriages by Auld Mac's team. Marcus had to help carry Callum back to his rooms, despite his protests. Callum had wanted nothing more than to stay with his men, to show his strength, even in his condition. But he was too pale, too weak to argue any longer. His fierce resolve had faltered when the pain became too much, and I could see the tension in Marcus's shoulders as he supported Callum's weight. The sight of my brother like this—it wasn't easy to bear.

I made my way down to the keep on the back of my mare, who had forgiven me for the ride earlier in the day. As we arrived at the keep, Aunt Genevieve was waiting. She greeted me with a hug that bruised my ribs. We took our horses and headed to the tunnels. We would bring our people home.

We rode in silence, the weight of the day's battle pressing heavily on my shoulders. The tunnels seemed endless, their dark, oppressive walls a stark contrast to the warmth we'd left behind at the keep. When we finally emerged into the caves above, the smell of Ms Mac's cooking cut through the fatigue. For a brief moment, I almost let myself relax, but the responsibility of what was to come quickly settled back into my chest. Genevieve opened the hidden door, and we rode through.

As we emerged into the cave, a few of the women gasped, their fear clear until Ms Mac saw us. "Och, it's naught but our Lady Genevieve and Lady Alix—come to bring us home. They've just got their war paints on, see?" Her words were light, but I could see the relief in their eyes. Still, I couldn't help but feel the weight of Callum's absence. We'd left him in the hands of Marcus and the healers, but I couldn't stop wondering how he was. We smiled as she handed us warm goblets of soup. "Take some, lassies, you likely haven't eaten since the gathering.

"Now, let's get ready, you hear? There's much to be done at the keep. Best make sure we get there sooner rather than later." She gave us a pointed look, as if time was already slipping through her fingers.

I must have fallen asleep on Genevieve as Ms Mac came over, startling me awake. "We're all ready to go, my ladies, would you do us the honour and bring us home?"

We both smiled and climbed on our horses. "*A dhion agus a dhion,*" we said together, leading our people back through the tunnels and to *Caisteal Moar*.

Chapter Fifteen

I STOOD ON THE WATCH TOWER LOOKING out over our lands. The familiar cold bite of the early morning wind froze me to the stone walls. The grey clouds were settling in, and the cold drops of rain ran down my face as I looked out. The walls inside the keep had been spared, and the castle hardly touched. The grounds were a mess of rubble and scorched ground, the well broken but easily mended. Most of the village crofts were burnt, but I reminded myself that most of the people were safe inside our walls. The glen and the woods were hurting, trees broken and knocked down. The ground was burnt, water was pooling in the dips, and there were craters in the ground from the worms or dragons. Men were walking around, clearing the dead and bringing them home. Tomorrow we would honour them. I could see the standing stones—the magic and secret they held unknown to all—as a faint glimmer of gold shimmered from them into the sky.

The dragons circled the keep and the glen, finding comfortable places to land amongst the trees. Their secret was no more; they had risked their safety to protect those who had feared them for centuries. Then, emerging from the mists beyond, was an image I had been longing to see. The dark silhouette ingrained in my memory was making its way in from the valley opening towards the keep. Time had paused, my heartbeat was the only sound I could hear, and it was in time with the steady beat of the wings in the distance.

And then I was no longer frozen to the wall. My legs burned as I ran, the cold rain stinging my face. The gates swung open, the guards stepping aside with bowed heads as I passed. But I barely noticed them, my eyes locked on the figures emerging from the mist. Cian's massive wings, gleaming in the dim light, were unmistakable. Malcolm and Liam landed their dragons on either side. But it wasn't them that made my heart leap. It was Tommy. The man I had feared I might never see again. He was there, alive, whole, and walking toward me with the same quiet intensity I had once loved, and still—desperately—did. I hesitated, just for a moment, my breath catching in my throat.

Whole.

Alive.

Safe.

A warrior of old returned from battle, his face covered in blood and dust, his armour battered and bruised. His head and shoulders held high, commanding the skies above. I ran towards him, tears and rain in my eyes. Flinging myself at him, he caught me tight in his arms, my legs wrapped around him. His warmth and strength engulfed me. I buried my face into his chest, breathing in the scents of earth and smoke, wild flowers and mountain air, the scent of the man I had feared I would not see again. His arms tightened around me in a fierce protectiveness that filled my heart. I clung to the solidness of his body. So very whole, alive, and real.

Eventually, I let go, holding myself back; I could see the darkness under his eyes, the shadows, and the horrors that lay behind him. His gaze was steady and intense. I was searching for the small spark of light buried deep within.

I looked at Cian, and his emerald eyes flickered toward me, ancient and knowing. He, too, had felt the pain of battle. I could see it in the way he stood, regal yet weary. Tommy looked at me, and in that instant, I saw the raw grief in his eyes. It was a weight I hadn't expected to see so plainly. He stepped forward, a hand trembling at his side, and whispered, "Sean." His voice cracked, barely above a whisper. "I couldn't save him."

I closed the distance between us, taking his hand in mine, my heart aching for him, for the burden he carried. I held him tighter, my fingers trembling as they gripped his armour. I should have felt only joy—he was home, he was safe. But beneath the surface, a part of me remained locked in fear.

Tommy pulled back slightly, his hands cupping my face. "Alix," he whispered, his voice hoarse. "I promised you... I promised I'd come back." And in that moment, I realised the promise had always been more than just words—it had been a pact between us.

***

As we passed through the castle gates, the sounds of celebration echoed from the great hall: laughter, music, and the clinking of mugs. The living were celebrating, giving thanks for their safety and the defeat of the Britannias and the Black Coats, though the names still felt strange on our tongues. We slipped through the secret passages, careful not to disturb the merrymaking, and made our way to the roof. There, our family had gathered, along with Liam, around a fire that crackled in the cool night air.

The warmth of the flames was a small comfort against the chill of the evening, but the weight of the loss hung heavy in the air. Niamh and Claire sang softly, their voices rising in the mournful ballads of warriors fallen too soon. The haunting melodies filled the space between us, honouring those we had lost. With each note, a pang of grief tightened in my chest, and I found myself passing the whisky more slowly than usual, savouring the warmth it brought against the coldness of memory.

We sat in silence, the stars above us distant and unfeeling. There was no grand victory here, no triumph to be celebrated. Only the quiet presence of those we still had, and the aching absence of Sean—and the others, so young, stolen from us in the prime of their lives. The fire crackled and popped, but all I could hear was the quiet echo of their names in my mind, and the soft murmur of the ballad still floating in the night air.

***

I stood on the parapet, watching dragons wheel overhead. In the distance, the crofts and village were being rebuilt. Children laughed and played in the meadows, while women hung washing on the trees. It was as though nothing had changed. Life, resilient and unbroken, went on.

I followed the familiar dragons as they landed, Malcolm and Tommy disembarking, jokingly pushing each other as they went to lift some wood for a croft. I could make out Marcus in the meadow playing with the children, Claire in a tree reading, her feet dangling out of the branches.

In a few days, she would head back to Skye, while Tommy and Liam would take their riders and dragons back to Storr or Eire, returning before the winter snow.

Soft footsteps came behind me. "When are you going to tell Da?" Callum said as he came to stand beside me.

"Aye, about what exactly?" I continued watching the crofts being rebuilt. Callum placed his hand on mine, turning it gently to reveal the ring. He smiled. "About being Lady Eire?"

I turned my head to look at my brother, and our mother's eyes looked back. I smiled. "How did you know?"

He looked at me, raising an eyebrow and said, *"For as long as my feet are on these lands, you have my protection and my sword. Should the day come I do leave, know I uphold this oath, in all decisions I make to protect all those who cannot protect themselves."*

"That was my oath to the MacLeod."

"Aye, and then a young Laird from Eire shows up in full regalia, refusing the oath, making another speaking of being kinsman, when his only kinsman is Niamh and Claire. Then, asking for a blessing to marry the Chieftain's daughter. At the gathering where the men could easily kill him for such a declaration and refusal to swear the oath." He paused, hand brushing over my ring. I looked down.

"Not to mention this ring..." Callum's voice softened as he gently brushed his fingers over the stone. "The Ring of Eire. Lost for centuries. Its last owner was Fayre MacLeod Patrick, Queen of Eire and the Fae."

"How?"

He tapped my nose and smiled, his eyes glimmering in the light.

"You forget, I studied at the great libraries, including the ones in Eire. I was curious when I found out about the MacLeod line. I've read many scrolls and tombs of the auld, and that ring was sketched in one of the most ancient scrolls I have ever read. In the starlight, its runes are clear. I took a closer look on the rooftop.

"It is Fayre's ring.

"Only a direct descendant would know where it has been hidden, and only her Heir would be able to give it to his betrothed.

"The stone is extremely rare. You will not find another the same, brought from the fairy realm, and the gold from Eire's deep lands.

"Uniquely beautiful." He smiled, holding my hand. "What I do not ken, is when?"

I was smiling then.

"Aye, well, that is assuming you are correct."

"*Mo chridhe*, my heart, you may have been able to fool Da and the others, but I ken you better than anyone. And magic was not the reason for your slight change when you came back from Skye or for the way Tommy looks at ye."

I laughed and shook my head. "Of course you'd figure it out; anyone else would only complement a bonny ring. Marcus hasn't even noticed either one I wear."

I paused and took a breath.

"A few days after the attack at Ewan."

"Malcolm?"

"Aye, he was there, we were handfast with the auld ones at the stones."

"*Sornaichean Coir' Fhinn?* The Kensalayre Stones?"

"Aye."

I looked out at the setting sun against the standing stone on the Healers Munro, so much like the day we were handfast not long ago.

*

We had flown from Ewan on Cian, Malcolm close behind on his dragon, and the small silver one followed behind. At the bottom of the valley, we looked back on the Quiraing, its timeless beauty of rugged cliffs softened by the lush greens that flowed over the edges. With the setting sun, shadows began to dance across its face, flickering in the ever-changing wind.

I stood in a ring of standing stones, each more than twice my height. Old and weathered like the stones on Storr, something about them felt alive, like their own magic was moving through them. The seven stones surrounded me, bathed in the glowing warmth of the sun, casting their own shadows on the lush grass below. The sun was following the direct line through the largest stone in the centre, facing the Quiraing. The scent of wild heather lingered in the air.

"There you are." Tommy brushed his arm gently across my back, then to my hand, and he lifted it, kissing it softly.

Shivers went down my back. He was wearing his full Eire warrior attire, both swords strapped on, and one ring on each hand. The stones matched his eyes. He looked up through glimmering emeralds. "Are ye sure, a chuisle mo chroi?"

"I have never been surer."

Malcolm came over to stand in front of the large stone, the sun slowly lowering to the top of it. He nodded at both of us, a smile broad across his face. Sean stood to Tommy's right, and the four dragons chose their space between the stones. Cian let out a breath, and mist covered our feet. Today, we would make a promise before the earth, the sky, and the auld.

Malcolm's presence was commanding, his voice steady and strong as he began to chant in the ancient language of the auld. Each word vibrated through the air, resonating with the earth beneath our feet. It was as if the stones themselves were alive, breathing, their magic pulsing through the ground like a heartbeat. The dragon's presence felt like a blessing, a connection to the magic of this land.

As Malcolm drew his dagger, the sound of metal rasping against the sheath seemed to echo in the quiet of the valley. My breath caught in my throat. The cool air felt heavier now, like the land itself was holding its breath, waiting for the promise we were about to make.

He reached forward, the blade sharp and precise. I barely flinched as the tip pressed against my skin, the first thin line of blood welling up. My pulse quickened, but I held my arm steady, meeting Tommy's gaze. His eyes were steady, but his jaw was clenched. I could see the slight tremor in his hand as he took hold of mine. The touch was reassuring, grounding.

The sting of the cut was sharp, then faded, replaced by a strange warmth that spread through my veins. Malcolm moved to Tommy, repeating the motion, his dagger slicing through the air with a swift, practised motion. When our blood mingled together, I felt a shiver of something ancient, something powerful, sweep through me. The earth beneath my feet seemed to pulse with it.

Malcolm took a length of silver ribbon, shimmering in the last light of the sun, and began to tie it around our wrists. The fabric was smooth and cool, the knots tight but gentle. With each knot, I felt something stir inside me—a low, vibrant hum. The magic was like fire, not burning, but warming, spreading through my skin, my bones, my very soul.

The words Malcolm spoke seemed to wrap around us like a spell. I could feel them resonate, not just in my ears, but deep within my chest.

I felt Tommy's grip on my hand tighten. His voice was steady, yet there was a rawness to it as he spoke the words alongside me. "You are Blood of my Blood, Bone of my Bone. I give ye my body, that we might be one. I give ye my spirit, until our life is done." We spoke together, our eyes meeting each other. We promised to stand by each other in laughter and sorrow, in peace and in battle. The protection of our names, our clans, and our lands, to protect and defend one another. Our voices echoed through the valley, the dragons let out a roar, and the mist surrounded us, binding our promises.

As Malcolm tied the final knot, I glanced around. The stones stood as silent witnesses, the dragons our guardians. Malcolm wiped away a tear, his face alight with joy. We stood in the fading light of the sun, its last rays sinking behind the stone.

Tommy's free hand brushed my face, his touch tender as he tucked a stray lock of hair behind my ear. His voice was low, sincere. "My Lady... may I kiss ye?" I smiled, my heart quickening. I nodded, and he leaned in, his lips meeting mine with a soft, lingering promise. Slow and tender, filled with promise and passion, gentle like the wind and as powerful as the ancient stones and dragons that surrounded us.

As we pulled away, I could taste salt and sweetness. I smiled and looked down at my brother. We were floating above the ground, turning slowly in a circle, a golden light visible through the mist below. There was a chuckle from the dragons, and my brother and Sean looked confused. I looked

up at Tommy. He smiled and shrugged. I laughed as we
slowly lowered back to the ground.

*

"Who else kens?"

"No one, no one alive."

We were silent, looking out over our lands.

"Aye, well, tell him. He will understand, you ken that."

"I ken, I came up here to find the words."

He placed his hand on mine and his other arm around me. "You are allowed to be happy, *mo phiuthar*, Da kens how precious love is more than anyone."

I leaned against Callum as we watched the sunset. A gentle breeze brushed my face, and the scent of wildflowers drifted by.

Chapter Sixteen

I ENTERED THE MACLEOD'S SPEAK-A-
word room, a room in the corridor that looked out into
the meadow towards the mountains and the stones. He
was sitting in his chair, whisky in one hand and a book
in the other. Da's silver eyes flickered with a knowing glint
as he looked up at me, his lips curving into a slight smile. He
didn't say anything right away, just studied me as if waiting
for me to speak first. I felt the weight of his gaze, the one
that always seemed to see through me.

"So," he finally said, his voice warm and teasing.
"You've come to tell me you've handfasted the Patrick lad?"
He chuckled softly, but his eyes held something more
serious, something I couldn't quite name.

I froze mid-step, as if the floor beneath me had turned to
ice. My mouth went dry, and I could feel my heart pounding

in my chest, but no words came out. I opened my mouth, tried to speak, but all I could do was blink at him, helpless.

Da didn't seem to mind. He just looked at me with those steady, silver eyes, his lips quirking into a knowing smile, waiting for me to find my voice.

"Did ye really think I would not ken? Come, lass, sit by me."

I sat down in the deep red chair, he poured me a glass, and I gulped it down. I turned to look at him.

"The lad came to see me with Malcolm a few months ago and asked. Then, yer Grannie saw it in her waters." He wiggled his eyebrows. "Standing stones, aye?"

I nodded. He leaned over, grabbing both my hands, his hands like a giant's holding mine, warm and callused from years of wielding a sword.

Da's voice softened, carrying a weight that seemed to fill the space between us. "Love, lass, no matter how long or short, is always worth the risk. Worth fighting for. It's a thing to cherish, because there's no telling how long we get to hold onto it. Those who never ken it... Well, they're the ones who miss out."

I swallowed, my throat tight. I thought of Tommy, of everything we'd been through. Was I ready for this? Could I risk everything I had left for this love, for him?

"Don't take it for granted," Da went on, his hand resting gently on mine. "Hold it close, every day. You'll never regret it."

He looked at both my rings and smiled, his thumb lightly brushing the stars. His expression softened with something I couldn't quite place. His large fingers reached out, gently turning it over as if testing its weight, its meaning.

"Where did ye find this?" His voice was quiet, almost reverent.

I glanced down at the ring on my hand, my fingers brushing over the cool surface. Da's question caught me off guard, pulling me out of my thoughts. "Niamh gave it to me, with a note"

"Do you remember what it said?"

The letter. Niamh's words. A rush of emotion surged in me as I recalled her handwriting, the carefully chosen words, the way they felt like a lifeline. I swallowed hard and nodded. I looked up, meeting his eyes.

"Alix,

Your mother left this in my possession to give to you when you were ready, and you are ready, a lennon. There is much you dinna ken yet, in time you will. Remember your lessons and the tales of auld, they will guide you. Know that when you do discover it all, ken how much she loved you.

Open your heart, it is strong enough to survive.

Auntie Niamh."

"Och, I thought, I had hoped, she had left it somewhere and it was not lost. She always wanted ye to have it should anything happen."

"Da…"

Da's expression shifted then, the playful glint in his eyes fading as he stared out the window. I could see the sadness begin to settle on his face, his shoulders slumping ever so slightly as if some invisible weight had fallen on him.

"Alix..." he began, his voice rougher than usual. "Get your brothers, lass," he said, his voice tight. "We'll meet in the family room. It's time you all knew. Bring Tommy and Claire, they also should hear it too"

***

We all sat on chairs or the floor of the large family room. Situated in the western wing of the castle, most of the chambers belonging to members of the family were in this wing. The room was used most in the winter because of its hearth, both large and warm. It was carpeted with warm rugs and furs, blankets and pillows. Tall bookshelves and paintings hung from each wall. In the winter, the sun blazed in from the large glass windows looking out to the mountains covered in snow. In the summer, the mountains were covered in blooming heather. Lit by candlelight, the room felt cozy, smaller than its size. As I sat on the floor, I felt uneasy. Marcus was pacing the room, Malcolm stared out the window, and Callum sat patiently in one of the larger chairs. We waited.

Grannie had fallen asleep, the closing door startling her. Da walked in slowly, sitting in his ash chair. He looked around the room, pulling out a worn parchment, and he laid it down on the table in front.

"I suppose the four of ye have questions?" His eyes darted around to look at his four children.

Callum and I nodded. I heard Mal grunt. "Aye, you suppose right," Marcus answered.

"Then I'll start at the very beginning."

He paused, inhaling slowly, then taking a sip from his cup. He placed his hands on the chair, pushing up, walking towards the fire, and he pulled something out of his sporran, sprinkling it into the hearth. A whisper under his breath, he was speaking a chant in an ancient language. I could barely make out his voice. Turning, he made his way back to his seat. After a moment, he began to talk. The fire was glowing deep and golden. Small flecks began to move, slowly hovering towards the table over the top of the parchment, swirling in a column to his voice.

"Long before any of ye were born, there was a war," Da began, his voice low, "Britannia invaded Caledonia, burning crofts and murdering clansmen in their sleep. The land was drenched in blood—disease and death followed in their wake."

I could see the weight of the memory on Da's face, and I felt a chill crawl down my spine.

"Those who fled the lowlands sought refuge here, but not all made it."

The fire glowed brighter, its flickering light casting strange, shifting shapes in the air. I watched, transfixed, as golden sparks danced like memories before my eyes: burning crofts, fleeing families, the terror in their faces as they ran through the woods.

My heart twisted in sorrow. The pain of their loss, so raw, lingered in the air.

"Caledonia was drenched in blood, but in the lochs of despair we found hope." His voice was a soft rumbling through the room. "The great chieftains met—my Da was one of them. I travelled with him to *Finnich Gorge*.

"Donnachaidh, Mackenzie, MacDonald, Dunkeld, Bruce, and MacLeod, each had travelled from across Caledonia and the Isles to this sacred place of kings, in truce to defeat Britannia. Each of the six chieftains brought with them a second, son or brother, all but one who brought his daughter."

The flecks merged into figures of the chieftains, resolute and fierce, faces fixed with determination. Donnachaidh's gaze burned with fire deep in rage, Mackenzie's thoughtful demeanour spoke of wisdom and calculation. MacDonald, amongst the chaos, was laughing.

"*Finnich Gorge* held not just a gathering of men but a convergence of destinies, a sacred place of kings, clans vowing to stand together. Fighting not just for their own lands and homes but for the legacy of our people, for the soul and fire of Caledonia itself."

The figures walked through the water to a flat stone above it, swords lay across it, and heads bowed in prayer.

"Together, the great chieftains forged a pact, a vow of honour, sealed with their oaths. Each one embodying the spirit of their people, symbolising not only warriors, but the hearts of their people."

The figure of the daughter shimmered into view, sitting on her horse cloak drawn high on her head, flowing down. She commanded the air around her, her sword raised high, a flame of defiance against the shadows. She was not merely a daughter among men, but a warrior in her own right.

The figure evaporated, turning into an image of a young Alastair MacLeod, head high, fierce and solid. Fearless, his kind eyes locked on mine. Da stood among those chieftains, his heart steady with courage. My heart paused. This was more than a tale; it was a call to arms.

"We left and gathered our men. The women, children, and those who could not fight we protected in the castles, deep gorges, and in secret paths into the mountains. The clan's road out to the Great Moor; Britania would have to cross here if they wanted to get to the Highlands. We waited for three nights before we heard their drums.

"Each of the chieftains led their men. I had set up healing tents within the trees, with two or three men from each clan, and we would tend the fallen.

"The Britannias were fierce but desperate. They'd burned crops along their march, leaving their men to starve. Their commanders wore dark cloaks, their faces set with cruelty. "As the Highlanders fought, their blood soaked the ground, turning the moor into a river of copper."

I felt my throat tighten. So many young men are dead. And for what?

"I don't understand it, Da," I whispered. "What brought this madness?"

Men fighting glimmered before my eyes, faces familiar, covered in mud and blood. The blue eyes of a young Brian stared back, his hair plastered to his face from rain or blood; horror filled them. The image changed again, the healers' tent, men screaming in pain, buckets of water at bedsides, bandages tried to arm and legs, other bodies lay underneath a tree, silent and still.

A hand glimmered, a small copper ring with a dark stone, reached out to cover a larger one. The large hand shook as it pressed firmly into a flowing wound with a cloth.

"*I'm here to help,*" I remember her words clearly; it was the first time I looked into the deep lochs of her eyes. Bright against the dark charcoal paint on her face.

"Valkyrie.

"She was dressed for war, broadsword hanging by her waist. Her hair matted with blood. She had come straight from the battlefield.

"She brought to the tent as many as she could, making a stretcher to hold the men who couldn't walk. She rode right out into the battle high upon her horse, tall as many of the men around her, flaming red hair flowing down her back. With her sword, she protected them, bringing them back to safety.

"Elizabeth Mackenzie, in all her fire, was a beacon of hope that dark day. She is the reason so many lived; not one man ran back on that battlefield for aid. She continued well into the night, carrying men, mending them when she could. She didn't stop."

My mother, high upon her horse, was riding through the battle, a bright figure in the middle of the room, and was now dragging a man to her stretcher to take back.

"On the second day of battle, the men continued to fight with everything they had. Unfortunately, they didn't have much strength left. Horses were exhausted, arrows were near gone, and hope had all but diminished.

"In the west, high upon a Munro was fire, the MacLeod Firey Cross had been lit."

The glittering sparks twisted together forming a figure on a horse, they were flying through the castle gates, across the river and climbing high upon the Munro behind Healer's Hill. The rider had a torch, lit in the castle and had made it to the cross. The figure was a woman with dark, braided, long hair, charcoal paint with white ruins, soaked, red material tight upon her right thigh. She was running, limping. Dropping her sword, she continued. Flame held high as she lit the Firey Cross. She looked up into the heavens, sending a prayer before turning at a run to her horse back to the keep.

Genevieve.

"Aye, Gen lit the cross. A call for aid. We had been attacked."

Men were riding back to the keep from the battle. Led by the Chieftain MacLeod. Brian was fighting on the main battlefield, the sparks were changing rapidly, faces, torn, grieving, fear, anger.

"I remember the horn, Da was blowing it. He was surrounded by Black Coats. Our men were fighting to get to him. It was an ambush; they had set a trap. Brian was trying to get to him, and I was mounting my horse, trying to decide whether to ride to Da or Gen.

I am the fastest rider. I will go to your sister. I will do everything I can. MacLeod, look at me. You canna be in both places, I promise I will see her safe.

Elizabeth held my hand tight and rode away. A flaming red against the darkening sky. I kicked off towards Da and Brian."

The figures were slowing, The MacLeod was surrounded by Black Coats, and he had three arrows in his back. He was pushing through them, meeting blow for blow. He was going to get to his daughter; there were flames in his eyes. A blast of fire came from behind, surrounding the Black Coats. They were taken by surprise, dissolving into the ground.

"Brian had pushed through enough to wield fire, hoping to clear the path. Not knowing the heat and the light would destroy them. I cut down the verra lest of them and we made it.

Get me a horse, he yelled at us. I could see arrows in his back; he had pulled one from his leg, ripping his shirt, and he tied it around to staunch the bleeding.

Go Brian! I grabbed my Da and tried as fast as I could to heal him. He wouldn't wait and climbed on the closest horse, riding out to Moar. Brian was ahead with some of the men, and we were close behind"

The sparks shifted. Elizabeth Mackenzie was riding through the river, an army of water behind her. Stags and wolves follow her towards the keep. She lowered her sword from above her head, and they overtook, slaughtering the army in their way.

Inside the keep, a few men were fighting, their leader fighting two Black Coats. She was wounded, the red material tied to her thigh. As Elizabeth reached the gates, she swung her sword high and around in the air, then, swinging it forward, the bared gates flew open.

She jumped off the horse and strode forward, sword ready. Genevieve had swung her sword; the strike would have killed a man, but the Black Coat just stood there. Genevieve fell to her knees as the enemy went to strike the rider's sword. Golden light beamed out from the clash. She sent her foot right into the middle of its chest, sending it backwards. The other attacked, she fought it, meeting it stroke for stroke, driving it back towards the other and far from Genevieve. They were the last two Black Coats remaining. Elizabeth pulled a dagger out and was now fighting both, golden light flying out with each strike.

"When we arrived, the grounds had water everywhere, and a silver wolf was walking back into the woods. The gates were pulled off their hinges and were lying on the ground. A large black horse stood eating the grass near a tree. Genevieve was on her knees, looking ahead. A fierce Valkyrie was fighting two Black Coats, her flaming hair behind her, sword and dagger alight in a golden flame. They both swung towards her. She slid across and under, getting up, she ran to the well, climbing on, she jumped somersaulting over the top of the attackers, as though she knew they would turn. She landed on one knee, sword and dagger flipped in her hands, stabbing the assailants in the chest. Light burned through them, spreading like a spiderweb. When it reached their faces, they exploded, leaving behind their coats.

She looked up slowly, her eyes went wide.

Appearing from the ground, a Black Coat right in front of her was ready to strike, green light building. Time paused. Then a sword came down, beheading the assassin. As it dropped back to the ground, Genevieve stood behind it, sword dripping in black blood.

An image of two Valkyrie, both so young, blood dripping from their swords, their eyes had seen too much horror. They nodded towards each other. Turning, Genevieve was swept into an embrace by her father and brothers. The Flaming Valkyrie stood and walked towards her horse. As she mounted it, she waited.

"I walked over to her to thank her. Before I could, she spoke: *I ask ye now for your help, I do not ken it will work. But I would like to try.* I mounted my horse as we were riding, fast towards the Healers' Moor. We walked towards the standing stone, and she looked at me. *I need your strength, Alastair and a little bit of your magic to hold me true. No matter what happens, I need you to hold on.* We stood right in the centre of the hill, in front of the stone, facing each other. She was chanting in an ancient language; whatever she was saying, asking or praying, it was beautiful. At last, her deep blue eyes looked at me with hope, a glint of light within. We lifted our swords, bringing them down into the earth at the same time. Light ran towards the stone, spreading out like a spider web. It shot out into the sky, spreading through the other stones and beyond. A soft golden light was falling from the sky above. *Let go, it's ok.* We pulled the swords out, and she fell to the ground. I held her. She was barely breathing, and her heart was slowing. Light was fading from her skin. I used every last bit of my magic, pulling from the deep well within. I willed it to work, I prayed to the auld gods to save her.

"Her eyelids fluttered, and then she opened her eyes— slowly, as if emerging from a deep fog. *I ken ye'd save me,* she whispered, a small smile curving her lips. But there was more than relief in her gaze. It was something deeper— something like recognition, as though she knew how much I had given to bring her back."

The images faded into nothing; the room was quiet.

"I do not understand it all, but she was able to create a shield through the standing stones across Caledonia and through to the Isles. It has protected the land since. But the night my twins were born, there was evil lurking. A moonless night, the Auld Ones sent a warning. We used as much magic as we could to shield the keep. We brought our people inside, a celebration we told them, but it was the only way to keep them safe. We heard later of great murders though Caledonia, babes slaughtered, the Black Coats had been searching. We believe they were searching for the two of you."

Tommy squeezed my hand tight. I hadn't realised I was shaking. I breathed, I am whole, I am safe, I am alive.

"Why?" My voice broke, and I couldn't hide the ache that had suddenly lodged in my chest.

Da met my eyes, his face heavy with sorrow. "We don't ken," he said softly. "But that's why we trained you—to survive, to protect. You'll understand, one day."

His gaze swept over us, filled with an unbearable mix of pride and pain. I could see the weight of everything he'd lost, everything he still carried.

"They did not come back until you both had turned five. There was an attack on the keep, your ma took all four of ye to the meadow, it was protected by the Auld Ones. She had made sure you all knew it in case of danger. She left you all guarded by their Auld Ones and their magic and rode to the standing stones.

"There was a great beam of light into the sky, and the Black Coats disappeared. I ken she would have gone there. I rode as fast as I could, but I was too late. She was disappearing into the stones. *Bidh gaol agam ort gu bràth. I will love you forever. They will be safe, Mo chridhe, I have made sure of it.* She smiled and was gone. And that was the last time I saw Elizabeth Mackenzie MacLeod.

"Orkadia—you must go as soon as the winter snow melts, Alix. Find her people; they may know where to look. Callum, they will recognise you as her son. Marcus, you will continue with Malcolm in Skye; there is much you both must learn from the Auld Ones."

The room was quiet, warm light burning from the hearth, candlelight flickering in the breeze. Snow was beginning to fall from the sky, bringing a chill in the air.

"Until we part then." He held his whisky high. "Slàinte Mhath!"

ACKNOWLEDGMENTS

To my son William, see, I told you dreams can come true. Thank you for bringing such adventures to my life., Never stop believing in yourself. You can achieve anything you set your mind to.

To my Mum, I can never thank you enough for giving me the greatest gift you could, teaching me to read. Without it, I could never have gone on the incredible adventures I have. From the Faraway Tree to Narnia and the Shire.

To Nanny, you made my childhood magical. Searching for fairies in your beautiful gardens and making crowns of flowers. Grampy, you always challenged my mind and encouraged me to read. I never went without a book.

Thank you to my friends and family who have supported me on this journey.

Holly, you made me write this down, believing others should read it. You were also my first book friend. I love our endless chats about them.

Bianca, thank you for always being my Person.

And most importantly, to YOU, the reader. I am so thankful you took the chance and read this book. All the comments, posts, support and reviews I receive are incredibly wonderful. It means the world to me that you jumped on this adventure with me.

And finally, to my husband Mathew, *a chuisle mo chroi.*

-Lisa-Maree

About the author

Lisa-Maree Patterson has always been captivated by the magic of
Scotland. After a life-changing visit, the country's rugged beauty and rich
history inspired her to put pen to paper and bring her own stories to life.
An avid reader and storyteller, Lisa-Maree's passion for the written word
shines through in her debut novel, *Skye*, the first book in the *Caledonian
Series*. Her work blends the enchantment of Scotland's landscapes with
unforgettable characters and thrilling narratives.

When she's not writing or reading, Lisa-Maree enjoys spending time in her
cosy library, baking delicious treats, exploring the outdoors, dreaming of
her next trip to Scotland, and sharing her love of fantasy with readers
around the world.

Follow on
TIKTOK @lisamareepattersonauthor
Instagram @lisamareepattersonuthor

The Caledonian Series

SKYE

Lisa Maree
Patterson

THE CALEDONIAN SERIES

ORKADIA

LISA MAREE
PATTERSON